LONG DARK NIGHT

A MICHAEL CARTER COLD CASE THRILLER

THE DARK SERIES BOOK ONE

SUSAN LUND

SUSAN LUND BOOKS

LONG DARK NIGHT

A Michael Carter Cold Case Thriller

The Dark Series Book One

Copyright 2022 Susan Lund

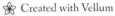

CHAPTER 1

DEAN BECKER WALKED THE PERIMETER OF HIS TWO properties — the family acreage with the old homestead near Deep Lake southeast of Black Diamond, and the small plot of undeveloped land to the west. He was pleased that finally, the two would be joined and he could build his and his wife Diane's dream house.

He'd hired Barton Excavations Inc., to remove the old wooden fence and row of cedars that separated the two plots of land so he could extend the yard and eventually build what people in the area called a 'monster house' because of the sheer size.

It would be a mansion compared to the old homestead that his grandfather had built back in the early 20th century when he acquired the acreage. With the two properties conjoined, there would be enough space for the magnificent house plans he'd chosen, as well as a circular driveway and a three-car garage for his various toys.

The property was on a lesser-used road bordering the lake. Tall fir and pine circled the property, hiding it from the road, offering the kind of privacy he had always dreamed of, growing up in Seattle. The old homestead was narrow and tall. The new house would be tall and wide.

There would even be room for Diane's garden and swimming pool in the small side yard where the excavators were currently working.

He walked over and watched the man work the small front-end loader, which had already pulled down the wood fence and was now digging up the cedar hedge.

The man operating the loader, a middle-aged guy named Salvador, stopped when he hit something that looked like an old carpet.

"There's some garbage under here," he said, pointing to the disturbed earth.

Dean peered closer and saw what looked like an old brown shag rug. He nodded at Salvador, who kept digging.

Then, Dean saw something that didn't belong — something long and white.

A bone...

"Whoa!" he called out, holding up his arm. "Stop for a minute."

Salvador complied and the shovel stopped in mid-air. "What?"

"There's a bone. Let me take a closer look. Might have unearthed a carcass. Or a body."

Dean knew that Salvador was up from Mexico working in the building trade and would be unhappy if work had to stop since his livelihood depended on it. He reluctantly got off the loader and stood beside Dean.

Dean bent down and used a stick to move the dirt around. The pointed end caught on something that offered considerable resistance. The earth around it was thick and wet.

Dean grunted, and the stick broke, but before it did, he

managed to partially remove what looked like a skull from the surrounding muck.

"Holy Mother of God," Salvador said and made the sign of the cross. "It's human."

Dean stood up and shook his head. "Guess we better call the cops."

Salvador nodded. "Should I move to another section and keep working?"

Dean regarded Salvador, who was no doubt worried about getting paid for a full day's work.

"Might as well, until the cops get here. Maybe try over there at the end of the fence line."

"Okay," Salvador said and moved the loader to a farther section of the hedge. He began digging, removing buckets full of cedars and dirt while Dean called 9-1-1 to request police assistance. When he was finished the call, he watched Salvador work the loader, worried that there might be more. Sure enough, within a few minutes, another bone was unearthed.

"Stop!" He held up his hand and made a slicing motion across his neck. "There's more. Better shut it down for the day."

Salvador nodded with clear reluctance, emptying the bucket, and moving the loader back to the driveway where a pickup with a small trailer was parked.

While they waited for the police to arrive, Salvador took out a pack of Camels and lit a cigarette.

"Can I have one?" Dean asked, pointing to the pack. He decided that finding at least two dead bodies on his property was a good enough excuse to have at least one cigarette, even though he'd given it up a few years earlier.

Salvador handed him the pack, so Dean removed one

cigarette and then accepted the old-fashioned metal lighter from the man. He lit up and took in a deep drag.

Yeah. That was what he needed. He'd never tell Diane, for she had been adamant that he quit before she'd agree to marry him. He promised himself he would have only one.

That was it.

The crunch of tires on gravel told Dean that the police had arrived. A black and white patrol car from the King County Sheriff's Office drove up the driveway and parked. Out strode two young officers dressed in their black uniforms. They put on their caps and came over to where Salvador and Dean stood smoking.

"Mr. Dean Becker?" the young cop on the right asked, his blue eyes narrowed.

"That's me," Dean replied. "This is Salvador Gomez, who works with the construction firm I hired to do some excavating on my property."

The cop nodded. "I'm Officer Bryant and this is Officer Webster from the Sheriff's Office. We're here to secure the scene for the Medical Examiner and detectives from the Major Crimes Unit."

"It's over here. We found two different locations with bones. They're definitely human. At first, I thought it might be an animal carcass. There's lots of deer and elk around here, but when I saw that," he said and pointed to the skull, "I realized it was human. There's another one over here."

He walked over to the second location where bones had been unearthed.

"We'll take it from here," Officer Bryant said, nodding. "If you could both wait for the detectives so they can take your statements, that would be great."

"Will do." Dean turned to Salvador. "You'll still get paid." Salvador nodded, and with that, Dean patted the man on the shoulder. "Let's go in the house and get a coffee or a drink. I came earlier and made sure the power was on and have some supplies in the old refrigerator."

"Thank you."

Salvador followed Dean to the house. As they mounted the steps to the front entrance, Dean watched as a white van drove into the driveway.

That would be the medical examiner, who would dig up the skeletal remains and determine cause of death.

Whatever the case, it would be an interesting diversion from the build. Dean hoped it wouldn't delay the work too long.

He had a dream house to build, although the thought that bodies had been buried on his property was a tad unsettling.

He shrugged and held the door open for Salvador.

They went in and after Salvador used the bathroom, the two men stood at the large picture window facing the yard and watched the proceedings.

The forensic team erected a cabana-like covering over the area where the first body had been found. While he and Salvador waited, a glass of good strong scotch in hand, a woman with grey hair in a bun and dark rimmed glasses put on a set of white coveralls, then donned a pair of goggles and a mask. She wore blue latex gloves and had blue coverings on her boots. She bent down and began photographing the exposed bones, then laid out some markings in the soil. With her back to them, she started her work uncovering the remains.

From what Dean had seen, the body looked almost fully skeletal. He had spent some time examining the bones, and they were mostly bare but there were strips of flesh at the end of the long bone, and so he figured it had been there for a pretty long time.

Finally, a dark sedan drove up and two plain clothes police got out and went over to the tent. They spoke with the medical examiner and then glanced over at the house.

"There's the two detectives now," Dean said. "They'll probably want our statements, and then you can go. It won't be long now."

Salvador nodded and the two men watched as the detectives walked over to the house.

It would make a great if somewhat macabre story to tell guests who came for the many barbecues he planned on hosting.

CHAPTER 2

MICHAEL CARTER SAT AT HIS DESK IN THE KING County Prosecutor's Office in downtown Seattle and looked at the box of files in front of him.

His current job was Investigator on the Cold Case Task Force, where he acted as the official liaison between the King County Prosecutor, the Seattle Police Department, and the Seattle City Attorney. He worked cold cases and reported to his superiors on the progress he was making—or not making, as the case may be.

It sounded more important than it was. After the police had arrested and charged members of the Pacific Northwest Sex Trafficking Ring, including Richard Parkinson and others involved in trafficking of young girls, the task force he'd worked on before had been shut down. Michael wasn't going to return to college and do a PhD, given the pandemic, so he was happy to stay on for the remainder of the year and work on cold cases instead.

Cold cases would give him the opportunity to keep involved in policing but would remove him from the field. He could use the skills he gained from his time in the FBI to profile potential suspects that might have been overlooked, and he could apply some of the newer geographical profiling techniques that hadn't been used as often in previous decades to give the cold cases a fresh set of eyes.

He had been working the cold cases for the past couple of months and had yet to find one with any real evidence that could be used to restart the stalled case. Many of the oldest cold cases lacked forensic evidence that could be used to identify possible suspects. All he could do was go over each case in detail, looking at what steps had been taken in what order, what statements had been given by which witnesses and which individuals had been put on or taken off the list of potential suspects, looking for something previous detectives had missed or just didn't have access to at the time. Some of the cases were decades old.

He'd arranged them in different ways to see patterns: by decade, by age and gender of the victim, and by location of the body. There were dozens and dozens of cold cases, and hundreds of missing persons cases in King County alone.

It was daunting.

The clearance rate for crime in general, and of murder in particular was poor. Much of the crime was gang or drug related, and that meant it was especially hard to find the perpetrators and bring them to justice. It was an insular world and difficult to get cooperation from witnesses. So many murders were done with guns, and so many were over drugs or money involved in the drug trade.

Those weren't the cases that interested Michael.

He couldn't help but gravitate to the others — murders that weren't gang related or connected to drugs or organized crime.

The runaways, the sex workers, the trafficked youth who went missing — those were the cases he cared about.

His first experience with law enforcement was personal. The girl from Paradise Hill, ten-year-old Lisa Tate, had been in his care while he and a friend had been babysitting when he was fourteen. Lisa went missing and was found alive years later, having survived years of sexual abuse in a pedophile ring operating in the Pacific Northwest. His contact with the local police as a witness and suspect had shaped his life from then on.

When he went to college, he studied criminology. When he joined the FBI after graduating with an MA, he was put on the Child Abduction Rapid Deployment team for the Western Division. He spent his six years with the FBI trying to locate children who had been abducted, hoping to find them before they were murdered.

It was a losing proposition. Most children who were abducted by strangers were killed in the first few hours. A small number were kept alive for longer — up to a few days. Rarely, a child might be kept alive for years, and used as a sex slave or trafficked as Lisa had.

He'd retired from the FBI after a particularly difficult case where he had failed to find the child in time and had suffered from PTSD after finding the boy's lifeless and sexually tortured body.

A boy about the same age as his own son.

That had been hard.

After he left the FBI, he worked for the Seattle DA's Office as an Investigator.

Now, he worked with the Cold Case Task Force. Which meant a whole lot of hurry up and wait. Forensic samples were backlogged. Video was backlogged. Everything was backlogged due to the pandemic and the need to social distance and work from home as much as possible.

Michael had been able to work at the office because

most of the rest of the staff were working from home or on paid leave. He was alone most of the time, which suited him fine.

Alone with the boxes and boxes of cold case files, he could use the boardroom to his heart's content, spreading out case files, filling the walls with maps and images.

There were few or no distractions, except for the cleaners who came in on a regular basis to keep the floors shiny and the dust off the window blinds. Alone in the office in the quiet building, he could focus.

When his cell phone on his desk rang, he startled, and jerked upright after leaning over a file, examining the photo of a body.

He grabbed the phone and checked the call display.

It was from the King County Sheriff's Office.

The man on the other end identified himself as Detective Paul Harris of the Major Crimes Unit. Michael had worked with the man before and thought highly of him. They'd shared a drink or two together after a case had been closed and the man was solid.

"Just thought you'd like to know we have at least three sets of remains down here on a property beside Deep Lake, and they're still digging in case there's more. Dr. Keller is here now and is working on the first set of remains. We found something on one body that might be of interest to you. A silver elephant pendant on a black nylon bracelet. Blue Adidas. Might match up to any cold cases or missing persons cases you're working."

"Elephant pendant on a black nylon bracelet?" Michael frowned. He had just recently gone through all the cold cases involving children and youth and there was one case that caught his eye. Two boys aged fourteen had gone missing over a decade earlier. One had been found by a hunter in some woods south of Newcastle in the ensuing weeks. The other had never been found and was one of his cases of interest.

The boy was presumed dead, since his friend had been murdered. All that was left was to find his body and to Michael, it sounded as though they finally had found him.

Ten years later.

"That sounds like Andy Owens," he said and reached over to a box of files on the ledge beside his desk. It contained all the cold cases involving children under the age of eighteen. "Hold on for a moment." He put down his phone and pulled out one file in particular. Nicolas "Nick" Dixon. Fourteen. From Newcastle. Went missing in 2010 with Andy Owens, also fourteen. He found Andy Owens's file and opened it, going to the page that included a description of Andy and what he was wearing the last time he had been seen alive.

Blue Adidas running shoes. A black jacket with a DC Comics character named The Comedian. A leather bracelet with a silver elephant pendant on it.

"Does it have a WWF insignia on the elephant? You said blue Adidas?"

"Yes, to both," Harris said.

Michael leaned back in his chair and rubbed his eyes. "It's him. His case has been in the Cold Case files for ten years. No leads. Presumed dead but no body."

"Looks like we found him. You want to come and see?"

Michael checked his watch. If he left now, he could get there in about fifty minutes.

"I'll grab some lunch and see you in an hour."

"See you then," Harris replied. "Might want to bring Dr. Keller a latte."

"Oh, I will be sure to. Grande Mocha Latte. I know the drill."

Harris chuckled and ended the call. Michael gathered up the files and stuffed them into his briefcase, then grabbed his jacket and made his way down to the parking lot where he'd parked his Range Rover. There was a Starbucks in Maple Valley that he could stop at and get Grace her requisite Grande Mocha Latte.

The first time he got one for her, she put him in her good books, where he'd been from then on.

He intended to stay there.

THE DRIVE to the Deep Lake location took about fifty minutes. Traffic wasn't too busy on the Interstate. He took Interstate 90 and then a secondary highway to where the property in question was located. When he drove up to the property, he saw the white van from the King County Medical Examiner's office and could see the tent that had been set up on the property to protect the scene from the rain, which had recently started to fall.

He pulled up his hood and left his vehicle, checking in with the police officer who was keeping control over the site, and then making his way along the approved path to the tent where Grace Keller was working.

She was dressed in her usual white suit, wearing goggles and gloves, and was bending down over the dirt which had been unearthed by the front-end loader parked in the driveway. A pair of portable floodlights had been set up to illuminate the scene.

Grace knelt on a pair of foam blocks and was brushing away dirt from some bones that looked to Michael like ribs.

He could make out a skull that was definitely out of place and located down below where he figured the feet would be. It had obviously been disturbed by the excavation. It was preferable to unearth the skeletal remains as they had been buried to get a better idea of the manner of disposal and clues about the cause of death, but you did the best with what you had. Luckily, the excavation had stopped soon after the first bone — a femur — had been found so there wasn't too much destruction of the evidence or scene.

"Hello," Michael said, holding up the cup of latte in his hand. "I thought you might be in need of this."

Grace glanced over her shoulder and saw Michael then nodded. "I was hoping someone would show up bearing gifts. The rain just started and it's damn cold."

She struggled up and left the site, coming to stand beside Michael. She took the cup from Michael eagerly and after removing her mask and goggles, she took a sip, sighing with contentment.

"That's more like it," she said. She looked back at the dig site. "This one of yours?"

"Yes." Michael nodded. "We think it's Andy Owens, fourteen, from Newcastle. Went missing ten years ago with his best friend Nick Dixon, also fourteen. Dixon's body was found soon after, but not Owens's."

"Harris called you about the elephant bracelet?"

"Yes," Michael said. "Both he and Dixon had them. Apparently, Andy's older brother worked as a canvasser for World Wildlife Fund raising money in the summer and gave both boys one of the bracelets. It helped police ID Dixon."

"So sad," Grace said and shook her head slowly. "You have boys about this age, right?"

Michael nodded. "Yes. Makes it all the harder to work a

case like this. I think of my boys and can't imagine what the parents went through. What they're still going through."

"You see your boys often?" Grace asked, tilting her head to one side. "They live in Tacoma, right?"

Michael sighed. "Not as much as I'd like. You have kids?"

"Never had any." Grace took another sip of her latte and was silent for a moment. "We wanted to, but things didn't work out in the biology department." She smiled sadly. "Then John died, and well, my work is my life. I see a few of John's relatives now and then when they're in town." She sighed. "We're going to be here for a while. There are three bodies that I can see so far. Might as well bring up a chair and watch if you're interested."

"You know me, Grace. I'm always interested."

She smiled. "I do."

Michael glanced up at the overcast sky and threatening clouds, which sent down a spray of rain that varied in intensity with the wind.

Three bodies? He glanced down the row of cedars and saw that police and the excavator were working to remove even more dirt. A body had been buried every ten feet. From the looks of it, there might be more.

It would be a long day and night.

CHAPTER 3

Dr. Grace Keller had been conducting an autopsy on the latest shooting victim to be brought into the morgue when the phone on the autopsy room wall rang.

Her assistant Annie Strickland took the call and after listening, called to Grace, her hand over the receiver.

"It's the King County Sheriff's Office," Annie said, her warm brown eyes wide over her N95 respirator. "They have some skeletal remains unearthed down near Deep Lake."

Grace exhaled. "Tell them I'll be there as soon as I can. I'm in the middle of this. Give me an hour or so to finish up."

Annie relayed the information and then returned to Grace's side.

It was an upsetting autopsy, for the young man was only about fifteen. He'd been shot while walking through a park outside of Seattle and had died on the scene. He was the city's most recent homicide. Given the park was in one of the worst neighborhoods for drugs and crime, it was likely gang- and drug-related.

No doubt it would go unsolved like so many others had

when it came to gang violence and the drug trade. No one talked. No one wanted to rat someone out lest they become the next victim of a drive-by shooting. There was little evidence to nail anyone for the shooting.

Grace felt incredibly sad for the parents, who mourned their dead children, no matter the cause of death.

She looked at the young man on the metal autopsy table, whose chest had been unzipped and whose organs she was now harvesting.

The bullet, a .44 caliber Nosler partition round, had entered the left chest at just the right angle to slice clean through the left ventricle, causing massive blood loss and death within moments. It was an unusual form of ammunition, which contained two bullets in one single casing. It was normally used for big game and not usually manufactured for use in handguns. They would have fun tracking down who sold the bullets and to whom. Whatever the case, it was unusual. Grace had only seen one other case of such bullets being used in her career, and it had been in a hunting accident over a decade earlier. The use of the unusual ammunition might help them solve the case.

At least, she hoped it would.

According to her records, this was the forty-second shooting death in the past twelve months, and only a few had been cleared.

She shook her head and removed the heart, preparing it for closer examination.

When the autopsy was finished, she let Annie finish up and after doing the minimal amount of paperwork, she prepared to travel to the Deep Lake site to the skeletal remains.

That was more to her liking. She'd trained as a forensic anthropologist as well as a pathologist, and there was nothing she liked better than digging up old bones. There was something about working in the dirt to unearth old bones that sparked pleasure in Grace. She had initially thought about becoming a paleontologist, unearthing old dinosaur bones in Montana and North Dakota, but had gone into medicine like her father, deciding on becoming a pathologist rather than dealing with live humans.

She was on the Autism Spectrum, and so working with things, even if they were dead humans, was preferable to those who were alive and who depended on her to save them.

She found that part of her medical training too stressful.

Finding out the cause of death in someone who had already passed away was a whole different kettle of fish.

That she could manage. No stress. Just curiosity and tests.

Science, in other words.

That made her happy.

As she drove south from Seattle, she thought about what she liked about forensic anthropology. You had to be careful when uncovering the bones to preserve as much of the scene as possible, taking your photos and samples in the process. Gradually, you revealed the way the body was lain down before being buried, and learned whether it was clothed or naked, if there were any signs of what killed the person — bullets, knife marks on bones, ligatures that survived being buried.

All of it was a giant puzzle that she loved to put together and solve.

Once she arrived on the scene and dressed in her white protective suit, donned her goggles, mask, and gloves, she was ready.

This crime scene had at least two bodies, and, as far as she could tell, they were both under age eighteen. Someone had either killed the two young people and dumped the bodies there all at once or had used it as a dumping ground for multiple murders over time.

That would be what she tried to figure out with her work. Absent an ID, there would be ways to determine when each body had been left in place. Soil samples taken as she unearthed each skeleton would give an idea — an approximate idea — of how long the body had been buried. Once they ID'd the body, they would know for sure but until then, the bones and the dirt in which they were found would tell them a lot.

"Can you continue along the hedge? There may be more bodies buried. Might as well dig it all up now that we're here."

"You want my guy to do it or your own?"

"Your guy is fine. Tell him we'll cover the costs. Just make sure to stop if you find anything. Bones, clothing, carpets, anything that shouldn't be there. Delicate. Delicate."

"Understood," the man said.

The man, the owner of the property, directed the contractor to set to work digging up the rest of the hedge, which divided the two properties. While Grace worked on the first set of remains, the police officer and owner watched the contractor dig up the rest of the hedge. She hoped they didn't find any other bodies, but if there were more, she wanted to know sooner rather than later.

She could call in reinforcements. Get her assistant, who

had trained in forensic anthropology from Washington State U, to come down and help.

After a few more moments, the owner called out.

"Got another one," he said, his expression shocked. "How many freaking bodies are buried here?"

Grace stood and glanced over to where the front-end loader was digging. It was about ten feet beyond the second body.

Three bodies.

How many more would there be?

It was going to be a very long day.

A WHILE LATER, Michael Carter from the King County Prosecuting Attorney's office arrived, bearing gifts. A much-needed steaming hot Mocha Latte.

Her favorite.

They exchanged pleasantries and discussed the first remains that Michael thought was one of his cold case victims from over a decade earlier.

After they found a fourth body, Grace called Michael over.

"Can you contact my assistant for me? Get her and a team out here. We're gonna need a bigger boat."

Michael laughed at her joke and nodded. "Will do."

He went off to the side and took out his cell, calling Grace's assistant and requesting that she and a team attend to help with the recovery of the remains.

Four sets of remains...

It was a graveyard.

The owner of the property was suitably alarmed.

"My family's owned this property for over a hundred

years. My great grandfather built this house, and my grandfather lived here, as did my father. I can assure you that none of them had anything to do with this. No one's lived here for almost twenty years, preferring to live in the city. It wasn't until I could finally buy the property next to us that I decided to build here. The place was abandoned. No one has lived here for twenty years."

Grace took a break, stretching her back after bending down for so long. "Don't worry," she said and put her hand on the man's shoulder. "The bodies were technically found on the other side of the property line. Given the remoteness and the fact it's been uninhabited for the past two decades, anyone could have buried these bodies here. It's well hidden from the road. Someone could have driven up the lane and buried the bodies and no one would have seen them do it."

The owner nodded and rubbed his forehead like he was relieved. "I mean, there are some pretty tough characters in my family, but we're not serial killers."

Beside Grace, Michael Carter nodded and waved his arm around. "Whoever buried the bodies knew this place was remote and likely abandoned. That's precisely why they chose it. Once we have the identity of the victims, we'll have a better idea of just how long this place has been used to dump bodies."

"You'll get to clear up a few of your cold cases, Michael," Grace said and went back under the tent to finish scraping some dirt into a tube for analysis, writing the ID numbers on the side of the plastic evidence bag.

"I hope so," Michael replied, his hands on his hips. "There's a lot of missing persons cases and cold cases on my desk. Hope we'll be able to reduce that by a few in the next while. How long will it take to get some idea of the timeframe?"

Grace shrugged. "Have to send samples of the dirt to the Washington State Lab for analysis. I'd say they've been here anywhere from a couple of years to a decade, given the state of the bones and the clothing. Some of it's pretty degraded. Could be over the span of a decade. Won't know more till I get the results back and until we get some dental records checked. I saw some fillings in body number two that can be used for identification purposes. I haven't even had a look at body number four. We'll see if there's any identifying marks or clothing."

Michael nodded. He seemed really interested in the whole forensic world and had spent some quality time with her over dinners of ribs and beer when they last worked together.

Grace liked Michael. He seemed like a serious but friendly man, who had a natural interest in the process. He liked to learn.

That was good because Grace loved to teach. What was the use of having knowledge if not to pass it on to someone else? She had taught for a while at the local college and had spent some time after her PhD in forensic anthropology teaching during a post-doc before she was hired as a medical examiner in King County.

She loved interacting with students — especially the eager beavers who waited around after class to ask questions.

Michael reminded her of one of those eager beavers — happy to stick around and watch, learn. He'd been in the FBI and apparently, was planning on doing his PhD and teaching at the BSU in Quantico, Virginia.

Grace thought he'd be perfect, but the FBI's gain would be King County's loss.

She turned back to the body in the ground beneath her.

"Let's see who you are," she said and took a photograph of the body, which lay face down, its head turned to one side. Around the neck was a thin metal wire that had been used as a garrote.

"Michael," she called out and waved him over. "Look at this. I think we have our cause of death."

Michael came over and knelt on some blocks that had been placed to allow him to watch but not disturb the evidence.

"What have you got?"

She pointed to the garrote, and Michael bent closer. "Oh, yeah. I see it."

"Follow me." She got up and went over to the second body and used her trowel to clean away mud from around the skull. Down below the neck was what she expected — another series of wires wrapped around the neck.

A classic garotte.

"Thin wire wrapped around the neck and a piece of wood used to tighten it. On this one, too. Same as the first body."

She glanced at Michael who was shaking his head. "Does that method of killing ring a bell for you? Any others you can remember that are the same?"

Michael shook his head. "Not with wire and wood."

Grace sighed. "Looks like you got yourself a new serial killer."

"Or an old one that we didn't know we had."

"That, too."

CHAPTER 4

Tess McClintock walked along the waterfront, a cup of coffee in hand, and considered where she should work.

The pandemic meant that most of her favorite coffee shops along the waterfront were closed except for takeout, and the streets were empty. Usually, at that time of day, there would be scores of people walking around the piers, taking in the scenery.

Not anymore.

She could have stayed in the apartment and worked, but she was used to getting up and ready for work and liked the routine of getting a cup of coffee and heading for the office.

Now that she was on leave, working on her book, she was free to set her own schedule.

Still, despite that freedom, she'd trained her mind and body to get up and go out every day to the offices at the *Sentinel*, and it was hard not to.

For the past couple of weeks, since she'd started her one-year leave to write her book, Tess had wandered around looking for a good place to park and write in her car. She'd picked one spot looking out over the bay, and that was where she decided to go and work that morning.

The book contract was decent, as far as first books went, and was enough to live off for at least six months.

Eugene Kincaid was going to make her some decent money, which was only fair, considering all the pain he'd caused her and everyone else in his wake. She planned on telling his story, how he'd gone undetected for decades, and had fooled everyone around him — except for Michael. Michael never liked his brother-in-law.

The agent who accepted her as a client and found a buyer for her book on Kincaid was excited for Tess to write a first-hand account of her brush with death at Kincaid's hand and how she tried to save the lives of his would-be victims. Most importantly, Tess would ensure that the girls who fought back and ended Kincaid's murderous career would be the real focus of her story.

With her laptop and cup of coffee in hand, Tess spent the morning writing the next chapter of her manuscript.

Around three in the afternoon, she got a text from Michael.

MICHAEL: *Going to be a long night. Probably staying late. At a scene near Deep Lake. Multiple skeletal remains. One of my cold cases. Several, actually.*

TESS: *Wow. Looks like you'll be busier than you thought.*

MICHAEL: *Yes. So far, four bodies. We've ID'd one of them, but the rest are still unknown. Will be late. Probably have dinner with Grace and be home late tonight.*

TESS: *Should I be jealous? What will you and Grace be eating? Ribs? I'll probably be having leftover lasagna.*

MICHAEL: *Probably if I can find a place. I like to keep in her good books.*

Tess smiled and thought about Michael and Grace —
what an odd couple they made. Grace was a woman in her
late fifties, with long grey hair that she wore in a bun, and a
very pleasant if wrinkled face and bright blue eyes. Tess
met the medical examiner once at a dinner hosted by the
former head of the task force Michael had been working on
in 2019. It was clear Grace felt affection for Michael and
the feeling was mutual. Grace was more like a mother to
Michael than a colleague but of course, she was that as well
— a very respected medical examiner, pathologist and to top
it off, a forensic anthropologist.

She was probably the most qualified in the entire state
of Washington and King County was lucky to have her.

*TESS: I suppose you can't tell me the identity of the
body you found...*

*MICHAEL: You know I can't, but I will say that it was
a young teenage boy who went missing ten years ago and
was presumed dead, although his body wasn't found until
today. If you can figure out who it is on your own, I can't
stop you.*

*TESS: Now you've done it — I won't be able to relax
until I know who it is. Can I ask if you know the cause of
death yet?*

*MICHAEL: Early days, but it wasn't natural causes or
an accident. That's all I can say.*

*TESS: Oh, so it's homicide. That's too bad. I'll see you
when you get in. XO*

MICHAEL: XOX

Tess smiled at his response and then sighed, her mind
immediately working hard to remember any famous missing
cases involving teenage boys. Instead of wondering, she
opened a browser and went immediately to the NamUS
website and searched for Washington State, and King

County in particular, to check on missing persons cases that fit the description Michael had given.

It took only a few minutes for her to find a couple of potential matches.

One was fifteen and had gone missing from his home in Renton in 2009. Jared Blake. He was a potential candidate, as was Andy Owens, age fourteen, last seen in 2010 in the company of Nick Dixon, also aged fourteen, from Newcastle. Dixon's body was later found by a pair of hunters east of Renton in the Cougar Mountain Regional Wildland Park. If Andy had been found near Deep Lake, the killer ranged widely.

Tess spent the next hour reading up on the case. Often, boys went missing from their homes and were later found to have wandered too far into the forest, requiring search and rescue to locate them and return them to safety. Sometimes, the lifeless body of the missing youth would be found in a reservoir or at the bottom of a lake after taking their own life. That was a very sad end to many missing young men in that age group and Tess's heart squeezed at the thought of their pain.

If Michael thought the boy hadn't died of natural causes or an accident, then it was homicide.

She searched online databases on the case, reading archived news reports written at the time the boys had gone missing.

The people of Newcastle had all joined together to search for the missing boys. They were reported missing in the summer before they started high school, and both boys had been working delivering papers and mowing lawns to save up money for the latest video game consoles. Neither boy was in any kind of trouble.

Tess watched an archived newscast from a local station.

On it, the distraught father of Nick Dixon pleaded with the public to help find the missing youth.

"They're good boys, from good hardworking families. Never been in trouble. We're asking everyone, if you've seen them, if you know where they are, please contact the police. Let's bring them home safely."

Everyone hoped that the boys had simply become lost while exploring the local wilderness. The boys had been known to take their bikes to Cougar Mountain Park, which was about eight miles east of Newcastle. The forests were thick in that part of the region, and it was always possible that the boys became lost and would be found, tired, dehydrated, mosquito bitten, but otherwise alive.

That had been the hope.

Search parties found the two bicycles several days later, abandoned on the side of a narrow hiking path. What alarmed the searchers was the fact that Andy Owens's backpack was left behind. Inside was a Gameboy, a water bottle, and some collector cards from a game the boys played — Dungeons and Dragons.

That suggested foul play. There was no way that the boy would have left his backpack behind if he and Nick had decided to walk deeper into the forest, leaving their bikes behind because the forest path was too narrow for bikes.

But what happened?

When Nick's body was found two days later by hunters in the Cougar Mountain Regional Wildland Park, miles away, the worst fears of all those involved in the search were realized.

He'd been sexually assaulted, then strangled with a ligature made from piano wire and wood. His half-clothed body, jeans pulled down around his ankles, had been dumped under a fallen log, with several branches from a nearby tree broken off to cover the remains.

At that point, authorities assumed that they'd find the other boy's body nearby, and an extensive search of the State Park was undertaken, lasting a week, with no luck.

If Andy's body was found on a property near Deep Lake, that meant he was killed and dumped in a different location.

Why?

Was Andy kept alive and killed later? If he was killed soon after Nick, why was he then dumped in a different location? Tess's mind went over the possibilities.

She felt haunted by the notion that Andy had been alive while his best friend was being sexually assaulted and then murdered. Had he been forced to watch? Had he been taken somewhere else and killed, then buried on the Deep Lake property?

The killer was taking a huge risk if so.

Tess felt slightly sick to her stomach, considering the different scenarios that the find made possible. It had been ten years since the boys had gone missing and Nick was found murdered. Tess was certain that the parents of the boy, Andy, would have held out hope that he was still alive somewhere.

This finding would crush them.

She went online and started reading on Websleuths to see what had been written about the boys. Sure enough, there was a whole thread devoted to the cases, and people familiar with the boys and the families, as well as those close to the police, had provided tips and information.

In one forum, someone wrote a cryptic message on a thread about the killer's identity.

From Questioning1:

You'll never find the killer. He's not your average run of the mill criminal. You're all just spinning your wheels, speculating. Cops are as in the dark as you all are. I laugh at you and your pathetic attempts to be armchair detectives and amateur sleuths, living in your mommy's basements. Leave it to the big boys. Even they can't find the killer, and they never will.

Tess figured it was from some disgruntled forum member, who didn't like how much interest was being placed on the case. There were what people called 'shit-posters' on all internet forums. People who loved to taunt the regular members and make fun of them.

It was either that, or the killer himself.

That made Tess shiver. The thought that an actual serial killer was monitoring the forums, watching what people said and what questions they asked made her uneasy. She decided not to use her professional account — the one she used to contact web sleuths for articles she was writing for the *Sentinel*. No, she decided to create a 'sock puppet' account so she could ask questions and remain anonymous.

She'd had enough run-ins with murderers in her time.

CHAPTER 5

THE NEWS ABOUT THE DISCOVERIES AT THE DEEP LAKE
site got Curtis to thinking.

What made him want to kill?

Was it something in his genetic makeup — some broken
part that was passed on from one generation to another until
it finally made itself known?

His family had been relatively peaceable, successful,
law-abiding types, with uncles in law enforcement and the
clergy, following the rules their faith laid out for them and
the laws of the land. Attending Mass, going to confession.
His father, a local attorney, had been strict but had used a
cane no thicker than his thumb to whip the children when
they disobeyed, which wasn't very often. He was struck no
more or less than the other four siblings.

None of them turned to murder to get their kicks.

Why him?

It was a question that absorbed him in his spare time
and popped into his head at random moments when his
mind wandered.

Why was he a killer?

In the end, why did it matter?

He just was.

But he couldn't escape the question, and that was why, when he went to college, he studied abnormal psychology and criminology. His father wanted him to be a lawyer and carry on the family tradition, but Curtis wanted to study himself.

All the better to control his baser urges so he didn't get caught.

At least, not doing anything really big.

He'd been caught when he was just a teen, exposing himself to kids in the small community in which he grew up, but that had been quickly swept under the social rug, so to speak. No one wanted to talk about it, least of all to the police.

You'd think that, growing up in such a religious family, he would never develop such murderous urges, such dark desires, but he had. He thought he'd finish his degree and leave town for Seattle or maybe Portland, Oregon, but that had been hard. His father would only support him if he attended college and lived at home. In the end, he was saved by the Iraq war, and the chance to sign up and leave home via military service.

During boot camp, he dreamed of killing enemies, but instead of getting his desire to kill satiated, he was assigned to drive vehicles, because it was the only real skill he had. So it was that he found himself in the Army, driving a truck, ferrying weapons and military equipment and supplies from one base to another. First in Afghanistan. Then in Iraq.

His dreams of killing enemies were quashed by his military occupation specialty—his MOS. The only thing he killed for the first two years of his deployment were random bugs on the windshield and the occasional rodent on the roads.

For the first year of his deployment, he generally kept to himself, rarely taking part in the games that his fellow soldiers played. During his second year, there was one young man, Elliott Scott, who seemed to understand his difference. A skinny, tall young man with the remnants of puberty in pockmarked scars on his face, Elliott was from somewhere in Utah, and had a similar religious upbringing except among the Mormons.

They fell in together and became fast friends, spending their time together talking about their similar lives back home in the USA.

"Why did you join up?" Elliott asked one day while they were working on the truck, replacing some spark plugs.

Curtis thought about how to answer. He remembered watching the towers fall on the television in town, while his father was at the office and there was a television in the window of the local hardware store tuned to CNN.

"To kill bad guys." He smiled at the expression on his friend's face. "Well? Didn't you want to after watching the towers fall?"

"I sure did," Elliott said. "I wanted to spill some blood. I still do. I think it's unfair that they make us drive a truck all the time. Why not swap us out with some of the soldiers who are seeing combat so we can get us some?"

"It all comes down to aptitude, according to my recruiting officer. And need. I thought that after two years of studying abnormal psych that they'd put me in planning, but they need drivers. My aptitude was driving a truck. I told them I could also shoot a gun. My father was a hunter and he and his brothers did a lot of hunting where I lived. Every fall, we filled up the ice chest with venison to keep us through the winter. But they needed drivers."

"Not me. I lived on a dairy farm and the most I ever did was shoot squirrels."

Despite their very unimpressive jobs in the Army, they both got their chance to "get some" in Iraq in late 2004. They'd been out moving equipment from one location to the next, and one of the vehicles ahead ran over an IED.

The battalion had been given orders to engage in what was termed '360-degree rotational fire' upon detonation of any IED that damaged the convoy. That meant that they had license to shoot anything and everything in a 360-degree arc around the convoy.

While Elliott drove, he grabbed a gun and shot his first Iraqi — a citizen standing at the side of the road, smoking a cigarette. With the gunfire going off all around him, he shot another and another.

"I got three motherfuckers," he told Elliott in an excited voice, his hands shaking.

It felt good.

"Next time, you drive, and I'll shoot," Elliott replied, angry that he didn't get to kill anyone.

"Deal," he replied, eager to get in some more killing as soon as possible.

It was also in Iraq that he got his first taste of illicit sex.

Most of the time, soldiers were on lockdown in their bases, stuck in their hot tents, eating MREs and being homesick while they waited for something to happen. There was nothing to do but play around with each other and there was a clandestine scene of sex in the showers, sex at night behind the latrines. Sex between men who usually preferred women, and sex between men and female soldiers for whatever money they could spare — if they had any. For rations, if they didn't.

It was then he heard about officers going into town on some 'mission' that the rest of the unit didn't need to know about.

They were secretly going in to take advantage of the local prostitutes.

A man had to get some relief and there were very poor peasants in the towns and villages in Iraq who needed money, now that the economy had tanked. There were many girls who helped their families by turning tricks with the US military.

He wasn't interested in the girls.

That had never been his thing. There were, however, boys he would be happy to pay for sex. There were several in the small desert villages who were more than willing to take some US dollars in exchange for sex and hung around the convoy when it had stopped one night outside a village because of repairs.

He met one of the boys behind the latrines after midnight. Before one even started servicing him, the boy called out to another, and they tried to rob him. He was fast, despite having his pants down to his ankles, and was able to stab the first boy before the second could react. The boy's eyes were huge. The boy fell to his knees and prayed for his life, but that only made him angrier.

That boy died as well with a quick thrust of his knife into the boy's chest. Then, he took them both, one after the other, in the darkness behind the latrine, using their dead bodies in a way that he had dreamed about again and again.

That was the first time he'd mixed sex and death, and when it happened, he knew it wouldn't be his last.

Then, he'd been sent back to Afghanistan and that was the end of his chance to shoot unarmed civilians.

Forced to drive endless miles across the desert of Afghanistan, without any chance of combat, he drank too much, and withdrew even more from his fellow soldiers. He missed Elliott and felt like he had no purpose any longer.

When his chance came, he did not re-enlist, and instead, went back to the USA and his old home in Washington State.

He'd killed five civilians in Iraq. That was it.

Hardly anything to brag about.

But it was in the darkness behind the latrine that he came into his own, so to speak.

Death and sex. In that order.

At the end of his first deployment, with an honorable discharge under his belt, he went back to college, this time on the VA, and studied Criminal Justice with the goal of finishing an associate degree and going to police college. He still had a burning desire to kill bad guys, and he figured one way to accomplish that was to become a cop. He wanted to work in the big city, maybe in Vice, where he'd get the chance to go after the worst of the worst — drug dealers, pimps, and other criminals in gangs. Lowlifes who had nothing better to do than take drugs, have sex, and steal for a living.

Instead, he ended up on the Washington State Patrol, driving endless miles like he had in Iraq and Afghanistan, pulling over speeders and drunk drivers. He figured he'd work as a Highway Patrol officer for a few years and apply to go into something more dangerous — and more exciting. He'd apply to a smaller police force first, and then, he'd work his way up to the Seattle PD.

That was his five-year plan.

It was during his time on Highway Patrol that he learned the highways and roads of Washington State. He worked several counties, including King, Pierce, Thurston, and Lewis. He got to know them like the back of his hand — isolated roads used by locals, abandoned buildings on remote acreages. Good places to take someone and use them, bury them so that no one ever found them.

The kids were unaware of how at risk they were — how easy it was to pull up to a couple of young boys riding their bikes on the back roads, show them his badge, and take them somewhere they wouldn't be able to escape.

Yes, the small towns and woodlands along the Interstate and on the secondary highways were prime hunting grounds.

And he was in the mood for some hunting...

CHAPTER 6

KAYLA WOKE up in the middle of the night and it was so cold.

She shivered and huddled down beneath the filthy blanket she shared with Chris, her boyfriend, a year her junior. They lived in a cardboard box. The hastily constructed lean-to was located under a bridge near the I-405 Expressway, the constant stream of vehicles a hum that interrupted her sleep.

Chris put his arm around her and pulled her closer. "Come here," he said, and she nestled in closer to him, his warmth barely penetrating her ski jacket. "Couple of hours and the sun will rise, and it'll be warmer."

She nodded, and closed her eyes, trying to fall back to sleep, but soon, the ache in her body became more insistent.

"I'm sick," she said. "I need something. Don't you have any left?"

Chris rustled around in the plastic bags beside him, searching.

"No, we finished it off. You'll just have to wait."

She squeezed her eyes shut and tried to think of something pleasant. In her mind's eye, she remembered a time long before everything went to shit, and she lived with her family in a nice house in the suburbs of Seattle. The whole family, including Grandma and Grandpa, went to Florida for Christmas vacation one year, and she remembered the white sand beaches and clear blue water. She drifted in that memory for a while, but soon, the ache was back, and she knew if she didn't get something soon, she'd start feeling really sick.

She sat up and rubbed her eyes, tears starting. "I need something. I'm going to the street, see what I can get."

If she had to, she could turn a trick, get some cash, get some smack, get straight.

"Don't," he said, grabbing her arm. "I told you, it's dangerous out there. Several girls have gone missing lately. You read about it. Let me go."

He sat up and scrubbed his face with his hands, smoothing back his ratty hair. "I'll go see if John has anything he wants me to do, and I'll get you some, okay? I told you I'd look after you, and I meant it."

"I need it soon," she said, feeling more desperate by the minute. "I can't wait long. If you're not back here in an hour, I'll go myself."

"I'll be working downtown. Come to find me first, before you do anything." He took her by the shoulders and leaned in, his eyes meeting hers. "Promise me you won't go out unless you come to me first. You know where John hangs. Come and find me."

"Okay," she said and rubbed her nose. "But I can't wait long. I'm sick."

"I know," he said and kissed her briefly. "I'll be fast. I promise."

With that, Chris crawled out from under the cardboard lean-to, adjusted his clothes, then grabbed his backpack. "Give me forty-five minutes. An hour, tops."

He gave her a crooked smile and she knew it was forced, but he always tried to make her feel better about everything. He had once been so cute, and would have been a looker, if he hadn't ever started doing drugs. Now, he looked like the rotting hull of a once-beautiful ship rusting on the beach.

"Okay."

He left her to shiver under the ratty blanket. She watched him walk away from their spot beneath the bridge, and hoped he was right — that John might have something for him to sell so he could get some smack for her. Even the thought of getting her gear out and preparing to inject made her feel better. She'd do it somewhere on her ankle because she'd damaged the veins in her arms so much.

She could imagine going through the motions, and just the thought of the needle approaching her vein made her feel both relief and even more desperate.

It was hell, life between hits.

This much she did know: her life as a junkie was measured by the time between fixes. What she craved most was the bliss as the opioid warmth washed away her chronic pain and the memories of her life before the crash and the injuries that sent her on the path to become an opiate addict. She went from bliss to sick need of a fix in a shorter and shorter time span.

She tried methadone once, when she was in treatment and met Chris, but then she lived in a constant state of gray.

She preferred the brief periods of warmth, even if they were followed by gray and then sick. If she could get back that warmth enough times, she didn't care about the rest. She'd met Chris while in treatment, and together, they planned on getting straight, cleaning up, living together as ex-junkies, but that fell apart as soon as they left the youth shelter and hit the streets.

The two of them were just junkies, plain and simple. They would die young, probably of an overdose when one or both got some bad junk and OD'd.

At that point, feeling the way she felt, death would be a relief.

She checked her watch and saw that he'd been gone only fifteen minutes.

She turned over and tried to sleep, but it was a hopeless case, so she sat up and checked her cell. She was lucky that her friend Kath still let her come by now and then for a shower and to charge her phone. The cell still was on her mom's plan, so she didn't have to worry about anything except another junkie stealing it and selling it for some smack.

Chris had a cell so he could work for John. He'd get a text that John had something for Chris to sell, and that would mean they both could get right.

They'd partied a bit too hard the night before and so they ran out of supply sooner than usual. They almost always had enough left to get them both through the night.

They'd overdone it and now, she was sicker than she'd been in a while.

Maybe Kath had some money...

Kayla checked her cell, and it was still only twenty-five minutes since Chris left.

She could always go to Kath's and knock on her

window, see if Kath would lend her some money, but she could already imagine Mr. Jones standing on the porch, telling her to get lost. That had happened once or twice in the past when she'd been desperate and tried to hit up Kath for some money.

She tossed and turned on the lumpy mattress Chris had found at a dumpsite, her whole body aching now, her head pounding.

She checked her watch once more and it had been forty-five minutes.

That was it. She couldn't wait any longer. She crawled out from under the cardboard, and adjusted her coat, smoothing her hair and grabbing her own backpack which held all her gear.

She'd go find Chris and if she had to, she'd stand on the street and smile at passing motorists, in case one of them liked her looks, even as filthy and hurting as she was.

There were a lot of men who cruised the streets in the downtown area looking for a fast blowjob. She could get enough cash to keep her and Chris high for the rest of the day.

She followed the path up to the street, passing the other young women who worked the streets.

"Hey, Kayla," Naomi said, waving at her, a cig in her hand. "Haven't seen you around for a while. You quit working?"

Kayla stopped and stuck her hands in her pockets. "Hey, there." Naomi was an older woman who befriended Kayla when she found herself working that section of town. She was in her thirties, but looked as old as Kayla's grandma, with her wrinkles and bad teeth. "Got a cig you can lend me? I'm all out."

"Sure," Naomi said and handed her the pack. Kayla

took two and held them up for Naomi to see. "One for Chris, when he gets back."

"Sure," Naomi said and nodded, her eyes moving to the streets to see if anyone was stopping to check her out. She handed Kayla a lighter, and so Kayla lit up and took in a long deep drag.

Kayla had tried to quit, because cigs now cost so much that the addiction was almost more expensive than smack, but apparently, nicotine was nearly as hard to give up as heroin.

"Have you seen Chris? He went looking for John, see if he could do some work."

Naomi shook her head. "I've been busy. Haven't seen him."

"Thanks," Kayla said and held up her cigarette. "I'll make sure to pay you back."

"Sure," Naomi said, nodding.

She likely knew Kayla would do no such thing. Kayla would like to be able to pay Naomi back, but it was unlikely. Any cigs that she got would be hoarded like gold.

Kayla walked on, checking the alleys and side streets, but Chris was nowhere in sight. She stopped and talked to several of the girls who worked the strip, asking if they'd seen Chris. He was a regular on the streets, selling dope for John, and they were all addicts.

Finally, she saw John himself, leaning against the brick wall in the alley beside a laundromat. He was smoking and was checking out his cell.

"Hey, John," she said and stood beside him. "Where's Chris?"

"I have no idea," John said. "I didn't have any work for him, so he said he'd go and see if he could turn a trick, get some money."

"Oh, damn..."

Kayla's heart felt like it skipped a beat. She didn't like the idea of Chris turning tricks. He'd been beaten up before, when some trick didn't want to pay, and Chris fought back.

"Where did he say he was going?"

"The Surrey Downs Park down the street is where some of the guys go," John said, flicking his ash. "It's either that or all the way down to the Killarney Glen Park, but he said he needed to be quick, so I'd say Surrey."

"Okay," Kayla said. "You wouldn't happen to have any extra on you? I'd be happy to party with you. I'm sick."

"Nah," John said and shook his head. "I'm waiting for my supplier to come through. Nothing on me. Not even a grain of dust."

"Okay," Kayla said with a huge sigh. "See you."

She turned and went back south, towards the park. If Chris was working the area, he'd be near the public washrooms.

She threaded her way through the streets until she arrived, just as the sun was rising. The park was empty, and when she went to the public washrooms, there was no one there. There were used condoms and needles littering the area around the building, but no Chris.

Where the hell was he?

She needed to find him, fast.

If she didn't, she would have to take care of business herself. It was almost too late to turn a trick because they'd have already all gone home. That meant she would have to wait until noon, when the businessmen and workers took a lunch break and roamed the streets, looking for a little lunch time fun, cruising the streets for hookers.

She could barely function now that the ache was becoming even more intense. Maybe she could beg John for some of his junk when his supply arrived, promising him she'd work the streets for him to pay him back. She'd done that before with other suppliers, and so she headed back to where John had been standing, hoping that he was still there.

Of course, he was gone. His supply had probably arrived, and he was home, getting it ready for distribution.

She felt like crying.

CHAPTER 7

Michael knelt beside Grace and tried to see what she was pointing to.

"You see this?" she said and held a small trowel against something white that looked like a rib bone. "That's the sternal end of the fourth rib. We use that to estimate age in skeletal remains. The less microporosity present, the sharper and more distinct the apex, the younger the victim was at death. This looks to be around puberty. Definitely under eighteen. Probably closer to sixteen would be my guess, but I'll have to check out the rest of the skeleton for other signs before I can conclude with any certainty."

Michael nodded and glanced around. Grace had packaged up several items found with the remains.

"What's in those? Anything we could use for an ID?"

"Check them out. I think there was a watch with this one. You might be able to identify the remains from that if a watch was mentioned. We'll check dental records once we get the remains in the morgue, but this one doesn't have any fillings that I can see."

Michael went to where Grace had bagged up the items

found with the body. He checked one plastic bag, which was labeled 'watch' and given an ID number. It was a Timex with a big face and a vinyl strap. Looked like it would fit a young adult or large child. Beside the watch were several other bags, with scraps of clothing, and some running shoes — Air Jordans. Whoever wore the shoes was a fan of Michael Jordan, the basketball player. The shoes were a child's size seven, so the owner was either a taller twelve-year-old or a shorter sixteen-year-old. Grace thought he was pubertal, which meant he could be between twelve and fourteen.

When he returned to Seattle, he'd spend time going over the cold cases and missing persons cases from the last thirty years, with a focus on boys between the ages of ten and eighteen. Until Grace had a better idea of the age of the remains, that would at least give him somewhere to start, if the watch yielded no results and if the dental records were of no help.

"Do you have any idea of how long these bodies have been in the ground? I mean, is there a difference between the three or were they all dumped around the same time? I'm trying to get a sense of whether this was a spree killing or serial, buried over a longer period."

"Can't say until I get some idea about the soil and what the chemistry says. If we can ID the remains, we'll have a better idea so that may come first. I checked victim number four, and it has fillings, so there will be dental records."

"I understand," Michael replied, feeling impatient to get to work. "Whoever used this place to dispose of these bodies, they felt comfortable being here. They know the area. Whether they dumped these all at once or over time, they knew this place was safe enough to dig here. It's isolated. And given that the house was unoccupied for nearly two decades..." Michael shrugged. "The murders could have been taking place over twenty years."

By the time the rain stopped, Grace and her assistant were just finishing up their work on the second body. They'd uncovered the skeletal remains, taken photographs to document the positions of the bodies, bagged up all the relevant evidence including clothing and other personal items, and had taken soil samples. But there were two more bodies to go.

"We're going to have to finish this tomorrow. I'm ready for some grub," Grace said and wiped her hands on her jeans, after removing her boot coverings. "Can we find somewhere close to eat? I don't feel like waiting until we get back to Seattle." She turned to one of the local cops. "Is there somewhere with good food around here we could go to?"

The patrol officer who had been keeping control of the perimeter nodded. "McLeans up near Black Diamond is pretty good. Chicken and ribs. Good roasted potatoes."

"Sounds great," Grace said. She turned to Michael and Annie. "Care to join me?"

"I thought you'd never ask," Michael said with a smile.

On her part, Annie declined. "I've got a husband and kiddies waiting for me. See you tomorrow, bright and early."

With that, Michael and Grace drove to Black Diamond, and found McLeans restaurant on a side street off the main road. There were several trucks parked outside the diner, and Michael thought that was a good sign. The busier a place was, the better the food, or so he'd found.

"Looks like a decent place," Grace said after parking her Volvo SUV and following Michael to the front entrance. "I like these old diners. Reminds me of my grandfather, who used to take me to one in Queens."

"You're from New York?" Michael said, surprised at the news. "I would never have considered you a New Yorker."

"I've been out west most of my adult life," she replied. "I guess you lose the accent eventually."

They entered the diner and took a booth by the window overlooking the street. Each booth had one of those old-fashioned juke boxes, which displayed a series of old hits from the 50s and 60s.

"This really is retro," Grace said. "My kind of place." She smiled at Michael and opened her menu, glancing over the offerings like they were treasures.

He took his own menu and glanced at it. Typical diner fare, but he did notice some barbecue ribs and hand-cut fries that looked good.

They ordered and sat back, Grace heaving a huge sigh. "That was quite the day. Not often I get to use my forensic anthropology skills. Any day I do I consider a very good day. I realize that sounds heartless, given the circumstances, but I'd rather find these bodies and give the families some closure than not."

"I feel the same," Michael said. "But I know there will be some families who would rather not know. That way, they can keep believing that their loved one or family member will just come home or be found alive somewhere living under a new identity."

Grace shook her head. "That's no way to live. Better a cruel truth than a comfortable delusion, I always say."

Michael sighed and took a drink of the ice water with lemon that was on the table. "Some people would disagree. I happen to feel the same, but then, I don't have someone missing in my life. Who knows how I'd feel if I did. I might prefer the comfortable delusion."

"True, but not me, and I have."

Michael frowned. "You have someone missing?"

She nodded. "Had. They eventually found him, but he was missing for years. That's a large part of why I do what I do. My cousin Chuck — Charles — went missing when we were kids. A group of us neighborhood kids were playing in a park. One minute he was there and the next, he was just gone. His bike and everything. No body found for five whole years." She rubbed her face and then took in a deep breath. "My aunt held out hope that he was kidnapped by someone who wanted a child, but that was crazy. No one kidnaps a boy of his age unless it's for some perverted sexual sadist reason."

"What happened to him?"

"Abducted, raped, murdered, buried in the dirt crawl-space of a house, discovered when the house was renovated. Him along with a half dozen other boys. You might have heard of the killer — Jack McBride. The Crawlspace Killer from the 70s."

Michael nodded. He knew pretty much every child serial killer in US history. "I know the case. I didn't know one of his victims was a relative of yours. So, is that why you went into forensic anthropology?"

She shrugged. "I was fascinated by how the medical examiner determined how long the bodies were buried, and who they were. I had initially thought I'd be a paleontologist, and study dinosaur bones, but then, when my cousin was murdered, I decided to become a pathologist and be a medical examiner. The rest, as they say, is history." She gave Michael a smile and dug into her plate of ribs after the waitress placed them on the table in front of her.

Michael watched Grace, smiling at how she attacked her ribs with clear gusto.

He really liked Grace. She was a true character. Smart. Competent. Sense of humor.

Someone who could be a mentor to him.

When dinner was finished, they went their separate ways, and Michael drove back to Seattle, his mind working to consider his next moves in figuring out the cases he had picked up due to the four new sets of remains unearthed at the site near Deep Lake. He'd probably return to watch Grace finish recovering the two sets of skeletal remains the next morning. Police would continue examining the yard with ground penetrating radar on the off chance there were more bodies.

He'd go over the Andy Owens cold case file and that of his friend, Nick Dixon, see what he could find, maybe set up interviews with the witnesses and family who were still available. He'd spend time looking at the forensic evidence and the police reports and talk with the detectives who were initially involved in the case before it was closed.

He arrived home just before eleven and found Tess still up and sitting at her desk, her laptop open. She smiled when she saw him and got up, removing her earbuds.

"Sorry, I didn't hear you come in," she said and went to the front entry, taking his briefcase from him while he removed his shoes and jacket. "I was sitting in on a livestream of some web sleuths talking about the case you're working on."

"Andy Owens?" Michael said with a frown. "They're already talking about it?"

"Yes," Tess said and followed him to the kitchen where he grabbed a glass and some ice for a cold drink of water. "Detectives contacted the family and the youngest son, who's been involved in the web sleuth community, started a thread to discuss the latest findings. It's out there."

Michael shook his head. "News travels fast. Bad news the fastest, or so they say."

"That it does." Tess sat at the kitchen island, her arms resting on the counter. "Well? What did your day of digging with the amazing Dr. Grace Keller result in? Anything juicy you can tell me?"

Michael chuckled. "Maybe I should ask you, since you were on the live stream."

She shrugged. "According to Andy's brother Tom, you found a bracelet from World Wildlife Foundation that identified Andy. Also, there was evidence found that the death was not accidental. That's all the family knows. Tom also said that there were three other bodies found at the site."

"They're going to bring in ground penetrating radar tomorrow and check to see if there are more bodies buried in the undeveloped lot next to the owner's homestead. He just bought the lot and was taking the fence and cedar hedge down when the excavator unearthed the bones. Who knows how many bodies we'll find?"

Tess made a face of pain. "I checked NamUS today. In King County alone, I found eight boys aged twelve to seventeen who are missing in the past two decades. Maybe you'll finally be able to bring some closure and some justice to the families."

Michael went to Tess and kissed her; glad she understood and shared his passion. "That's my hope. I'm heading up to hit the sack. I have an early morning. You still on the livestream?"

"Yes, it's still going strong. I'll be up when it's done."

"Okay. Good night. You can fill me in on all the juicy details over coffee in the morning."

Tess nodded and went back to her laptop, slipping on

the ear buds so she could continue listening to the livestream.

Michael went to the bedroom, tired after a long day of watching, waiting, and wondering how many more bodies they'd find after the ground penetrating radar was used and just who had been killing young teenage boys for the past decade.

Maybe even longer.

CHAPTER 8

FOURTEEN-YEAR-OLD BEN COLE HAD BEEN WAITING AT the skatepark for the past fifteen minutes, eager for his best friend Aaron to arrive and for the two of them to take the trail deeper into the park so they could smoke the joint he'd managed to sneak from his older brother Cam's backpack.

Cam would freak when he found one joint missing, but he had a job and steady money. He could buy pot whenever he felt like it and smoke as much of it as he wanted. A joint here and there was no big deal.

At least, that's what Ben told himself.

It wasn't like Cam didn't sneak their parent's alcohol on occasion.

In fact, years earlier when Cam was Ben's current age, Ben had seen Cam and his friends sneaking vodka from the bottle in the basement bar and replacing the liquid with water.

"Dad won't notice," Cam had said when Ben found him in the bathroom refilling the bottle with water one night when their parents were out at a concert in Portland overnight and Cam had his friends over for a party. "He drinks the vodka with 7 Up and ice."

"You're going to get in trouble if he finds out."

"He won't. I've been doing it for the past year, and he hasn't noticed."

Ben reasoned that Cam wouldn't miss a joint. There were seven in the small metal Altoids container that Cam carried around with his rolling papers. He'd probably be so drunk or stoned when he went to get a joint that he'd forget how many he'd rolled.

Ben hoped so. Whatever. He'd deal with it and remind his older brother about all the vodka he'd pilfered over the years.

That would shut him up.

Finally, Aaron arrived at the skatepark, driving his own BMX bike, his helmet on and a black backpack carrying whatever he could scrounge from his kitchen pantry for them to munch on. His parents were well-off compared to Ben's and so they always had extra-large bags of nacho chips and salsa, plus popcorn and other treats. The two of them would smoke some pot, maybe drink whatever alcohol Aaron could find, and then munch down before riding back to Aaron's place where Ben would spend the night.

"There you are," Ben said. "What took you?"

"I took some extra booze. My dad only had dark rum and some of this cherry brandy," he said with a face of disgust, "so when I put the water in to replace it, the color changed. I had to improvise. I put some Red Bull in and that made the color better." Aaron shrugged. "I doubt they'll notice. Dad said he was going to the liquor store to get some new stuff, so they probably don't drink dark rum very often."

"What does it taste like?" Ben asked as the two took the trail deeper into the forest.

"Like poison, but who cares? Weed smells like a skunk's ass and you still smoke it."

They drove for a while and then emerged onto a secondary road that snaked through the park and led to the Newcastle Highlands Forest Park.

They took a secondary road and then parked their bikes a dozen feet away in a clearing. They could watch the road from where they sat and had a good view of the huge houses in the distance.

"My brother says this is where the wealthy people live," Aaron said when he passed the bottle of dark rum and coke to Ben.

"Your family's wealthy compared to mine," Ben replied. He took a mouthful from the bottle and squinted at the taste. The coke almost masked the flavor of the dark rum — almost. Not quite. He washed it down with some Red Bull.

Ben removed the joint from his pocket and licked it all over as he had seen his brother do. Then, he took out the black Bic lighter and lit the end, sucking in the smoke and then coughing immediately.

He'd smoked a joint before and had the same initial trouble with having smoke in his lungs, but he was determined to persist.

He wanted to get high.

"Here, give me that," Aaron said. Aaron had more experience and was able to take in a big lungful of smoke and hold it in for a few seconds before coughing it out. "That's some good shit," Aaron said.

Ben tried once more to take in a big toke, but he had childhood asthma, and his lungs were hinky. He coughed and coughed until his eyes watered.

"You better stick to the rum." Aaron handed the bottle to him, taking the joint away from Ben.

"No, I can do it. Just gotta practice," Ben said with a smile.

Aaron laughed. "Yeah, right."

Ben tried again and had the exact same result — coughing the smoke out of his lungs before it had a chance to saturate his blood with THC.

He'd never get high that way.

They heard the crunch of feet on the gravel path and realized someone was coming towards them on the pathway. They both hunkered down, trying to be quiet, but of course, Ben had just taken in some smoke and had to cough no matter what.

"Quiet," Aaron hissed and took the joint away from Ben, tapping it out and stuffing the rest of the joint into his pocket. He hid the bottle in his backpack.

From the path emerged a Washington State Patrol police officer, his hands on his hips. He had a broad face, longish dark hair, and was wearing dark sunglasses, his hair poking out from under the patrol hat. A black KN95 mask covered the bottom of his face.

"What are you two boys doing? I smell cannabis..."

"Nothing, officer, honestly," Aaron said. "We were just resting after biking over here from Newcastle."

"I'm going to have to ask you both to stand up. I suspect that you're in possession of some cannabis and are not permitted given your age. I also smell alcohol and suspect that you may be drinking underage. You both should also be in school, so we can add truancy to that list. I have to search you both."

Aaron glanced at Ben; his eyes wide.

"Fu-u-uck," he muttered under his breath.

"Come stand over here on the path," the patrol officer said and pointed to the path where he stood. Ben complied and glanced over to the road, where he saw a black patrol car parked, the engine still running.

The officer took the two backpacks from them and searched through. He found the bottle of dark rum and coke and removed the lid, sniffing the contents.

"That's alcohol," the officer said. "I'm going to have to search you both. Put your hands on top of your head and spread your legs."

The boys both complied and stood silently while the officer ran his hands over their bodies, checking their pockets for contents. The officer seemed to take a long time searching Ben, his hands roving over Ben's body in a way that creeped him out, lingering over his crotch. The cop stood too close, pressing his body against Ben and it felt really sexual.

He moved to Aaron and Ben could see he was getting a little too familiar with him, too.

The cop found the half-smoked joint in Aaron's shirt pocket.

"What's this?" he asked and held the joint up in front of Aaron's face. "I'm going to have to arrest you both for possession of cannabis while underage. Place your hands behind your back."

At that, Aaron complied, and the officer cuffed him, Aaron's hands behind his back.

Ben didn't want to be handcuffed or arrested. He took off running.

"Hey!" the officer shouted and chased him. Ben thought he might be able to outrun the much larger cop, but he was wrong, and the man grabbed Ben, throwing him down on the ground.

"Think you can get away, do you?" the officer said, his face next to Ben's, which was crushed into the dried leaves on the forest floor. "Think again, asshole. Now, I can add resisting arrest to the list of crimes you're going to be charged with."

Again, he lay on top of Ben, pressing his hips into Ben's ass. It was clearly sexual.

He dragged Ben up and pushed him over to the police car but found that Aaron was gone.

The cop cuffed Ben and locked him in the cruiser and took off, running into the forest. When he came back, he was alone.

"Where's Aaron? Where are you taking me? Can I call my parents?"

But the officer didn't respond. Ben thought that the cop would radio in that he was bringing in a suspect, but strangely, the cop didn't use his radio at all.

"Where are we going?"

"None of your goddamn business." The cop went into the trunk and then came to the back seat where Ben was sitting. He had a roll of duct tape in his hand.

"What are you doing?"

"Shut the fuck up."

Then, to his surprise, the cop ripped off a length of duct tape and used it to cover Ben's mouth. He then pulled Ben out of the vehicle and stuffed him in the trunk.

Ben struggled, but what could he do? The man zip-tied Ben's ankles together.

It was then Ben realized that the cop wasn't going to take him to the local police station, which wasn't too far from where he'd been picked up. All the sexual touching was exactly that.

The man was a pedo.

Instead of going to the police station, the car drove south on the Interstate. Ben knew because he could hear cars zipping by them.

He was fucked...

CHAPTER 9

EARLY THE NEXT MORNING, GRACE KELLER BENT OVER the freshly turned earth and surveyed the scene in front of her. In a deep hole in the earth where a cedar hedge had once stood were the remains of a young boy, who was perhaps ten to fourteen years old, based on the length of the femur and the state of the ribs.

She would collect the skeletal remains and take them to the morgue, where she would conduct a more thorough analysis of the remains and what story they would tell about the time and manner of death. It had taken hours to carefully remove the dirt and garbage that was piled on top of the bodies, so Grace could expose the skeletal remains and clothing, take photographs, and then collect the bones and samples of the surrounding earth for examination in the lab.

With all four bodies at the site, it was painstaking. She wanted to preserve as much of the physical evidence as possible so that the police could do their work. She also wanted to be able to see how each body had been placed before being covered over. That could tell the police something about the relationship — if any — between the dead and the killer. Grace knew that a killer who felt guilt would often cover the face and place the body in a respectful position. If the killer was a psychopath who took pleasure in hurting his victims — and it was almost always a man — the killer would either pose the body in some grotesque and often sexual position to show his disdain, or he would carelessly dump the body and not care how it fell.

Because of that, Grace took extreme care when uncovering the skeletal remains. Unfortunately, the excavator had disturbed the first and second bodies when using the front-end loader, but only a few bones had been disturbed, their actual location changed. The rest of the skeletons had been pretty much undisturbed, so she could photograph the remains and police would have a better idea of the killer's MO.

These bodies had been dumped unceremoniously into the ground and then covered with dirt and garbage. In other words, the killer had no relationship to the dead except for the fact that he killed them.

Grace pondered the darkness that some humans were capable of while she worked to unearth the young man's remains.

Not long after, Michael Carter arrived and came to stand beside her, two cups of coffee in hand.

"Got this for you," he said and held up one of the cups. "Your favorite."

"You're a godsend," Grace said and stood up, removing her gloves and mask, and then taking the coffee. It was delicious, and so she took a break, having a few sips.

"What have you found out about the first two sets of remains?" she asked, curious about the police work.

"The first boy was definitely Andy Owens."

Grace shook her head and sighed. "Well, at least there's closure, although I'm sure the parents were probably wishing he'd been taken and kept alive somewhere." She shrugged and then stepped back to the excavation and put her cup of coffee down. She replaced her mask and gloves and picked up a trowel, continuing to remove the dirt and muck from around the skeleton.

On his part, Michael seemed happy to just watch as she photographed the remains once they had been completely exposed.

"Look at how the body was just dumped face down in the dirt," she said and sat back on her knees. "Like trash. There were old food containers and empty plastic bottles and other junk on top of the body. The killer didn't know the victim, right?"

"Most likely not," Michael replied, his voice soft. "Most of the victims who were killed by someone close to them show more reverence for the dead body. They might fold the victim's hands, place them on their back or in a fetal position, depending on the situation. They might cover the face. Adjust the clothing if there was a sexual assault involved."

"This one appears to have been sexually assaulted," Grace replied. "The pants are down around the ankles, the belt unbuckled."

"Most likely," Michael replied. "We're talking about a violent pedophile who prefers pubescent boys aged ten to fourteen. I checked and there's at least eight boys in that age range missing over the past two decades from King County alone."

"Spread far enough apart to not raise any suspicions of a serial killer, am I right?"

"Correct," Michael said. "Which suggests that our killer is smart and has some idea of how to escape detection. We ID'd the other boy— Peter Cummings — thirteen, from Renton. Went missing three years after Andy and Nick. Different part of King County. Whoever the killer is, he felt comfortable returning to this property to dump the bodies."

"He must have known that the house was unoccupied. It's pretty remote. At night, no one would notice if you drove into the yard and parked. You can't see inside from the road."

"Exactly. He knew what he was doing. Smart. The worst kind. A stupid killer will get caught soon after. A cunning killer can escape detection sometimes for decades."

Grace sighed and took a photo of the remains now that they were fully exposed.

Her knees ached, and she adjusted her position. "Looks like there was a broken right arm on this body, old fracture, healed. That should help in identifying him."

"Old fracture on his right arm?" Michael repeated.

"Yes, you can see here," Grace said and lifted a bone from the boy's arm. "The radius and ulna were both broken near the wrist, suggesting quite a fall." She held the bones up for Michael to view. He bent down and frowned as he examined the bones. "I've seen this on skateboarders. It's quite common. This boy might have been a skateboarder."

"That should help ID him."

Grace stood and stretched out her aching knees. Then, she motioned to Annie to come over and finish packing up the remains. She moved to the other excavation site and began the work all over again with the new body.

She took a photo of the ground where the fourth body

had been unearthed. This one had been done with more care when Annie took a shovel and gingerly dug down until she hit something hard. It was an old tin can, and beneath it was more garbage and then, some rotting fabric that suggested a body. Grace placed the blocks of rubber on the ground on which she would kneel and then bent down, adjusting herself until she was comfortable.

Then she began digging, using a specially designed trowel and paint brush to remove the dirt and debris from the remains a little at a time. She paused when she got close to the bones and took several samples of the dirt closest to the remains so she could get some idea of the chemical composition.

That would help determine approximately how long the body had been buried.

What she knew of the Andy Owens case was that he and his friend had gone missing a decade earlier. This body looked to be newer than that. Grace could tell by the amount of adipocere and the state of the tendons and ligaments, which were the last to decay. Depending on the type of soil the bodies had been buried in, complete decay of the skeleton would take up to twenty years.

This body had been buried less than two years.

Like Andy, this boy had been dumped face down, like he was nothing more than trash. Like Andy, the boy's jeans were pulled down to his ankles. His feet were bare and there were no running shoes in the grave. There was also nothing on his torso, so he might have been shirtless when dumped. There was still some hair on the skull.

"This one's pretty recent," Grace said, avoiding the word she would have used — fresh. "There's still hair. Longer, dark. Thick hair. He was killed in the past two years. Maybe the past year, given the state of the hair."

"Good to know," Michael said and entered some info into his iPad. "I'll check my missing persons cases for the past couple of years and see who his age was reported missing." While Grace watched, Michael swiped on his iPad, obviously checking some documents on it. "Here we go. Here's one possible." He read something to himself and then shook his head. "Daniel Moore, thirteen. From Tacoma. Went missing after visiting a skatepark." He sighed heavily. "Jesus. My boys live in Tacoma. They skateboard."

Michael glanced up at the sky, and Grace felt bad for him. He'd been part of the FBI's Child Abduction Rapid Deployment team for the Western Region. He'd quit because of the trauma of failing to find and save children who had been kidnapped by strangers.

The current case would be hard for him.

Grace continued her work uncovering the remains, photographing each step in the process, and taking samples when she could. When the body was fully uncovered, she took a final photo and then stood, stretching her aching legs and back.

"Well, that's it for me unless the guys find signs of more bodies," she said to Michael who was reading something on his iPad. "Frankly, I haven't unearthed this many since I started this work. This is the biggest crime scene for me since I started working for King County. The most was three people who died in a fire and building collapse back in 2014."

"I remember that," Michael said. "They thought the building was empty, but there were some homeless people living in it."

"Yes," Grace said. "We went in to check just in case and found three sets of remains."

"Not a good record to break."

"No, it isn't," Grace replied. "I hope the guys don't find any more."

For the rest of the morning, Grace helped Alice package up the bones and document the soil samples. By noon, she was hungry and ready to go back to the morgue.

"I'm heading out if you're done. The guys don't seem to have any other remains to dig up," Michael said as he got into his Range Rover. "I'll be by later to watch you do your magic."

"I look forward to it," Grace said and removed her white coveralls and protective gear.

She watched as Michael drove off and then got in her own vehicle.

It was going to be an interesting afternoon, going over the bones to see what there was to see.

Maybe they'd find something to identify the two remaining victims and figure out what kind of monster they were dealing with.

He was a monster — of that there could be no doubt. He raped and strangled the young boys, then dumped their bodies in the wet earth, covering them up with garbage and soil. Then, he'd replanted the cedars that grew over the spot, making it appear as if nothing had ever happened.

It took a certain kind of evil to carry out that kind of task...

CHAPTER 10

Michael drove back to Seattle, his mind working on the new cases that Grace had unearthed that morning.

Two more boys, both under age eighteen by the size of their bones and other bone markers, according to Grace Keller.

He'd grab lunch and then read over the missing persons cases from the last few years and see who was missing and what kind of info was in their files to see if there was anything to identify the remains, such as broken bones, fillings, and other characteristics. He knew that one boy had a broken right arm, likely from some fall. He also knew that one of the boys had fillings in several adult teeth.

There were some items of clothing with the remains that could also be used to help ID the other victims. One of the boys had a leather belt with an intricate belt buckle. That would be useful, and so he hoped the files contained rich detail of what the boys were wearing when they went missing so he could compare and hopefully, identify the remains as quickly as possible.

He felt a vague sense of unease as he arrived back in

Seattle. He drove to a local coffee shop drive-through and ordered a sandwich and coffee. Then, he went to the office and parked his vehicle, bag of lunch and fresh coffee in hand. The sun was now shining, the clouds parting as the system of rain passed out of the region, but his mood was not sunny.

It was too close to home that one of the sets of remains potentially belonged to Daniel Moore from Tacoma. The boy had been last seen at a skateboard park. If he was the body at the Deep Lake site, he was murdered and probably sexually assaulted based on the position of the body and the fact the boy's jeans had been pulled down around his ankles when he was unceremoniously dumped in a pile of trash.

Why the trash?

Had he buried the bodies in trash to confound anyone searching using ground penetrating radar?

That suggested someone who knew quite a bit about hiding bodies.

What else it suggested, Michael wasn't sure.

Disdain for his victims?

Was he making a statement that the boys were trash?

When Michael arrived at the building, he was one of the few people at work since most of the staff were working from home. Only a few were there — the security guard at the front, a KN95 mask on, a bottle of hand sanitizer at his side.

"Hey, Steve," Michael said after slipping on his own KN95 mask to sign in. "Pretty quiet today?"

"You said it," Steve replied and took the clipboard back. The administration was keeping track of everyone who entered and left the building in case they needed info to track cases of Covid.

When the pandemic first struck, Michael was hesitant

to go into work but had decided that his work required he spend as much time as possible in the archives, poring over old cold cases and missing persons cases. With so few people in the building, he felt pretty safe to go into the office.

He took the elevator to his office and spread out his lunch on the desktop after switching on his computer and logging in. While he ate, he read emails and reviewed the files that someone had forwarded him on a case he'd asked about from a neighboring county.

When his phone rang, he was just finishing up his sandwich, and so he hastily swallowed and answered.

"Michael Carter," he said, wiping his mouth with a napkin.

"Hey, Michael, this is Detective Joe Mendez from King County Sheriff's Office, how are you?"

"Hey, Joe," Michael replied, smiling as he thought about the round-faced detective. "I'm fine, all things considered. What's up?"

"State Patrol just found a boy, aged fourteen, running along one of the roads bordering Newcastle Highlands Park. Get this: he claims a cop stopped him and his friend while they were in the woods smoking some pot. The cop handcuffed him and the other boy. The kid ran and managed to get away. He says he doesn't know where his friend is, and when we checked, there were no reports of any boys his age being arrested or brought in for questioning. When we found him, he was still handcuffed and pretty scuffed up. Apparently, he fell numerous times trying to escape the man, and cut himself up badly on thorns and fallen trees. We have officers searching the area for the vehicle, which the boy says appeared to be an unmarked police patrol car."

"He was handcuffed?" Michael's pulse rate increased. "Newcastle Park?"

"Yes," Joe replied. "The two boys live in Newcastle just west of the park and skate there regularly. Only, State Patrol had no unmarked patrol cars in the vicinity, and no officers wearing the kind of uniform the boy described because we updated them in the past decade, so the uniform was old. Seems like we got someone posing as a State Patrol officer trying to abduct boys. I knew you used to work on the CARD Team with the FBI, so I figured I'd call you. You're on that cold case task force, right?"

"I did and I am," Michael said with a sigh. "Sounds like we need to call the Feds."

"Already did," Joe replied. "Their guys are down in California on another case, and everyone else is busy right now. Maybe you want to come down to our office in Bellevue and talk to the boy. I know you did this work, and so it would be useful to have your input, if you're available, at least until the Feds can send someone."

Michael glanced at his watch. It would take fifteen minutes to get there if he left right away.

"I'll be there in twenty, give or take."

"Great. See you soon."

Michael ended the call and leaned back.

He'd left the FBI several years earlier because he found working the cases to be too hard on him. Few stranger abductions of children ended well, and these boys were close to the same age as Michael's oldest boy, Connor. Part of him wanted to turn down the request. He had every right to do so but given that the Feds were delayed getting agents out to the scene because of workload and Covid, Michael felt honor-bound to go and help.

At least until the Feds had someone available, but that might be — was probably — too late.

He took out his cell to call Tess and let her know. He dialed the number and exhaled heavily, sure that she would be wary of him becoming involved.

Still, he couldn't sit idly by knowing that every moment counted when it came to missing children, especially those abducted by strangers.

When she answered, he considered his words. "Hey, I'm heading to Bellevue to assist with a case that King County Sheriff's Office has. It's to interview a young boy whose friend was abducted by someone posing as a State Patrol officer. The boy escaped, but his friend is missing. I got a call from Bellevue because the Feds can't send anyone until later and that might be too late."

"They're lucky they have you," she said, her voice sounding hesitant. "Are you sure you should go?"

"I really can't say no." He gathered up his files and stuffed them in his briefcase, his cell to his ear. He stopped in the hallway next to the elevator. "Both our agents are down in California working an active case and it will take hours for another team to get here. Maybe not till later tonight."

"As long as you're sure..."

"I'll be fine. If I sit by and do nothing, I'll feel worse."

"Okay. Let me know how it's going — whatever you can tell me of course."

"I will."

He ended the call and took the elevator down to the lobby.

Steve was reading a newspaper when Michael approached the front desk. "You gone already?"

"Got a possible child abduction case down in Bellevue and they want my advice."

"Oh, Jeeze..." Steve shook his head. "Take care."

"I will," Michael said as he signed the sheet. He handed the clipboard back to Steve. "See you later or maybe tomorrow, depending on how it goes."

Steve touched his forehead in a salute. "Good luck."

Michael nodded and then left the building, wondering what he'd find when he got to Bellevue.

THE DRIVE TOOK ABOUT fifteen minutes, and when Michael arrived at the King County Sheriff's mobile field office in Bellevue, he went through the same routine of putting on his mask and signing in, thanking the officer at the front desk for the fresh mask.

"We're asking everyone to use them," the officer said. "Cases are really rising this week."

"I'm happy to comply." Michael slipped the fresh mask on and threw his old one in the trash bin beside the front desk. The King County Prosecutor's Office made sure they had enough in stock for workers to use fresh ones daily or when they went to a new venue, but he was happy to use one of the new masks provided.

He was met at the elevator by Detective Mendez, a man in his late thirties, with a shaved head and dark piercing eyes under thick dark eyebrows. Mendez wore a mask as well, but Michael could tell he was smiling by the crinkle around his eyes.

"Welcome to our humble abode," Mendez said and ushered Michael into the elevator. "Sorry to drag you from your work, but this would be a big help if you could talk to the boy and see what you can get out of him, what you think our next steps should be."

"I'm happy to help," Michael replied, although he was quite hesitant to get too involved. If all he did was offer advice and left the rest to the detectives, it would be fine.

They went to a meeting room at the rear of the building where young Aaron Baker was waiting. Aaron, fourteen, was a skinny kid with a mop of black hair and hazel eyes. The boy had been seen by the local ER and had his scrapes and cuts bandaged. Other than that, he had a haunted expression in his eyes over the mask on his face.

He knew his friend was in danger and that he was lucky he escaped.

Aaron looked like he could be an older version of Connor, dressed as he was in a black jacket, t-shirt with a Punisher image, jeans, and black boots. Typical attire. Beside him sat a man who looked like he'd just been taken off a construction site, wearing work clothes and a reflecting vest. Mendez introduced him as Aaron's father, Ted Baker.

"Hi, Mr. Baker. Aaron," Michael said and sat across from the boy. "My name is Michael Carter and I'm an Investigator with King County."

"Hello," Tom Baker said, his voice somewhat muffled by the mask. Beside him, Aaron sat up like he had just woken up.

"Hello," Aaron said, his voice cracking like he had only recently gone through puberty. He was scrawny and looked younger than fourteen.

"I worked with the FBI's Child Abduction Rapid Deployment team before I worked for King County, so I'm here to talk to you, see what information you can provide us while we wait for the FBI to arrive."

Aaron nodded, his arms crossed over his chest.

"What I want you to do is walk me through everything that happened from the time you first saw the man who took Ben to when you were picked up. I know you've already done this, but if you wouldn't mind going over it again, in as much detail as you can remember, it would really help me understand."

"You're one of those FBI profilers?"

Michael shook his head. "We all train on profiling unknown subjects, but we're not all profilers. The team I worked on went to locations where a child under eighteen was abducted by a stranger, to see if we could find them as soon as possible. The more information we have from you now, the better. Everything you can remember is critical to helping find Ben."

Aaron sighed and stole a glance at his father. "We skipped classes for the morning and were smoking some weed when we heard someone in the forest. It was a tall man, kinda fat, wearing a blue police uniform. He had on a hat and a mask. I saw a badge on his shirt and a yellow patch on his shoulder. He looked legit."

Michael nodded to encourage the boy to continue. "What did he say to you?"

"He asked us what we were doing. Said he could smell cannabis and that we had to come with him to his vehicle. It was a black Ford sedan with a dark interior. It looked like it had lights on the dashboard. He was wearing a uniform but was in an unmarked car. I thought only undercover cops used those. You know, it had a black thing on the front fender, like you'd use to ram something, so I knew it was a cop car."

For the next half-hour, Michael sat with the boy and asked questions, going over every detail. He placed some images of unmarked police vehicles being used by the

Highway Patrol and Aaron identified one in particular. It would allow them to track which vehicles from the Highway Patrol had been retired and junked or sold.

The boy then worked with a sketch artist to draw an image of the man which would be used to help identify the perpetrator. They would use it in a police bulletin and Amber Alert as well as any press conference on the case.

When he could tell the boy was getting tired and frustrated, Michael ended the interview, thanking Aaron and his father for their patience.

"You'll probably be asked all these questions again when the FBI arrives, but it will really help us get started looking for Ben, so thank you."

Mr. Baker stood and shook Michael's hand. "We're only too happy to help. I hope you find him. He's a good boy. They're good boys and this is terrible."

"It is," Michael said. "I have two boys myself, close to this age."

Michael walked them out of the building and said goodbye, watching as Mr. Baker and Aaron walked down the sidewalk to their vehicle.

He sighed and returned to the office, his mind working on what steps they could and should do next.

CHAPTER 11

Tess spent the morning searching the online archives, reading old newspaper articles from when the boys Michael found near Deep Lake were abducted.

She should have spent the time working on her manuscript, but she found her mind was occupied with the case Michael was working. Poor Andy Owens, fourteen when he went missing a decade earlier. The discovery of his body in a plot of vacant land near Deep Lake had been made public, and Tess read an article written by her replacement in the Seattle *Sentinel*.

Part of Tess felt envy that the guy who replaced her, Cliff Freeman, wrote the piece and not her. Another part of her found it hard to go over the events that led to her book deal, writing about her time with serial killer Eugene Kincaid.

They were difficult memories, and rehashing everything that happened back in Paradise Hill had given rise to a new bout of insomnia and anxiety.

Learning that Michael was asked to act as a stand-in for

the FBI CARD Team while they found someone to take over the case only added to her anxiety.

Michael had seemed to thrive working Cold Cases and Missing Persons Cases for the King County Prosecutor's Office, in tandem with Cold Case detectives in the Seattle PD. There was still a sense of urgency in dealing with the cases but given the time that had passed between the disappearances or since the bodies had been found, Michael knew the victims were likely dead.

In other words, there was less pressure on him to find someone before the killer could murder them.

The case near Deep Lake threatened to change all that.

If there was a serial child killer still active in King County, everything changed. The sense of urgency became overwhelming.

Michael had been practicing his shooting since he recovered from the injury he received when Eugene had shot him with the crossbow, and he was improving as more time passed.

He still wasn't ready to go into the field after bad guys. He might never be, so working as a stand-in for the CARD Team wasn't good.

She knew he did it out of a sense of duty and loyalty to the Bureau.

He had to put his own health first. He'd be no good to anyone — working cold cases or in grad school doing his PhD—if he ruined his health by taking on the same kind of work that had made him leave the FBI in the first place.

She didn't want to fight him on the issue. He knew himself and his strengths and weaknesses. She had to trust him that he could handle the work.

She also knew that any case involving children was hard

for him, considering what happened with the CARD Team and the fact he had two young boys of his own.

~

SHE GOT a text from Michael later that afternoon.

MICHAEL: Sticking around here for the day and I have the autopsy tonight, so I'll be late. Spoke with the boy who escaped the abduction of his friend. Have to develop a response plan and make sure every resource is deployed to find the boy if possible.

She read over his text and chewed her bottom lip, trying to decide how to respond. Part of her wanted to tell him to come home and let the FBI respond. The other part knew that was a waste of energy and would only upset him.

TESS: This must be hard for you. If you need to talk about it, I'll wait up. They're lucky to have someone with your experience there to get the ball rolling. When is the CARD Team scheduled to arrive?

MICHAEL: Not until later tonight, so I want to make sure everything is in place. We've already lost several hours. That's critical in a case like this.

TESS: Take care of yourself, and don't drink too much coffee. I'll see you when you get home. I'll probably be up late working on the manuscript.

MICHAEL: Okay. Just wanted to let you know I'd be late.

TESS: Bye.

She put away her cell and sighed, hoping he would be able to leave the case to the Special Agents when they arrived. He might get sucked into working with them, and she worried that it would not be good for his mental health.

She turned back to her laptop and her browser, which

she used to access old news stories from the time the Andy Owens boy had gone missing, and his friend Nick had been found murdered.

Clearly there was a serial child killer at work in King County... What was it about the Pacific Northwest that seemed to produce serial killers of the most heinous kind?

Was it the gloominess of the rainy season that seemed to stretch on for weeks and weeks at a time during the winter?

Tess didn't know and thought that perhaps there really wasn't anything special about the PNW. Maybe the killers had just been more macabre. Westley Allen Dodd. The Green River Killer. BTK. Kincaid. Even Bundy. Up north just past the border into British Columbia, Canada, there was the pig farmer who killed prostitutes and ground their bodies up, feeding the meat to his pigs.

Robert Pickton.

Yes. She'd read a lot about him. There was also Clifford Olson — the "Beast of BC" who killed eleven children and sent letters to their families. Another American serial killer operating in BC was Bobby Jack Fowler, who killed up to twenty women on the Highway of Tears, as it was called, between Prince George and Prince Rupert, most of them First Nations women.

Who was this new killer? How many victims? Michael said there were four bodies found at the site, and at least one of them was from over a decade earlier.

Tess had the feeling that four would not be the final total.

She went back to the web sleuth forum and read over the latest posts on the Andy Owens case, eager to see what had been written.

One caught her eye for the sheer nastiness of it, not to mention the guy's forum handle: DIEveryone18. The forum was decent, but there were the occasional trolls there who liked to post inflammatory material to see if they could get a response from the forum regulars, who took web sleuthing very seriously. Maybe too seriously, for some.

DIEveryone18: He was probably one of those boys who got it on with other boys in the woods outside of town. He was asking for it.

The response was to be expected.

Canterbury4: Why are you here if you don't want to see justice served? Andy was just fourteen and starting his life. You should be ashamed of yourself for your homophobic rant.

There was more like that, with varying degrees of anger and attempt to shame DIEveryone18.

Finally, one of the forum moderators stepped in and shut it down.

MOD2: Victims don't ask to be raped and murdered, DIE. You violated the rules AGAIN so your latest profile will be removed like the others, and you are banned permanently from posting. We know your IP so if you want to keep shitposting, you'll have to get a VPN.

Such was life on a web forum. The regular members were a mix of the curious and dedicated, who came to learn the latest news and post their theories.

One of the most popular theories was that the two boys were taken for the sex trade, but that Nick fought back and was killed outright, while Andy was more cooperative and went to some other city — or even country — to be sold into the child sex trade.

Given what Tess knew about the pedophile rings operating around the country, she could believe that might be the case. Usually, however, the boys and girls who were taken were ones most vulnerable — coming from impoverished homes torn apart by substance abuse and violence, who were experiencing substance abuse issues themselves and were forced into the business out of necessity. They were hungry, homeless, or were hurting for their next fix or hit and were willing to do whatever it took to get it.

The young children had no choice. They were abused by adults who they depended on and who they trusted. The older children may have just graduated from passive victims to active victims because of their substance abuse issues or homelessness.

It made Tess so sad to think of them all — what kind of monsters were some humans?

Then, she thought about Eugene Kincaid, and she knew exactly what kind. Like his father, Daryl, Eugene had no empathy. He did what he wanted with no shame or remorse. People were objects to be used and thrown away when they were used up.

Eugene got away with it for so many years because he was smart enough to put up a good front, wear a mask of the good father and hard worker.

She sighed after reading another whacko theory that the discovery of his body put to rest. This theory suggested that Andy killed Nick and ran away to another city. Maybe hitchhiking and then becoming a 'rent boy' as they were called. One poster, D3vilInPNW, was a proponent of this theory.

D3vilInPNW: *I always knew he was gay. I met him once and my gaydar went off like crazy. He probably made the moves on Nick and Nick shut him down. Andy might have lost it and then did the dirty deed before running off and starting a new life somewhere else.*

The response to D3vilInPNW was very disapproving and forceful. '*Proof or it didn't happen*' was one response from a forum regular. D3vilInPNW was not backing down, nor did he provide any proof that he met Andy at any time.

D3vilInPNW: *I don't have to prove anything to you losers. I have a right to post my ideas and that's what I did. You can accept it or not. But if you remember, Nick was found with his pants down around his ankles and had been butt raped. He was fourteen, so he probably knew what he was getting into, and it went too far. That's all.*

D3vilInPNW had likewise been put on moderation, so he couldn't post any longer, but he could visit the forum.

Tess wondered if some of the shitposters and trolls weren't the same person with multiple forum handles, who just couldn't stay away. Web sleuthing could become an obsession.

She also wondered if the real killer wasn't watching the forum, and the threads that dealt specifically with the schoolboy murders, as they were being called. Whoever killed Andy and Nick, and the other boys found near Deep Lake, had so far not been caught. Or, if they had been caught, perhaps they hadn't been connected to the previous murders.

There were fewer serial killers who preyed on young boys and men, but they were out there.

There was Dennis Nilsen in the UK who killed twelve in the 1970s and 1980s. Dean Corll killed more than thirty in Houston in the 1970s. John Wayne Gacy killed thirty-three in the 1970s. More recently, there was Jeffrey Dahmer, and Larry Eyler. Not to mention Westley Allen Dodd, who killed young boys.

Given that the remains of four boys were found at the site near Deep Lake and that Andy was tied to another murder a decade earlier, Tess knew that they had a pedophile serial killer on their hands.

One who preferred young boys.

That would be hard for Michael to deal with. He'd had problems when he worked on the CARD Team. Most specifically, the last case before he took a medical leave. It had involved the abduction of a young boy, who was later found to have been murdered only hours earlier.

The killer, Blaine Lawson, was still at large, as far as Tess knew, and so Michael felt a deep sense of failure that the team had been unable to find the boy before he died, and then, the FBI team failed to find the killer and stop him.

For all Michael and the FBI knew, he was still at large, perhaps having moved somewhere else to continue his killing unabated.

Tess knew that's what motivated Michael, and kept him involved in fighting serial killers, even if now, he was doing it from deep in the police archives, one cold case at a time.

She couldn't help but join him in that fight, except for Tess, it was from a crime column in a newspaper or in the pages of her book.

CHAPTER 12

KAYLA WAITED for Chris at the lean-to. She checked her cell every five minutes, hoping for a text, but received nothing.

Where was he? Had he done some smack and was sleeping it off in some flophouse downtown?

He'd done it before, after getting an extra-large supply. He'd always promised to let her know if he was delayed, but he was just as desperate as she was.

In the end, as good as he was to her, he was still just a druggie, like her.

An addict.

Who would do almost anything for their next hit.

She took out her cell and sent him another text.

KAYLA: *Where are you? I'm sick.*

Nothing.

No response. That wasn't like him. He was always so

fast with texts, responding as soon as he heard his cell chime.

When the sun rose and he still hadn't responded, she pulled up her hood against the drizzle that seemed to perpetually fall, and started to walk the streets again, checking all the places where he had often stayed.

Maybe his cell battery was dead? Maybe that was why he hadn't contacted her. Sometimes, it took him a few hours to get some stuff for them. He had to run errands for the dealers, pick up stuff, drop stuff off. Whatever he could do, especially when he was short on cash, as he was now.

She went to every street corner where they often hung out and spoke with people who knew Chris. She talked to every hooker who was out early, standing on the streets bordering the park, looking for some money to feed their addiction, umbrellas in hand.

"Have you seen Chris?"

Nothing.

She was almost in tears when a vehicle pulled up beside her and a potential trick leaned over and looked at her from the driver's side. He rolled down the window and smiled, his eyes obscured by dark sunglasses.

"Hey, babe, how you doing?"

"Great, now," she said and pasted on a smile. If Chris had abandoned her, she'd have to take care of business herself. "You looking for some fun?"

"I surely am," he replied and patted the seat beside him. "Hop in."

She did, glancing left and right before opening the door and sitting inside. The vehicle was an old black Mercury Montego that Chris had shown her one day when a convoy of them had driven through the streets. This one had a fresh paint job and faux leather seats that looked brand new.

Whatever. If the guy could afford to buy an old car and fix it up, he had money and that was all she cared about at that point.

"What are you interested in?" she asked, giving him the once-over to see what kind of trick he was. Heavy-set, shaved head, aviator sunglasses. A nice suit, however.

He had money.

"Just a quick BJ. How much?"

She thought for a second. Usually, she charged $50, but this guy looked like he was worth a lot more.

"You a cop?"

"Do I look like a cop?"

"That's not an answer."

"I'm an investment banker. So, how much, sweetie? And how old are you?"

"How old do you want me to be?"

He smiled. "You tell me the truth, and I'll give you extra."

She hesitated, not liking the fact he was being so chatty. "I'm fifteen."

"Fifteen?" he asked, frowning. "You look eighteen at least."

"I try," she said and shrugged. "I charge $80 for a quick BJ. More if you want me to spend more time."

"You shouldn't be walking the streets," he said, reaching into his wallet. "You should be in school studying world history and biology."

"Yeah, well, that ended a while back when my parents kicked me out," she replied, reaching out to accept the four twenty-dollar bills from him.

He didn't give them to her, and then she knew he was a cop.

"You are a cop, aren't you?"

He smiled sadly. "No, I'm not a cop. I'm with a group who saves children from the streets. I'm going to take you somewhere, get you cleaned up and working in a better environment, okay? You'll get drugs, and a place to sleep, clean clothes. All you gotta do is perform and you'll be good."

She reached for the door, hoping to escape, and run down the back alley so she could avoid being abducted, but he snapped the locks shut on the old vehicle. She'd heard about sex traffickers who took kids and farmed them out to wealthy clients.

A lot of them ended up dead, or so she'd read.

"Please, let me go," she said. "I don't want to go with you. I'll just run away again."

"No can do," the man said and drove on. "I'm taking you to the house and will get you clean and set up with one of our minders, who will teach you the ropes. You look rough. You need to see a nurse and get some treatment."

She didn't say anything. Instead, she leaned her head against the door and cried. "You're abducting me."

"I'm saving you from the streets. Believe me, where you'll be staying is much better than where you were staying before."

"You don't have any right to take me against my will."

"I don't, but you're a child and need a responsible adult to make decisions for you. Don't you worry. We'll do what we can to get you back on track. What's your full name? Do you have any family who will be looking for you?"

"Kayla. As to family?" She shook her head. "Only my boyfriend, but he went missing," she said, deciding to tell him everything. "He was supposed to get us some stuff, but he never came back. I've been texting him, but nothing. I'm afraid something happened to him."

The man shrugged. "You deal drugs as a street worker; you get in trouble. What's his name? How old is he?"

"Fourteen like me. His name is Chris Rogers."

"We need to know if any family will be checking up on you so we can let them know you're okay. What's your father's name?"

She glanced at the man. "You don't get it. My father doesn't give a shit about me. He kicked me out for doing drugs."

"Doesn't matter," the man said. "He's legally responsible for you until you're sixteen and so we need to make sure he doesn't come looking for you. We need to contact him. What's his name?"

"Drew. Drew Weber. My mom's name is Lauren Ross, but she moved away. I don't know where she lives."

They drove through the streets of Bellevue as the sun peeked through the clouds. She expected to be taken to a shelter, like the Sisters of St. Mary, but instead, she was taken out of the city to a large mansion-looking house set in a wooded area off the main roads. It looked like it was worth some serious money.

"You're not going to have to worry anymore about anything, sweetheart," the man said. "We're gonna take care of your every need here."

"Why?" she asked, confused and scared at the same time. "Why are you doing this?"

"We have a lot of people who pay good money for a sweet thing like you. Believe me, this is going to be better than anything you've experienced for a while. Pretty soon, you'll be glad you got in my car. I promise you. Good food. Clean clothes, drugs when you need them. Your own bedroom."

He smiled at her, and she tried to smile back, but something in the back of her mind was screaming, *when you get the chance, run!*

So, she did.

When he unlocked the doors, she ran.

She ran back down the lane that they took from the main road, screaming and crying the entire time, waving her arms when she reached the main road, hoping that someone would drive by and see her, help her escape.

The road was empty, so she just kept running, glancing back now and then to see if the guy was following. Sure enough, she saw the car turn onto the road and follow her, so she ran into the woods and tried to pick her way through the underbrush, getting as far away from the house as she could without losing sight of the road.

She didn't want to get lost in the woods and die of exposure or something. She'd watched Survivor on television back in the day when she lived in a foster home. People survived eating grubs and worms and weird looking plants, drinking water from streams.

She didn't want to risk that, so she kept a few feet from the road, but deep enough into the woods that the man couldn't see her.

In fact, he drove right by the place where she was crouched. He had the window open and was shouting.

"Hey, Kayla, it's pretty far from civilization out here. You're gonna get cold and wet and mosquito bitten if you stay here. Better come with me now. You won't regret it."

But there was no way. No way she was going to go back to that house, however nice it looked on the outside.

It was a brothel. Maybe high class, but that was what it was.

The girls inside? They were all sex trafficked. That much, she could tell.

The man drove up and down the road, shouting at her to come back, get her drugs, a nice hot bath, and some food.

Really, she'd be happy if she did, he promised.

She'd rather take her chances and so she kept it up, walking through the underbrush, deep enough in the woods to remain unseen, but close enough that she could follow the road.

Eventually, she'd get back to civilization.

Eventually, the man would give up and let her go, figuring that she wasn't worth the effort.

Then, she'd go to the road and try to flag down a passing car, ask for help. She wouldn't say anything about the mansion and what happened to her.

She'd just say she was lost and needed a ride back.

For the next hour, she kept up her pace, until she came to a fork where the two roads intersected. Now, she had to think about what to do. The man had given up trying to follow her, as she expected, but she still had to remain hidden for as long as possible.

She was tired and wet from the recent rain. Her running shoes were soaked. Her hair was plastered to her face under the wet hood.

She was hungry, she was tired, and she was hurting badly for a hit.

But she was free.

CHAPTER 13

Grace went home to her cottage overlooking Puget Sound and threw her keys into the dish on the table in the entry. She switched on the lights and sighed as she thought about the day's work.

Four sets of remains, all of them young boys aged between twelve and sixteen.

Only one had a preliminary identity so far — Andy Owens, fourteen, from King County. They had lucked out that he was wearing the nylon bracelet from the WWF. It was a pretty good clue to his identity, but they would do other tests to make sure it was Andy. They had a tentative ID on Peter Cummings from Renton, and a possible in Daniel Moore from Tacoma, but so far, only Andy was positive. The fourth body was still unidentified.

Grace felt for the poor parents, who were probably still in shock. From her experience with parents of the deceased, they would be walking around like zombies, being forced to accept if they hadn't already that their beloved child was dead — and not only that but was the victim of a serial child killer who most likely brutally raped and then killed them, before dumping their bodies like so much trash.

That angered Grace in a way that few other horrible things angered her, and it was also what drove her to want to do the absolute best job she could at recovering and then identifying the remains of those poor boys.

Grace went right to her dining room, where she had her computer setup and logged in to check any emails that might have come in while she was driving back from the Deep Lake site.

Before she could open the first, her cell chimed. There was an incoming text message from Michael Carter, so she opened it and read.

MCARTER: Hey, Grace. Just wanted to say thanks for everything you do. I checked with the recruiter for the WWF when Andy's older brother worked for them. While there were a number of those elephant bracelets given out, they were only a dozen in total. All except the ones given to Andy and Nick are accounted for. So that means the remains you recovered today were almost certainly Andy. He was known to have been wearing it when he went missing as was Nick.

She texted him back right away.

GKELLER: Thanks for letting me know, Michael. We'll do some more tests tomorrow to make sure. I think we have enough material to do a decent DNA profile that should conclusively ID Andy. I'll be at work first thing in the morning if you plan on joining me to watch the proceedings. Bring coffee.

MCARTER: Mocha latte. Grande. I know the drill. See you tomorrow.

Grace smiled to herself. Michael was such a decent type. Serious, but also able to be lighthearted when the moment called for it.

She sat at the desk and read her work email for the next half hour, and then, when she felt she'd done enough, she turned off the lights in the main living area and went to the back of the cottage where her bedroom and bathroom were located. She eyed the huge jacuzzi tub but didn't have the energy to fill it and soak, so instead, she took a quick hot shower and then slipped into her pajamas before brushing her teeth and taking her meds.

Finally, at near midnight, she fell into her bed, the distant sound of the water lapping against the shore filtering in through the screen on her window lulling her to sleep.

IN THE MORNING, she had another quick hot shower, dressed in her usual work attire of a pair of khakis, a t-shirt, sweater jacket and silk scarf, pulled her long grey hair back into a tidy bun, and then grabbed a slice of cinnamon raisin toast with blueberry jam before heading out, her briefcase in hand.

Once at work, she checked in with her team to see what had come in while she was out at the Deep Lake site and was assured that they had everything well in hand. There had been several deaths the preceding day that her assistants handled, and so all she had to do was check them over and approve the conclusions. It would take an hour or less of her time, so she'd get those out of the way during her lunch. Unless, of course, Michael Carter was there watching the examination of the bones they'd recovered the previous day. If he was, she might convince him to go with her for a quick lunch down by the waterfront.

She changed into her protective gear, donned a mask

and gloves, and then went into the autopsy suite where the boxes of recovered bones were waiting.

One by one, she removed the bones from the plastic bags in which they were placed and laid them out on the dissection tables according to their location in an intact body. Once that was complete, she examined each bone, looking for evidence that would confirm one of four issues: the victim's sex, their age, the cause of death, and how long they had been buried.

Based on her examination conducted at the Deep Lake site, Grace was certain that all four were young males under the age of eighteen. Probably closer to puberty than adulthood, based on the length of the femur and the lack of fusion of the medial clavicular epiphysis, which usually occurred between age eighteen to twenty-one.

She had taken care to retain all the ligatures and other devices used to restrain the victims, so they could reconstruct how the bodies were left when buried and how they were killed. It seemed to Grace that all four had been killed in the same manner — strangled with a ligature of a similar fashion — wires with wooden pieces used to tighten the ligature. All four had their arms fastened with nylon rope and had bare feet. There were some items of clothing left on or beside the victims — running shoes, jackets, and all four had their pants down to their ankles or were bare from the waist down, suggesting sexual assault. Grace would be unable to tell whether they had been assaulted pre- or post-mortem. What she did know was that they most likely were sexually assaulted.

Probably raped.

What kind of monster...

So many deaths that Grace dealt with were meaningless — gang shootings, drive-bys, and then there were the heat-of-the-moment shootings and murders that resulted from an argument getting out of hand, or an unlucky punch that led to the victim's death.

This — this was planned and executed. It was full of meaning, but only for the killer.

Figuring out what their purpose was and how they killed was important for profiling them and then, ultimately, bringing them to justice.

That was Michael's job. Grace's role was to ensure that she provided Michael and his counterparts in the police and prosecutor's office with the evidence they needed to find and stop the monster as quickly as possible.

This current monster had been at work for at least a decade. Probably longer, given that his MO seemed well established by the time poor Andy Owens was murdered a decade earlier.

She sighed and examined the neck bones, but she knew what she'd find because she'd already seen it at the burial site — evidence of fracture in the hyoid bone.

Andy had been garroted, the wire with two wooden handles. Looked like piano wire. As someone who took music lessons as a young girl, she was familiar with piano wire. Her parents owned an old baby grand that her father had inherited from his father, who bought it from the local conservatory of music when they were getting rid of the old pianos.

She knew the wires were of different diameter and were a metal alloy of some kind. Older pianos like the one her family had back in the fifties would have different composition than those made today. Depending on the composition of these wires, the garrote would be a useful clue for Michael to use to try to track down the killer.

Michael arrived around ten in the morning, a cup of

much-needed coffee in hand from her favorite place — Starbucks.

"Mocha Latte, Grande, as the lady demands," he said, holding it up from the doorway.

"Oh, good. Time for a break anyway."

She left the metal slab with the bones of Andy Owens laid out and followed Michael into the office just off the autopsy suite. She removed her mask and goggles, then sat down at her desk, happily accepting the cup of coffee from Michael.

"So, how goes the battle?" Michael asked. "I had to brief my boss about the case before I came over and clean up a few loose ends at the office. I was checking on the abduction of that teenage boy. The division is hopping, working that case, as you can imagine."

"I can imagine. I was wondering when you'd show up. The battle rages, as ever. I did discover that the garrote is made of piano wire, and it looks thick, so not your usual wire for other purposes. It looks specifically like that used in pianos, in other words."

"You can buy that at any hardware store, can't you?"

She shrugged. "It depends on how old it is. The old stuff is specific and was probably bought in bulk from the manufacturers. I'll send it to the lab, and they'll look at it more closely, determine the composition and get an idea of its provenance from that."

"Sounds like a good lead," Michael said and sipped his own cup of coffee. "Anything else unusual about the remains of Andy Owens?"

"No, just that my examination of the neck shows clear fracture of the hyoid bone. Given the presence of the garrote, I expect that was used to kill the victim. Uncertain whether he was sexually assaulted prior to or after death.

That's about all I can tell you at this point. Soil samples have been sent to the lab for analysis, and we should confirm based on the results that the burial happened close to when Nick was found, although why the killer would have dumped them at two different locations, I have no idea."

"Nick wasn't really buried. Very shallow grave that was predated and the bones exposed, which was how the body was found."

"Why would a killer use two different burial sites if he killed the two at the same time?"

Michael shrugged. "Who can say what evil lurks in the hearts of men? Maybe he planned on burying them both at the Deep Lake site but was interrupted and decided to bury Nick somewhere else or vice versa. Maybe he was going to bury Andy in the forest with Nick but was interrupted. Maybe he kept one of them alive longer than the other and changed locations due to access. If we can find the killer, he might be able to answer those questions. Until then, it will help to know if they were buried at the same time, so those soil samples will be useful."

Grace nodded and finished the last of the latte.

"Well, let's get back to it, shall we?"

Michael stood, a smile on his face. "Let's."

He was as eager as she was to learn more about the four sets of remains waiting in the autopsy suite.

CHAPTER 14

Ben remembered something he'd seen on an episode of Criminal Minds. You could be rescued from a locked trunk by kicking out the brake light and waving your hand at passing motorists. They could call police and police would give chase.

He could tell they were driving on the highway by the speed of the car and the sound of passing cars, which whooshed by.

Would the kidnapper hear him kicking the brake light and get off the highway, come back and kill him outright?

Ben didn't know, but what he did know was that if he did nothing, he would be dead within a few hours at most. He wiggled down in the trunk and tried to angle his heel in such a way that he could kick out the brake light, but it was hard.

He kicked and kicked, and finally, the plastic was pushed out. Next, he stuck his foot out of the hole, and was cut in the process by the sharp plastic rim, but it was a superficial cut and so he kept waving his foot, hoping that a passing motorist would see and would call police.

He felt the vehicle slow and then turn — was the kidnapper getting off the highway?

That wouldn't be good. Even if someone did call police, would they be able to find the vehicle?

The car kept driving and now it sounded as if they were on a dirt road because the tires crunched against something like gravel.

Finally, the vehicle came to a complete stop.

"Son of a bitch," he heard the kidnapper say. He then heard a garage door open, and the car drove inside, the sound muffled compared to when outside.

He heard some voices and then a scuffle. The next thing he heard was a loud bang.

Was that a gun?

In a few moments, the trunk popped open, and Ben squinted from the brightness of the light. He glanced around and saw that they were in a large double car garage. Out the side window, he could see a house surrounded by trees. The kidnapper was standing over him, gun in hand. He was wearing a mask, and a black ball cap and dark sunglasses.

He grabbed Ben and dragged him up and out of the trunk, then pushed him over to the other vehicle, which was a late model Mazda. On the garage floor lay a man, a bullet wound in his left temple, blood seeping out of the wound onto the floor.

"Now look what you made me do," the kidnapper said. The last thing Ben saw was a fist as it approached his face.

Then, blackness.

WHEN HE WOKE, he was in the back of the Mazda, on the floor, his arms and legs tied behind his back in an awkward position. There was a heavy tarp thrown over him.

They were driving fast again, on their way to who knew where.

All Ben knew was that his attempt to escape had resulted in another person's death. Some poor man got a bullet to the head as a result.

Ben cried to himself, tears running down his face.

It was his fault the man had died...

If he hadn't tried to escape, if he hadn't kicked out the brake light, the man would still be alive.

He had no idea how long they had been driving, but it seemed like hours. Eventually, they came to a stop. He noted that the ground still sounded like a mix of gravel and dirt, so they were some distance away from the highway. The tarp was removed from over his body and the man grabbed Ben from under one arm and dragged him out of the Mazda, letting Ben fall to the ground, his head hitting the dirt. From where he lay, he could see they were in a forested area and the road seemingly came to an end in a clearing. It looked like an area that had been logged or cleared for some purpose, and there was an old building in the distance, the wood weathered gray with age.

"Off we go," the kidnapper said and after closing the Mazda's door, he lifted Ben up and half-dragged him to the building, which looked like an old cabin with windows that were covered in plywood. The kidnapper opened the door and threw Ben onto the bare floor. Ben glanced around. The place was a mess, with old furniture piled in one corner and a table with what looked like empty food containers on it. On the floor not far from where he lay, Ben saw what looked like drop sheets of the kind you'd use when painting a house interior but stained a dark reddish black.

That was not good.

He didn't think it was dark red paint on those sheets…

When the kidnapper's back was turned, Ben tried to stand, hoping that he could head-butt the man and knock him out. He was almost on his knees when the kidnapper turned and saw him. The man came over and kicked Ben in the ribs. Ben fell onto his side, his ribs aching so badly that he almost blacked out.

He heard one crunch.

"Don't even bother to try to escape," the man said. "There's a reason you're hog-tied. It's impossible to run, so give it up. If you try again, I'll do you incaprettamento-style, which means you're hog-tied, and you eventually strangle yourself. So, behave."

Ben didn't want that. He'd heard that the Italian Mafia did that to its victims.

He decided to be quiet and not anger the man any further.

He wanted to live.

CHAPTER 15

"What do you think?" Michael asked, after he returned to Mendez's office.

Mendez sat at his desk, leaning back, his hands clasped behind his head. "Someone has an old Highway Patrol uniform and is posing as a police officer to abduct teenage boys. Highway Patrol stopped using the old ones in 2016, so if he worked with us, it was before then. As to the vehicle, our unmarked patrol vehicles don't have push bars or lights on the dash. Whoever is doing this has a decommissioned patrol vehicle and has modified it."

Michael nodded and looked over his notes from the meeting with Aaron. "He may have worked for the force, or he may have obtained the old uniform in some way. The big question is whether this is his first time or whether he's been doing this for a while. Considering that the boy escaped, I'd think it was his first, but it's also possible that he's experienced and is just getting sloppy. Won't know which until we have more info."

"So, we got one missing teenage boy, aged fourteen, and

a possible former or current Washington State Patrol officer who is the unknown subject. What are the stats?"

Michael flipped through a screen on his tablet and pulled up a table. "Between three hundred and three hundred and ninety children under age twenty-one are abducted by strangers each year in the US. About three quarters die in the first hour. Approximately eighty-nine percent within the first twenty-four hours. The majority are abducted for the purposes of sexual assault."

"Those are some grim statistics," Mendez said and rubbed his bald head. "We have to haul ass if we want to save this boy. What's our first move?"

"Amber Alert and APB to every patrol out there to be on the lookout for an unmarked police vehicle in the county. We need to check every security camera and traffic camera for the hour around the time of the abduction. If we can find the vehicle, we might be able to track it to a location where the boy is being kept. We need records of every retired state trooper who worked prior to the uniform change. We might even have to consider looking at current troopers who were off duty at the time of the abduction."

"I'm on it," Mendez said. "Let's go talk to the team." Together, they left Mendez's office and went out into the main room where the other detectives were sitting, waiting for the briefing. "Okay, listen up," Mendez said. "We have limited time, so we need to get right on this." He pointed to a detective who sat at a desk against the wall. "This is Detective Gord Fields, who is our tech wizard. Gord, we need you to track down any security footage from the area around the park and any highway cam footage. We need to find the black sedan Aaron described and track it, if possible. Terry, I need you to handle the Amber Alert. Let's send a squad to the location in the park to see what we can find.

If this is like most child stranger abductions, the boy's already dead. If we're lucky, he's still alive and we have twenty-four hours to find him and bring him to safety. Also, Terry, get me a list of every former trooper who retired prior to 2016 who is still in the county and state. Let's go."

As Michael watched, the officers in the room turned to their desks and phones and got right to it. Good. That meant they would have a fighting chance of finding Ben.

Mendez turned to Michael. "What's your preference? You want to stay here and do paperwork or come to the field? I'm heading out to the site to see what's up. Hopefully, Gord will get the security footage for us to review when we get back. Want to come with me?"

"Sounds perfect. I'll follow you in my vehicle."

"Great."

Michael grabbed his briefcase, slipping his tablet into the side pocket, and followed Mendez out of the office and into the elevator. They went to the lobby and signed out before heading to their respective vehicles.

"You know your way there?" Mendez asked.

"I already have it programmed into my GPS. I'll stop and get us a coffee on the way if you want one."

"Great. Two creams and two sugars."

With that, Mendez jumped into his vehicle, a late model dark grey Ford Interceptor. Michael got into his own Range Rover and drove out of the parking lot and to the nearest Starbucks. He went through the drive-through and ordered the two coffees for them, and then entered in the GPS locations on his cell, using it to navigate to the park where the abduction took place.

WHEN HE ARRIVED, there were several patrol vehicles near the path into the woods, the officers fanned out in the local area checking for any evidence. Michael slipped on some gloves and took the narrow dirt path deeper into the woods to a location where Mendez was standing, his hands on his hips.

"This is where the boys were sitting," he said and pointed to a fallen log. Beside it were a couple of cans of Red Bull, one of them tipped over, the contents having spilled onto the ground. "There's a pack of rolling papers and a Bic lighter, just like Aaron described. We found Aaron's backpack."

Mendez held it up, and Michael nodded. "Does that mean our guy is pretty green at this? Wouldn't he have removed all this stuff to prevent anyone from finding it later?"

"He had one kid run off, so that probably threw off his plan. He likely chased Aaron but gave up and went back to the vehicle, figuring he had one boy and had to get the hell out of the park as quickly as possible."

Mendez nodded and glanced around the forest. "Aaron ran that way," Mendez said, pointing to the west. "Highway Patrol picked him up on the west side of the park, about fifteen minutes after he escaped. He's damn lucky he was able to get away, considering he was handcuffed. It must have been hard running through this thick brush."

"Yeah, he's pretty scratched up, but nothing major. The trauma will be the worst, especially if Ben isn't found."

Mendez nodded. "Let's go. See what Fields has tracked down in terms of video. Let's hope we catch the vehicle and can track it to where he's keeping Ben."

"I'll be right behind you."

~

THE DRIVE back to the field office in Bellevue took fifteen minutes, which meant that, according to Michael's timer, five full hours had passed since Ben was abducted. He kept the timer on his cell running, just so it was a constant reminder of how much time had passed to motivate him to work hard.

By the time he got back in the station, Gord Fields had already accessed the traffic camera feed from near the park and had video ready to view in a windowless room filled with computer and video equipment. Several detectives were huddled around a computer with a large screen watching the video feed. Mendez stood behind Gord, who was operating the computer.

"We're just tracking the vehicle now. It circled the park and went back inside. Either the perp has the boy somewhere in the park, or he's ditched the vehicle and will leave with a different vehicle to throw us off the track."

Michael shook his head and watched the replay of the video. On the black and white feed, he could see a dark Ford Explorer leave from a side road close to where the abduction had taken place. The video briefly caught the vehicle as it turned north and west, then lost it when it went out of the camera's range. Gord next cued up another traffic cam video, which showed the same vehicle enter the park via one of the secondary roads to the north and east of the initial location.

When the video feed was finished, Mendez turned to Michael. "What's your assessment?"

"It's a big park. There's a maze of roads and trails inside. There are too many entries and exits to watch. The Squak Mountain Natural Area is south and east of the park and bordering that is Tiger Mountain State Forest. It's a lot of ground to cover and too many locations where he could hide out. The only thing we can do is send in patrols to monitor activity in the three areas, but he could just as easily go farther south-east and get lost in the woods and Cougar Mountain area."

Cougar Mountain...

That sent a chill through Michael. It made him think of his other case that was active — Andy Owens.

He didn't want to make any connections in his mind too soon, because that could throw him off track.

But it was there, and his mind refused to ignore it completely.

Mendez turned to Michael. "You guys found remains near Deep Lake of a missing persons case from 2010, right? Connected to that case back in 2010? Two teen boys abducted from a park?"

Michael nodded. "Andy Owens. His best friend was also abducted and murdered. His body was found several months later in the Cougar Mountain area, but the Andy Owens case is cold."

Then, Mendez said what Michael was thinking. "Looks like it might have heated right back up. What's the chance that some other perp just happens to abduct two boys alone in a park with the obvious goal of sexually assaulting them and killing them? In nearly the same area? It's gotta be linked..."

Michael didn't respond, but that was his thought exactly.

He thought about the timing of the abduction — just hours after news broke that the remains of Andy Owens had been found at the Deep Lake site. It could be a copy-cat, who was inspired by the case and all the publicity surrounding it. Or, it could be the same killer, who just decided now was as good a time as any to do it again.

Whatever the case, they had limited time to find Ben before the second window of opportunity closed.

"What can we do now?" Mendez asked, when they returned to his office and sat down to discuss the video.

"Just the press conference. We need to focus on the Amber Alert and get Ben's image and that of the vehicle and the police sketch of the suspect out there. Someone might have seen the vehicle and have more information. They may have seen the vehicle in the park or elsewhere. When is the news conference scheduled?"

"At 5:30PM so it's in time for local news. I'll be making a brief statement and I'd appreciate it if you could be there as a stand-in for the FBI CARD Team. I think it would make people feel better knowing that you're there to assist with the investigation."

Michael hesitated. "I'm not with the FBI," he said, trying to carefully frame his words. "I'm with the task force looking into Andy Owens's murder. Do we really want me to be so visible? We don't want to make the connection between the two cases before we have a better idea if they are connected, whether a copy-cat or the original killer."

"You can just say you're with the King County Prosecutor's Office if you think it's better at this point."

Michael nodded. "I think so. I don't want us to get off on a track of thinking the two cases are connected until we have some more concrete evidence. Otherwise, we might overlook something important. Some connection we don't make because we're already assuming the cases are linked. For example, we need to talk to the family and Ben's friends. Most children are abducted by someone known to them — whether immediate family or friends of the family, acquaintances, people with a direct connection to the child. We should ensure we thoroughly vet the family and friends, the neighborhood first before we go there."

"Agreed," Mendez said and sighed. "I have to spend some time in the neighborhood talking to family and friends. It's a dirty job, but someone's got to do it and until the FBI team arrives, it's me."

Michael smiled ruefully. "I have an autopsy to attend tonight that I'll go to after the press conference, but I'm free until about seven. I can help if you want company."

"Good," Mendez said and grabbed his jacket. "I'm just happy to have you for as long as I can."

With that, they left the building, a sense of urgency filling Michael that they get in as much work as they could before the day ended.

CHAPTER 16

HE TOOK THE BOY TO THE HUNTING CABIN HIS FAMILY owned on the side of Mount Rainier.

He'd used the place on many hunting trips with his buddies, but also used it to scout out places to stash things — and people. The woods were thick at that part of the state, and there were few curious explorers to the isolated area. No one wanted to explore that part of the mountain because there were no trails, and the brush was thick. There were also bear and cougar warnings.

The vehicle could manage the rough dirt road and he was strong enough to haul the boy onto his shoulder and carry him to the cabin. He'd taken over the property a decade earlier after his father passed, and it had served him well over the years, both as a place to decompress with his friends, and as a place to escape and enjoy his very specific pastimes.

He would have liked to stay and have some fun with the boy, but instead, he had to return to Bellevue, change vehicles and clothes, and go to work so he had an intact alibi.

No one would know he'd been gone for the hours it took

to grab the boy, take him to the cabin, and return. He'd already told everyone at work that he would be in a conference call for the morning and could not be disturbed, no matter what. Then, he'd simply walked out the side door and left with no one noticing his absence.

After making sure the boy's restraints were secure, Curtis drove back to Bellevue. While he was on the highway back to civilization, his cell vibrated and then an emergency alert sounded.

An Amber Alert.

He checked the message and sure enough, there was an image of Ben on the page. It was a photo of him from a year or more earlier, when he looked more like a ten-year-old, smiling up at the camera, the familiar gap between his two front teeth.

They must have found Aaron and he'd provided them with a description. There was a police sketch, but of course, the image had him with longer dark hair.

He shrugged mentally, unworried that anyone could link him to the abduction. He didn't know the boys or their families personally, although he had occasion to watch them during his patrols of the neighborhood and local hangouts. He'd watched the two boys on several occasions and knew they liked to skip school, and then go off into the woods near their homes and smoke pot, drink alcohol. There was once when he almost took the boys but changed his mind at the last minute when a car drove by the usually deserted road.

That stopped him.

He tried again that morning, but it hadn't gone as smoothly as he planned. The one boy — Aaron — got loose and ran. He chased Aaron but had been unable to catch him, his bulk impeding his ability to jump over fallen logs and thick brush. Aaron had gotten away.

Ben had still been in the vehicle, so he decided to cut his losses and get the hell out of the park, take the boy to the hunting cabin, and dump him there. He'd return later to claim his prize.

The boy could stew in his own juices in the cabin until late that night. He planned on keeping the boy for a while this time, because it had been over a year since his last hunting trip, and he needed a diversion from the deathly boring middle class life he led.

He pulled over on a side road and checked the Amber Alert to read the press release attached. There was a notice of a press conference at 5:30PM outside the King County Sheriff's office in Bellevue. It would be televised, and so he decided to stay at the office until the press conference was over.

He'd told Joyce he was going to head to the cabin for a hunting weekend with the boys on Thursday night. He planned on enjoying himself, taking care of business, and then returning on Sunday.

Joyce was the perfect trophy wife. She knew barely anything about his business or his friends, and he aimed to keep it that way. The less she knew, the better. Besides, she wasn't interested in the daily business. She was only interested in the monthly revenues and whether his profit and loss statements were in the black.

It was good to keep her at arm's length from the business. He could make up a dozen excuses for his intermittent absences from home that way, and she would never be the wiser. Joyce was as blonde as she could be. She often joked that he liked her only for how good she looked at business functions, and she was partly right. It wasn't only because she looked good to the rest of the men he dealt with. She was also vacuous enough not to question him about things

— if he was able to keep her happy with unlimited credit cards and shopping sprees to LA now and then.

She was pretty easy to please, which was one of the reasons he wooed her and married her. She was a very important part of his well-crafted and maintained front he showed the world. The upstanding businessman and pillar of the community. Church attender, frequent donor to all the right causes. Even had a charity to provide homeless youth with funding for mental health and counseling.

Each summer, he even taught wilderness survival skills at the local youth center.

He was the guy who attended all the functions, donated enough to keep his name up in the list of community leaders, and was someone no one would ever suspect could be keeping a teenage boy alive in a cabin on the side of Mount Rainier for his later enjoyment...

People were in general trusting and impressed by external appearance.

He'd learned that early on in life, and had used it to ensure that his darker impulses were under control, hidden, and well-fed.

So long as he didn't slip up and let the mask fall, he was sure he could continue on his merry way, duping the plebes who had no idea of the monster in their midst.

He was the supreme predator — the smart one who took what he wanted when he wanted, and none of them could do anything about it.

Once he was back in Bellevue, he abandoned the stolen vehicle a few blocks away from his office where he'd parked his regular vehicle, changed clothes in a nearby public washroom in a park, and took his uniform to a nearby laundromat, where he popped it into a washing machine, giving the attendant a pleasant smile and good afternoon.

Mr. Nice Guy.

Then, he drove back to his office, parked the Denali, and slipped inside the side door once more. It was a complicated game, setting up everything in advance, but it served him well over the years.

If the Army did anything for him, it was to teach him how to prepare.

If any highway cam caught him, they'd see a different man with a stolen vehicle wearing different clothes. A wig changed his appearance enough to fool anyone who did catch a glimpse of his face through the windscreen. Wearing a KN95 mask was useful, for it covered up his facial features and the sunglasses did even more to hide his face from any cameras that might capture him driving by.

No problem.

As he sat back behind his desk, he tucked his duffle bag containing his disguise in the closet. In reality, he had a shaved head, which he found to be cooler than letting his hair grow, and it made him look badass in a Kojak kind of way that he liked.

He wiped sweat off his face and head, and then checked his computer for any emails. There were several, so he answered them one by one, and then sent them off.

He'd spend the rest of the afternoon catching up on work, his mind going back every so often to the boy who was waiting at the cabin.

He went to the door and stuck his head out to speak with his assistant, Patricia.

"Hey, I'm finally done the conference call. Took longer than I expected. Can you bring me a cold bottle of water?"

"Will do," she said with a smile.

Good. The stupid bitch was none the wiser.

None of them were. Now, all he had to do was finish up

at work, let them know he'd be gone until Monday and give them the long weekend off, and he could take the Denali, run a few errands to complete covering his tracks, and go to the cabin.

It would be a weekend to remember.

CHAPTER 17

Tess spent the afternoon working on her book, but her mind kept returning to Michael's case. Her cell chimed, indicating an incoming text from him. He wrote that he'd be attending the press conference. She frowned. He really was getting pulled into the case.

He seemed like he was mentally strong but being involved in an active child abduction case could wear him back down, depending on how everything turned out.

Part of her thought he would be so much better off teaching at the local university or even at the FBI Academy than doing the work he was now involved in.

These cases were too close to home. The young boys were close to the same age as Michael's own sons. That had to be hard for him.

She decided to attend the press conference and watch to see how much he was involved. Plus, it would be good to get out of the house for a change. Everyone would be masked up, but the venue was outside so they would all be safer than if it were being held indoors. Hopefully, the weather would hold out.

She grabbed her jacket and notebook and headed out, taking her vehicle through the streets of Seattle to the venue outside of the Bellevue police station.

The press conference was held in the parking lot near the rear entrance to the building. Several vehicles from local TV stations were parked along the street, and she saw several reporters she knew from various papers in Washington State.

She parked her car and then walked over to where Pete Quinn, a reporter with the local Fox Network, stood with his camera operator. Pete was an old-school reporter who had been with the network for two decades and reminded Tess of her father, with the same thinning gray hair and bright blue eyes.

"Hey, Pete," she said and nodded to the camera operator.

"Hey there, Tess," Pete said and nodded back. "We're not supposed to shake hands, but we can elbow bump, if you like."

He held out his elbow and Tess laughed and reciprocated, bumping elbows. It felt a little silly, but it was done in a good spirit.

"I thought you were on leave from the *Sentinel* to write your book?"

"I am," Tess replied, glancing around as several people looked her way. "But old habits die hard, and I would have been here to cover this. It's good background for my book."

"How's the writing coming?"

"Good. I've got it outlined and I'm finishing the first section."

There was a buzz from the reporters as people from the police station emerged. Michael stood behind the main detective, a bald man in plain clothes wearing a dark grey raincoat.

Tess stepped back to stand next to a tree, hoping that Michael wouldn't see her. She didn't want to distract him from his work or make him concerned that she was out following the case.

The detective went to the microphone and cleared his throat. Another man carried a portable easel with a large poster board used to display images. Two uniformed officers from Highway Patrol stood on either side of the main group.

"Good afternoon. I'm Detective Joseph Mendez of the King County Sheriff's Office on the Major Crimes Unit. This press conference will give us the opportunity to update you on a case you've been informed about that started approximately seven hours ago. To my right is Detective Gord Fields, who also works in our Major Crimes Unit. To my left is former FBI Special Agent on the FBI's Child Abduction Rapid Deployment Team, Michael Carter, who is currently an investigator with King County. He can answer any questions you might have when my statement is finished. Now, I'm going to read a prepared statement on the case."

Detective Mendez shuffled some papers and cleared his throat again.

"This morning at approximately 10:30AM, officers with the Washington State Patrol came across a young boy, Aaron Baker, who had been with a friend, Ben Cole, in the Newcastle Highlands Forest Park." Beside him, Detective Fields turned the top page on a poster, showing two enlarged photos of the boys. The top image was of Aaron, who had been found, and the bottom was of Ben, who was still missing. The two boys looked out at the crowd, Ben's gap-toothed smile engaging. Aaron's tousled hair fell in his eyes above a wide smile. Tess thought that the photos were chosen wisely. They would elicit sympathy in viewers, who would want to help two such innocent looking teens.

"The two boys were approached by a man wearing an old Washington State Patrol uniform, driving a dark unmarked Ford Escape police vehicle with a push bar. The suspect handcuffed Aaron, and when he had the chance, Aaron ran from the scene and managed to escape, finding his way through the park to a side road where he was able to flag down a passing motorist. The motorist called 9-1-1 and a nearby Highway Patrol vehicle was dispatched to the scene, where they found Aaron. An ambulance responded and provided immediate medical care for Aaron, before taking him to the local hospital emergency to be checked out by ER doctors. When he was released from the ER, he was taken to the police station to be interviewed by our officers, including Investigator Carter. Based on his interview and description of the assailant, we put out a BOLO for the vehicle and the individual who abducted Ben. As well, we issued a state-wide Amber Alert. We have provided a police sketch to all police stations in the State and ask that if anyone has any information on this abduction or has seen something they believe might be connected to the case, please call our hotline. As always, we are committed to finding Ben as quickly as possible and bringing him home alive and well to his family and community. We are also committed to finding the man who abducted Ben and bringing him to justice. And now, I'll turn it over to Investigator Carter for any specific questions you may have."

With that, Detective Mendez stepped aside, and Michael stepped up to the podium and adjusted the microphone. He removed his mask and cleared his throat.

"I'm Michael Carter, Investigator with the King County Prosecutor's Office, currently working as a liaison officer between the Prosecutor and the local police. As Detective Mendez indicated, I spent six years working for the FBI on its Child Abduction Rapid Deployment Team, before retiring to work in local law enforcement as an Investigator. I'll provide support to the local police until FBI Special Agents from the CARD Team arrive later to take over. If you have any questions, I'll be happy to answer them."

He glanced around and a man in the group of reporters raised his hand. Michael nodded and pointed at him.

"Cal Rivers from Local 42. Investigator Carter, can you tell us the likelihood of recovering Ben alive? My research suggests that most children who are abducted by strangers are killed in the first hour."

That elicited a few gasps and a quick bubble of conversation among the reporters and onlookers.

"While it's true that the first hours are critical in finding abducted victims alive, a considerable number are found in the first twenty-four to forty-eight hours alive. That's why it's so important to get this information out into the public, so people can think of what they were doing this morning when this event began. If you saw anything and were concerned — a man with a young boy that struck you as being in any way unusual or odd or a vehicle that appeared to be an unmarked car behaving strangely — please contact the tip line and provide us with the details."

He glanced around and pointed to another reporter, this time a woman, who had her hand raised.

"Cherry McMillan, Channel 7 News. Investigator Carter, is the Internal Affairs bureau looking into this, considering that the perpetrator appears to be a Washington State Patrol officer?"

Michael shook his head. "We don't yet know whether this offender was a former or current officer with the State Patrol or whether he obtained the old uniform from someone who was. Until we have more information, we are considering all options and will be looking into any former or current officers who may have any connection to the case."

Michael pointed to another reporter, a man in the back.

"Lance Trent, Action News 11. Investigator Carter, what kind of person abducts a fourteen-year-old boy and why? You worked for the FBI. What is your profile of the man?"

Michael nodded and paused a moment as if considering. "Thanks for your question. This has been of interest to me since my university days when I studied Criminology and from my time working with the FBI CARD Team. What kind of man abducts a fourteen-year-old and why? I can't tell you about this perpetrator in particular, but from previous cases I worked, such as the Colin Murphy case, perpetrators like Blaine Lawson enjoy the power they have over a younger person. They are likely to be pedophiles and have fantasized about abducting young boys for sexual purposes and have planned on acting on it. They may have a history of starting fires, abusing animals, molesting relatives, and many started out as Peeping Toms. Until we know more, that's about all we can say about this case and type of perpetrator, but we are looking at other missing persons who fit the victim profile from King County and surrounding states for the past decade. My profile suggests that the perpetrator is in his late thirties or early forties, and likely has a history with law enforcement. He might be married, but it would be only to fit in and provide him with cover for his darker urges. These perpetrators are arrogant and think they are smarter than everyone else, but eventually, they make mistakes, and that's how we'll find them and this perpetrator in particular. If he's listening to this broadcast, let me say this to him directly: now is the time to turn yourself in. If that's everything, I'll let Detective Mendez take over."

Michael stepped away from the podium and Mendez stepped forward to answer further questions about who people should call and what the next steps in the investigation were.

All in all, Tess thought that Michael looked pretty confident standing at the podium answering questions. He didn't seem troubled when bringing up the Colin Murphy case, but she did hear the lingering acid in his voice when he said Blaine Lawson's name.

Michael did well. When the conference was finished and the other reporters started dispersing, Tess decided to let him know she was there, so she went up to where Michael and the other officers stood answering specific questions. Michael saw her and raised his eyebrows, smiling. He came right over.

"Tess," he said and kissed her briefly on the cheek. "You're here."

"Couldn't keep me away," Tess replied, smiling. "You did well."

"I'm fine," he said, as if he knew what she was thinking and worrying about. "We're going back to the office to review more video and will be busy most of the evening, as you can imagine. The CARD Team is scheduled to arrive at nine, so after I brief them, I should be home soon after."

"Okay," she said and squeezed his arm. "I'll be up, waiting."

They smiled at each other, and Tess watched as

Michael walked back to Detective Mendez and together, they walked into the building, leaving the reporters and bystanders behind.

Michael seemed really in a good place, so she tried to switch off her concern and decided that he knew his limits and had been wise enough from the start to take leave and then retire from the FBI. He would know whether he could handle the case.

Besides, the FBI would be arriving soon, and that would mean Michael could go back to the cold cases which he seemed to love so much.

That was a good thing, in Tess's mind. She liked the idea of Michael working cold cases rather than dealing with a live case and especially a case dealing with a child abduction.

She saw a couple of reporters she knew from working at the *Sentinel* and stopped to chat with them about her book contract and her leave from the paper.

"That was your significant other at the microphone, right?" one of them asked.

She nodded. "Yes, he's working for King County at the moment, before returning to finish his PhD and maybe do profiling work."

They talked a while longer about their jobs, and when the conversation ended, she said goodbye and walked back to her car. When she got inside, she checked her cell for any texts.

There was one from Michael.

MICHAEL: Checking up on me, were you? :) Don't worry. I'm fine. Seriously. I feel fine dealing with this. At first, I was concerned, but after working with Mendez, I realize I'm better.

TESS: I'm glad to hear that. I love you.
MICHAEL: I love you back.

With that, she smiled and put her cell down. She felt a sense of relief that maybe, finally, Michael was back to his old self.

CHAPTER 18

Kayla sat in the auditorium with her work spread out in front of her on the table. Once a week, she volunteered at the local homeless shelter, and did whatever office work they had on hand. Most of the time, it was filling out orders for the kitchen, filing receipts and invoices, arranging the payroll for those employees who worked for pay. She'd gotten clean a few years after Chris went missing, and had gone back to school, getting her high school diploma, and then attending the local community college to take an office management course.

She'd been working steady for a local restaurant, making enough money to afford her tiny studio apartment. It was hard, but she was clean.

Well, except for her nicotine habit.

That, she couldn't shake. Like other recovering addicts, nicotine was her one vice. She would likely smoke until it killed her as a sixty-year-old woman, like her grandma. She could still see the beloved woman sitting in her chair, her eyes wide, breathing heavily, the cannula feeding her oxygen threaded around her head and into her nostrils. The old woman had died slowly and painfully, getting skinnier and skinnier.

"Quit smoking," Grandma had said to Kayla, even as she lit a cigarette, smoking herself right up until the last few months of her life when she was unable to get around anymore and couldn't buy cigarettes. No one else would so Grandma had quit out of necessity.

But she kept asking Kayla for a cigarette.

"Come on, I know you smoke," Grandma would say. "Give me one. Just one..."

Yes, nicotine had proven harder to quit than heroin, but heroin killed you a lot faster.

Kayla wanted to live.

She took a break from her work and checked her email.

There was a headline from the local *Sentinel* that caught her eye.

MULTIPLE BODIES TURN UP IN MASS GRAVE NEAR DEEP LAKE

She was intrigued and so she clicked on the link and read the news article at the website.

Police have recovered the skeletal remains of four young men who went missing over the past decade buried on an abandoned property near Deep Lake, in south King County. Two of the remains have been identified and the forensic anthropologist is currently working with police to identify the other two sets of remains. Both are thought to be young men in their early teens.

That made her sit up straighter.

Chris went missing ten years earlier, and there had never even been a missing person's case connected to him. He simply disappeared that night he left her and went in search of money for their dope.

Kayla wasn't sure, but she wondered if Chris was one of the two remaining victims.

Chris's family had never reported him missing—primarily because he didn't really have one. As far as his stepfather was concerned, he was one less mouth to feed. Kayla tried to convince someone to take it seriously, but to no avail.

It was as if Chris never existed.

She'd always felt that the world had failed Chris. He'd dropped out of school when he turned fourteen and no one tried to find him and put him in juvenile hall, where at least he'd finish his high school. He'd gotten hooked on drugs because he was homeless, and there were no good Samaritans to help him out and put him back on the right track — no loving father or uncle, no grandfather. Not even a mother who cared about him.

Poor Chris...

They'd both been destitute and homeless, but at least she was able to get free finally and start a new life.

Chris had just disappeared, and no one ever bothered to look.

They didn't even know he was gone.

That made her feel sad, and for a moment, she felt tears well up in her eyes. She had tried hard not to dwell on the past, which she couldn't change no matter how much she regretted it, but every now and then, the past came up and she had to deal with it.

Every time she passed by the last place she'd seen Chris, a deep sadness filled her, and she had to fight the hopelessness that threatened.

This was one of those times the sadness just wouldn't pass.

She turned on the flatscreen and switched to a local

station, hoping to get some more news about the four dead young men found near Deep Lake. They were calling the killer the Deep Lake Killer, which reminded her of Gary Ridgeway. She'd read about the Green River Killer, but he killed young women, not young men Chris's age.

On a local station, the reporter was standing near a forested area, microphone in hand. Behind her were police cars and a white van, and in the distance, she could see a white tent which probably kept the medical examiner from getting rained on and the prying eyes of the news media from watching what was going on.

It wouldn't be pleasant to dig up dead bodies.

Chris had been gone for a decade. He'd be nothing more than a skeleton if he was one of the bodies.

She tried to remember what he was wearing the night he disappeared. She could picture him in her mind's eye: not very tall for his age and underweight. He looked younger than fourteen — maybe twelve if she didn't know better. He'd had scraggly light brown hair and brown eyes. He had on a padded blue jacket he'd gotten from a local charity store, and faded jeans. He wore Nike running shoes he got from a friend, and a belt with a special buckle. He said it was his Uncle John's belt, and that Uncle John had given it to him because Chris's pants always fell down because he was so skinny. What was the belt buckle again? It had the Wyoming logo on it with a rodeo rider on a bucking bronco, because his Uncle John had been to the gift shop at a Dude Ranch in Wyoming and had bought the belt there as a gift.

Chris loved that belt buckle. It was one of the few gifts someone gave him spontaneously.

It made him feel like he really mattered to someone, even if it wasn't his stepfather or mother, who had pretty much abandoned him when he turned twelve, preferring the bottle or drugs to being a parent.

Despite it all, Chris had been so positive all the time. Always smiling, always wanting to share his food or his drugs or his sleeping bag.

Chris had been a really good person when it came down to it. A nice guy, who would give you the shirt off his back if you were cold, even if it meant he'd be cold.

Why would he have just run off without telling anyone?

It was just not like him to leave and never come back unless something bad happened to him. That was what Kayla feared. Something bad happened to Chris that night when he went in search of some drugs and money for food.

She stopped for a moment and considered what to do. She could call police and let them know about Chris, see what they thought. It might help them identify the bodies. At least it would give her some peace of mind to think that Chris wasn't one of the four found in the ground near Deep Lake.

She googled the local police department mentioned in the article and spoke with someone in reception, who forwarded her to an officer's number. She was instructed to leave a message, including her name, her number and the reason for the call.

Hello, this is Kayla McDonald from Bellevue. I read about police finding the bodies of four young boys under age eighteen near Deep Lake and think I might have some information about one of them. Chris Rogers. He's a friend of mine who went missing ten years ago. There was never a missing persons case about him, but I thought he might be one of the bodies you found. My number is...

Then, she waited, wondering if anyone would call her back.

Sure enough, within half an hour, her cell rang and when she checked the caller ID, it was the Bellevue PD. Officer Hawkins was on the other line. After he introduced himself, he asked her to give him more details about why she was calling.

She told him that when she saw the news report about the four bodies dug up near Deep Lake, how she thought about Chris, and how he'd gone missing one night almost a decade earlier. She was wondering if he might be one of the four.

"Was there anything you can remember about what he was wearing the night he went missing?"

She told him about the belt buckle that had Wyoming on it and about his black and white Nike running shoes and the blue padded jacket he'd worn.

"Anything else you can tell us? How tall was he?"

She tried to think about it, but it was hard to gauge height. "Maybe five foot six? I know he said he broke his arm when he fell down some stairs as a kid, but it was really his stepfather who broke his arm. Chris always said he fell so no one would take him out of his home and put him in foster care because of abuse."

"That's good information," Officer Hawkins said. "Thank you for calling us."

"Will I find out if it's him?" she asked before they said goodbye.

"If it is your friend Chris, his family will be notified first, and it will probably be released to the public at some point in the investigation when the ID has been confirmed."

"Thanks," she said and ended the call.

Well, she'd done her duty.

Now, she couldn't get Chris out of her mind, and wondered what happened to him that night he went missing. Was he abducted by some pervert and murdered, his body dumped near Deep Lake with other victims? Or was it over some drugs? That happened enough on the strip when she'd been living on the street. There were always stabbings and shootings over drugs.

She hoped not. She hoped he simply met someone who offered him a way out of the hard life he'd found himself living and he was now happy, living somewhere, employed, and married with kids.

But she didn't think so...

CHAPTER 19

On his way to the laundromat to put his now-clean Highway Patrol uniform into the dryer, Curtis decided to go get a coffee at the local donut shop. He got into his Denali and drove off. The drive was about ten minutes away, which would give him time to get his coffee and drive to the laundromat.

It was while he was driving along Lake Hills Connector that his car was T-boned by a vehicle running a red light.

The last thing he remembered before he blacked out was the crunching sound of metal on metal and bang as the car's airbag blew up in front of him.

When he came to, he was sitting in his vehicle, the passenger side of the car crunched in almost in a "V". The airbags had deflated from the metal edges of the car door's frame. He reached up and felt blood flowing from out of his nose and felt numb. His hearing was muted, and he tasted blood in his mouth. Beside his SUV was the front end of the car that struck him. The two vehicles were pinned against a lamp post on the far corner of the intersection. The car's engine hissed and sizzled.

"Are you okay, Mister?" someone asked. Curtis turned his head to the sound, which was muffled. It was a man wearing aviator sunglasses, a worried expression on his fat face. "You got crunched pretty good. The ambulance is on its way," he said and held up his cell. "I can already hear the sirens because the station's real close. Just a mile away."

Curtis nodded, not wanting to speak.

Damn...

Now what the fuck was he going to do? He could try to unbuckle the belt and climb out the back of the vehicle, but then what?

He couldn't just run from the scene of the accident. He'd have to stay and give his details to the police, who would investigate the accident. He'd have to provide details about his insurance and probably they'd want him to go to the ER. Maybe the EMTs who came with the ambulance could check him out and treat him on scene. The last thing he wanted was to go to the hospital.

He had his old uniform in the laundromat washing machine. What would the clerk do when he failed to show? Put his stuff in a plastic bag, and leave it to molder in a corner in case he came back?

Which Curtis planned to do as soon as he could get away from all this.

Finally, the ambulance and firetruck arrived on scene, and one of the EMTs from the ambulance came to the vehicle and spoke with Curtis.

"How are you feeling, Sir?" the EMT asked. Curtis wanted to downplay any pain he was starting to feel so they didn't feel a need to take him to a hospital. That wouldn't do. He needed to get out of the situation as fast as possible with as little contact with the police as possible.

"I'm fine," he said, wiping his nose, his hand coming back smeared with blood. "Nose might be busted. Maybe bit my tongue. Other than that, I feel okay. Nothing broken, in other words."

"Can you move your arms and legs? We're getting the Jaws of Life out to pry the door open so we can get you out."

"Yeah, I can move both arms. One leg seems trapped under the dash, but it doesn't hurt too much."

"Any pain in your chest or abdomen?" The EMT shone a small light in Curtis's eyes. "Any dizziness?"

"No, feel fine, actually," he said, squinting from the light. "My hearing was a bit dull at first, but I can hear fine now."

They worked away on the door, which was damaged and wasn't opening properly. The side of the car had been crunched and bent inward when it struck the light standard. The Jaws of Life were strange. He'd been at crash sites before as a Highway Patrol Officer and had seen many a bad crash on the interstate highways. Dead people, their bodies crumpled into odd positions, arms and legs broken, decapitated, blood everywhere.

He was lucky they were in the city and the speeds weren't as high as some on the Interstate. The car was a write-off, but he had good insurance. He could get another one easy enough since he wasn't at fault.

"How's the other guy?" he asked, wondering if the guy who did this was okay. Not that he cared. He just wanted to know how much of a production this whole business would be and how soon he could get the hell out of there.

"He's being taken care of. You worry about you. Right

now, we're going to try to get you out of the vehicle so we can treat you and see how you're doing."

For the next fifteen minutes, the two firefighters worked on the door of his SUV, using the Jaws of Life to pry the door open and then they spent even more time trying to extricate him from the driver's seat. His leg was pinned under the crumpled dash, and when he finally was free, the pain was incredible.

He heard a scream and was shocked to realize that it was, in fact, him.

"You've got a bad cut," the EMT said as he lifted Curtis onto the gurney and began working on the leg. "Don't know if the bone is broken, but the cut is pretty deep."

"Do I have to go to the hospital?"

The EMT glanced at him like he didn't believe the question. "Do you have insurance?"

"Yes, but I'm really busy with work right now."

The EMT shook his head. "You need to worry more about blood loss than work, Sir. Just relax."

"As long as I'm not kept in all day or overnight," Curtis said. "I have work, important meetings..."

"Your life is important," the EMT said. "We'll get you to the Overlake ER and they'll fix you up."

Curtis lay back on the gurney and rubbed his eyes while they strapped him down and applied a tourniquet and bandage on his leg.

He didn't want to bleed to death, but at the same time, he didn't want to spend the rest of the day in a hospital. He left the damn uniform at the laundromat...

The trip to the hospital took a brief ten minutes and then he was wheeled into the ER treatment room where a nurse took over and did his vitals, while the doctor examined the wound.

"You'll need stitches for this. We'll do a quick x-ray to make sure we don't have a fracture. But I'm more concerned about your head injury. We need to do some scans to make sure you're okay."

They rolled him into a room for an x-ray and then for a CT scan, before rolling him back to the treatment room.

The doctor shook his head when he came into Curtis's room. "No break. Just some tissue damage that will need stitches. But I am concerned about your concussion. I think you should stay in overnight for observation."

"Are you sure? I have a lot of work to do…"

The doctor shook his head. "Seriously, Mr. Holloway. You need to stay in overnight so we can watch how your brain responds to the trauma."

Curtis sighed. That sure threw a monkey wrench into his plans. The boy would be fine overnight, but he had been planning this for a while. Besides, he wanted to get out of town quickly to reduce his risk of exposure. There was a dead body and the vehicle he'd used to abduct the boys hidden in a garage.

Loose ends…

There was nothing to do but give in, so for the next hour, the doctors cleaned and stitched the wound, gave him antibiotics and other drugs for the inflammation, and had him hooked up to all kinds of medical telemetry to monitor his vital signs.

If he called Joyce to let her know he'd be in the hospital overnight, he'd have to contend with her fawning all over him like he was in danger of dying — which he wasn't.

This was all just precautionary.

So, instead of telling her he had been in an accident, he said nothing. She was expecting him to be out of town until

Sunday. She didn't need to know about the accident until later.

Next, he called his secretary and let her know he wouldn't be in for the rest of the day due to a meeting, and that he'd stop in on the weekend to check on things. There was no problem, given that he had an assistant who could practically run the show on his own, so Curtis wouldn't have to worry about that end of things.

It wasn't the first time he'd spent the weekend at the cabin on short notice and it wouldn't be the last.

OF COURSE, he only remembered the laundromat the next morning when he was discharged from the hospital. The doctor had warned him there might be some short-term memory loss associated with the crash. Maybe the short-term memory loss was a real thing. At least he didn't forget about the boy.

Man, he really was falling down on the job.

He took a taxi to the laundromat, where he expected that the uniform would be waiting but he was in for a shock.

The clerk behind the desk shook his head when Curtis asked about the load of laundry he'd left the day before. The man's eyes brightened. "When you didn't show yesterday, I put your laundry in a bag to wait in case you turned up. I heard about the accident this morning from another customer. I figured you were a cop, because of the uniform, so I called police this morning and let them know that I had your laundry. Someone came by and took the load not long before you got here. They said they'd make sure to return it to you." The man smiled, like he was proud.

Curtis exhaled heavily and glanced around the laundro-mat, checking to see if there were any security cameras.

Dammit.

There were two.

"How did you know it was me?" he asked.

The clerk shrugged. "The accident happened at the intersection a few blocks away, and someone told me when they came in. Said it was a big black SUV — a Yukon Denali — and I remembered that you had one. When you didn't come back, I put two and two together. The police sent a patrol car over right away."

The clerk smiled like he was a fucking genius.

"Thanks," Curtis said.

Then, he left the laundromat and got into the taxi.

Jesus...

The Denali would have been taken to the Washington State Patrol impound until he claimed it and insurance was settled. Since he wasn't at fault, it would be the other driver whose insurance had to pay.

But the very last thing he needed was the police knowing that he had his old uniform at the laundromat. Especially if the other boy — Aaron — told police that some Highway Patrol Officer was the one who tried to abduct him and who did abduct Ben.

This whole thing was fucked up from the very start.

"Where to now?" the taxi driver asked.

"Just stop at the nearest bank machine. I need some cash."

The taxi driver complied, stopping at a drive-through automated teller. Curtis removed as much money from his account as he could — three thousand dollars — and then decided to go directly to his mother's place where he could take the second car she kept there for him — an old Audi — and then leave for the cabin in the mountains.

He needed to get the hell out of Bellevue. If police connected the dots, they would go right back to the laundromat, get the security video footage, and have proof that he had been there to wash the uniform.

It was only a hop, skip and a jump from that to Curtis being the suspect.

If that was the case, they'd come knocking to interview him, and while he had an alibi for the time covering the abduction, there might be some camera somewhere that recorded his vehicle.

He took out his cell and opened the browser to check the local news, but even doing so could alert police that he was in the city and where, if they checked his records.

He had to know what the police were saying about the abduction.

Nothing much, but there had been an emergency Amber Alert sent out for the boy and a description of the vehicle and of him.

Wrong, of course, and the said vehicle was currently parked in a garage, safe from public view, but still...he shot a guy and took his vehicle, which was now parked not far from his workplace.

There was a trail leading directly to him if police could find the right crumb.

Nothing to do about it now, except to try to clean up his tracks as much as possible, and then get out of the city, the state, and the country, if necessary.

He hated the idea of leaving because he had a nice life in Washington State. He had a solid rep and was operating under the radar for years.

Still, he could start over somewhere where the police weren't quite as competent or well-funded — like Mexico.

So many targets. So many easy targets.

A target rich zone, as his buddies in the service used to say when they'd drive through the streets of some dusty town in Iraq or Afghanistan.

Yeah, Mexico might be right up his alley. All he had to do was get as much cash as possible, take care of the boy, and then leave.

When he thought of it, he didn't really care if he never saw Joyce or the girls again. They had been nothing more than a smokescreen, giving him cover for his real life.

The life he lived in darkness. In the shadows.

Right now, in Washington State, there was just too much damn light...

CHAPTER 20

Grace spent some time laying the bones of the fourth victim onto the examination table. She also placed the items of clothing and personal effects found with the body at the foot of the table, examining each one.

"Here's what remains of a nylon jacket, looks dark, maybe navy blue. Padded. Some running shoes. Nikes. Interesting belt buckle with "Wyoming" on it and a rodeo rider. That should help identify the victim."

Michael stood a foot away from the table, wearing a mask and coveralls. He wore gloves and goggles but had his cell out and he was calling someone.

"Hey, Tom," Michael said. "Can you do a quick search of our MisPers files for a belt buckle with the name Wyoming on it and the image of a rodeo rider? Yes. Thanks. Will do."

He ended the call. "My colleague will search for anyone with that buckle. Hopefully, it's unique enough that it will ID him."

While Grace examined each bone, commenting on them for the recording, she came to the left arm.

"Uh, oh. Looks like an old parry fracture here," she said, pointing to the ulna. "The research isn't conclusive, but it suggests that an isolated parry fracture to the shaft of the left ulna is the bone most likely to be fractured in child abuse."

Michael leaned down. He'd likely heard about parry fractures before. They were common in children who had been abused and occurred when the child raised their left arm to protect their face.

"Let's get an x-ray of these two," she said and placed the two bones from the left arm, the radius and ulna, in a plastic bag, labeled them and then placed them to the side. "If it's a parry fracture, it suggests the individual was abused as a child. We can run the x-rays against any on record and see if we can get an ID that way."

"Let's hope."

Grace called out to Annie, her assistant, who was in the adjoining room working at her desk. "Annie, can you get me x-rays for these right away? Thanks."

Then, Grace turned back to the remains and continued examining the bones, one at a time.

"You don't mind how slow I'm going?" she asked Michael, who was standing beside her like a med student at an autopsy.

"Not at all," Michael replied. "I enjoy it. Always keep learning is my motto."

"Good motto to have. There's always something new to learn."

In about ten minutes, Annie returned to the autopsy suite with her iPad in hand and the bags of the victim's bones.

"Here," she said and opened an image of two radiographs. "You can see the fracture of the ulna shaft. The radius is fine."

Grace went over to examine the radiograph displayed on the iPad.

"I want the radiograph," she said and pointed to the lightbox on the wall where radiographs were typically read. While she could see the image on the iPad, she preferred using the old method of radiographs on a lightbox to examine more closely.

Annie complied and soon, the two radiographs were on the twin light boxes on the wall. Grace bent closer and sure enough, she could see the transverse fracture line on the ulna that was located just below the mid shaft.

"Yep. Just as I thought. Parry fracture of the left ulna. Pretty sure this poor guy was abused as a child. Have to look more closely at other bones for signs of healed fractures."

"How can you be sure it's from abuse and not, say, playing football or other innocent causes?" Michael asked. He likely already knew why but wanted Grace to explain.

"You can imagine if some big adult has struck the child or threatens to. They'll raise their left arm to protect their face and when they do, the ulna is the bone most likely to be struck."

Michael nodded like he was satisfied with her explanation.

Grace next began examining the ribs, checking for signs of healed trauma. Often, ribs were another source of evidence for child abuse. She picked up and examined each rib separately, and then set aside two on the left side of the body. "Annie, can you x-ray these as well?"

Annie took the two ribs.

"Looks like this poor kid was abused quite a bit. I'll check the scapula next so you might as well wait."

She picked up the scapula — the triangular shaped bone that attached to the clavicle or collarbone as it was commonly known. She examined it closely and then nodded. "Yep. Looks like we got another one. Here," she said to Annie, who was standing by, waiting. "Take this as well."

Annie took the bones and left the suite. Michael bent closer.

"What else can the oracle of the bones see?"

Grace laughed and then turned back to the autopsy table. "Let's see. Next to the ulna and ribs, scapula, what else is often damaged in child abuse cases? The spine."

She went about examining each of the vertebrae in turn. "Did you know that we're all born with thirty-three vertebrae, but some fuse as we grow and usually, an adult has only twenty-four?"

"I did not know that," Michael replied, his tone sounding humorous.

"Yes, occasionally, someone may have an extra vertebra, called a transitional body, located at L-6. The sixth vertebra in the lumbar region. I checked all this young fellow's vertebrae for obvious signs of past trauma, but I think I'll get Annie to x-ray them all. When you see a couple of signs of abuse, you're bound to find more, if you keep looking. This poor kid seems to have experienced quite a lot of abuse. Then, to be murdered on top of it?" She exhaled heavily and shook her head. "Doesn't seem fair, does it?"

"Life's not fair," Michael replied. "Not by a long shot."

"Ain't that the truth? I bet the killer is walking amongst us unknown and undetected."

Michael sighed. "That's my job. I'll do my best to find the monster who did this, who killed these boys, and bring them to justice."

"Good man." Grace's affection for Michael just kept growing. If she'd ever had a son, she would have wanted one like him.

Annie came back with the radiographs and slipped them into place on the light box readers. Grace went over and bent close to examine each radiograph.

"Yep," she said. "Just as I thought. Look at this. Clearly damaged. Looks like the scapula was fractured."

"What would cause that kind of injury?"

"External force of some kind. Punch, kick, use of something to strike the victim. Painful. Wouldn't be able to move the shoulder much for weeks. Would require stabilization, but not surgery. Poor kid. There should be hospital data, ER data, medical records of this. Someone would have reported it."

"Not necessarily," Michael replied. "You might be surprised at the number of kids whose injuries are left to heal and never reported. Teachers are mandated to do so if they suspect abuse at home, but it sometimes slips through the cracks."

Michael's cell rang and so he left the autopsy table and went off to the side of the autopsy suite to take it.

He spoke in a quiet voice for a few moments. Grace tried not to listen in, but it was hard not to. She did watch his face for his expression, but because of his mask, she could only see his eyebrows were raised. Whatever he was being told was interesting.

He put his cell away and came back over to the side of the autopsy table where Grace was now busy examining the long bones of the leg.

"We have an ID, strangely enough. The boy is Chris Rogers from Bellevue. Never reported missing. Assumed to be a runaway by the family so they didn't even bother to report to police. Get this — his old girlfriend read about the Deep Lake bodies and called in with a description of what Chris was wearing the night he went missing. Of special note is the Wyoming belt buckle. Not very many of them lying around, so I think the ID is pretty certain. She told the police officer who took the report that he was abused as a child, was a runaway, and went missing when he was fourteen after being homeless for a while."

Grace shook her head. "Poor bastard, pardon my French. It's like heaping insult on injury. Abused as a child, then homeless and finally murdered by a pedophile serial killer."

She took a moment to breathe in deeply. Nothing made her angrier than child abuse and child murder. Nothing.

She felt tears spring to her eyes because she now had a name, and a history to this set of remains. They were no longer just bones on a table with a mystery attached to them. They were the final remains of a real live person who lived and breathed and laughed and cried and who had his life taken away from him, violently by a murderous monster.

She tried hard not to let the personal stories of the remains she examined affect her, keeping it professional and distancing herself from the trauma the bodies experienced, but sometimes — especially with children — it was impossible. The boy would have been the same age as her own nephew, and she couldn't imagine how she'd feel to learn he was the victim of a pedophile serial killer.

"You okay?" Michael asked, his hand on her shoulder.

She blinked several times and took in a deep breath to get control over herself.

"Just thinking of my own nephews and unable to imagine how the family must feel, except, I guess the family didn't care in this case. Just the old girlfriend. Thank God for her coming forward."

"Yes, thank God for that. Although we might have ID'd him through the x-rays eventually. Now, we can start digging into his past and what was going on in his life at the time he went missing. It makes my life a lot easier."

"You going to be leading this case?"

Michael shook his head. "No. Just the liaison between the Feds and local law enforcement and the Prosecutor's Office."

"Still, you get to be involved directly."

"That's right. It gives me access and I do have a role."

She nodded. "Keep me informed as the case progresses." She turned and examined the boxes of remains she had left to examine. "I'm hoping you'll be able to find the monster who did this to these poor boys and bring him to justice."

"I'll do my best."

Then, she moved on to the next set of remains, which Annie had laid out on the second autopsy table, each bone in its proper place.

It was going to be a very long night.

CHAPTER 21

Tess spent the early evening in the room she used as an office, where her book's manuscript awaited.

She was torn between working on the manuscript and digging deeper into the Deep Lake case that was all over the news. Since the press conference, she'd been obsessed with the case and had switched on the television, spending the evening and that morning moving between the local news channels, waiting for the latest news on the case.

That evening, police reported they had identified a second set of remains and were waiting to notify the family before releasing the name to the public.

That was hopeful. The more names they had, the better able police would be to identify the killer or killers. Michael was spending time at the medical examiner's office, watching the ME go over the remains to see what could be gleaned from the bones and other evidence found at the burial site.

Once they had more information about the victims, Michael could do victimology, and get a sense of what connected them. That would go a long way to identifying who might have abducted them. What police knew already was that the young boys were all under age 18 and above puberty, but that was all.

Their names would help a lot, so she was eager to learn who the second victim was.

It made Tess wish she was still working for the *Sentinel* and wasn't on leave to write her book. She ached to get out there, talk to other reporters, and see if she could contact police and other people in law enforcement who she knew to get tidbits of info. Maybe interview the families of the victims. Tell their stories.

That was what she loved about reporting and writing about crime. She loved being able to tell the stories of the victims and their families, of the friends who lost loved ones. She enjoyed the whole story of the case, and how police went from a body to a suspect to a final convicted murderer.

Her book was supposed to be about her own experience with a serial killer — Eugene Kincaid-Hammond from Paradise Hill — but she was putting in as much information about Kincaid's other victims as she could, to take the focus off her.

Yes, she was one of Kincaid's victims. She was supposed to be the first victim, but she was alive, while over twenty girls weren't.

That felt like a weight she could never escape.

Around seven that night, Michael texted her.

MICHAEL: We ID'd another victim from the Deep Lake site and the next of kin have been informed. Boy was never reported missing, but a friend called in and said the last time he was seen was ten years ago. We interviewed her, and she provided info that helped identify him.

TESS: *That's good. It will help figure out who the killer is. Where was he from?*

MICHAEL: Bellevue. *Was homeless at the time and was an addict according to the witness. Fourteen, looked younger. From an abusive home, based on the autopsy and the statement of the witness.*

TESS: *In other words, he was a vulnerable youth and was likely preyed upon by the serial killer precisely because of it...*

MICHAEL: *Exactly. Same old story. He was easy pickings because no one cared where he was, and those who did were just as vulnerable. The woman who provided the info is a recovering addict. They were homeless together.*

TESS: *Oh, she must be heartbroken to learn he was a victim.*

MICHAEL: *Yes. Thankfully she came forward when she heard about the remains of teenage boys being found near Deep Lake or we might have had a hard time IDing him. Our next avenue was x-ray records, because he had several old, healed fractures.*

TESS: *Glad you didn't have to resort to that. So, why are you texting me instead of coming home?*

MICHAEL: *The CARD team member is in town and I'm meeting with him in Bellevue to update him on the cases. I'll be home late, in other words. Same as usual.*

TESS: *Okay. I'll probably be up late anyway, because the Websleuth crowd is busy at work speculating on the cases.*

MICHAEL: *Okay. See you later. XO*

Tess smiled and sent him back an OX reply as was their usual practice.

She turned back to her computer and refreshed the thread she was watching, discussing the latest news in the Deep Lake case.

There were all kinds of speculation about who the serial killer might be. People made links between the current abduction of Ben and Aaron. Given that the abductor wore a police uniform, forum members suggested that it was a bad cop who was using his knowledge of police procedure to abduct, kill, and bury bodies and that it was just a fluke that the homeowner near the Deep Lake decided to dig up the old fence to expand the yard.

Tommy12689: If he didn't dig that fence up, the bodies would have remained there for decades. The killer would keep killing until he made some other mistake.

Tess nodded as she read that. It was indeed one of those flukes of luck — for law enforcement — that the homeowner decided to expand the yard. If he hadn't, they would be none the wiser about Andy Owens's murder or the new boy, who the local news station had identified as Chris Rogers, who had been fourteen at the time that he went missing.

She switched on the local news and watched the latest report, which showed a photo of a young woman, who must be about twenty-five, who looked quite sad, her dark eyes haunted. The caption identified her as Kayla Ross, who was the girlfriend of the dead boy, Chris Rogers.

"He was always positive, despite everything," Kayla said, standing at the doorway to the apartment where she lived. "He had such a hard life, what with the abuse and drug addiction, but he always tried to look after me, look after us." Tears formed in Kayla's eyes as she spoke, and she wiped away a tear before continuing. "I'm glad they found him. I heard about the bodies found by Deep Lake, and I thought that maybe Chris might be one of them, so I called the police tip line. They found his belt buckle, so they know it was him. From Wyoming. His uncle gave it to him. His uncle was one of the few adults in his life that he trusted."

Tess felt her own eyes tear up at the sight of Kayla's face, now wet with tears. It must have been horrible for her, homeless, wondering where her boyfriend had gone, and no one seemed to care.

She searched on Facebook for Kayla Ross and found one profile. It showed that Kayla's profile was private and so Tess sent Kayla a private message.

Hi, Kayla: This is Tess McClintock from the Seattle Sentinel. I write the weekly crime column and would really like to speak with you about Chris and what happened. We could do a zoom meeting or meet in person, social distancing of course, if you want to talk more about Chris. I feel like his story should be told, because there are others like him, forgotten boys and girls who no one seems to care about. If you're interested, please send me an email or call me. My number is...

She didn't know whether Kayla would want to talk about Chris to her, but it was worth a try.

Sure enough, within fifteen minutes, a chime sounded on her cell, indicating an incoming text.

KAYLA: Hi, Tess. I have read some of your columns before. I would be pleased to do an interview. I work at the Lake Café. If you want, we can meet tomorrow before my shift, which starts at 11:00. We could meet at 10:00 and sit on the patio. Is that enough time?

Tess replied immediately, wanting to secure a time before Kayla changed her mind.

TESS: That sounds perfect. I'll see you at 10:00. Thanks for agreeing to meet with me. I really want to tell Chris's story — and yours.

Tess put the meeting into her calendar with an alert to remind her to leave with enough time to get to the cafe, which was located near downtown Bellevue. On Google Earth the café was quaint, in the side of an old warehouse, and had a small patio that overlooked Lake Washington.

When she went back to the Websleuth forum, she saw that the news about Kayla was now the talk of the moment, and people were speculating that Chris was a sex worker and had been abducted and killed by a police officer working Vice.

Canter89: A Vice detective would know all the sex workers on the strolls and would know the young ones like Chris who were especially vulnerable because they were homeless. You know, instead of arresting these kids and putting them in juvenile detention, they could give them a place to live and some money for food. And decriminalize drugs so they don't keep getting arrested. They're drug addicts — it's a medical issue not a moral issue.

In reply, someone with a handle JoeBlow4223 wrote:

JoeBlow4223: It's the moral decay of the country that's responsible. Parents have to teach youth better ethics and values, and they won't use drugs...

The discussion continued like that, with some posters on the side of decriminalization and better care for homeless youth, while others were blaming the youth for taking risks and doing drugs.

Tess grew frustrated with that whole debate and turned to other sites, hoping that instead of moralizing and political fights, people were more interested in police procedure and profiling the potential killer.

She couldn't wait for Michael to arrive home after meeting with the CARD Team member who would be handling the new abduction case.

She was glad that Michael felt better — good enough to meet with the family and discuss the abduction, but she would be happier when the FBI Special Agents took over the case.

Michael had enough on his hands dealing with the cold cases that had become hot.

CHAPTER 22

THE FBI SPECIAL AGENT ASSIGNED TO THE BEN COLE abduction case arrived at the Bellevue Police Department around seven. He'd flown in from California and had driven directly from SeaTac airport in a rental car. Michael went down to meet him at the front desk and watched the SA get out of the black SUV and walk up to the entrance.

"Hey, Michael," Alan Conway said and extended his hand, smiling in recognition. "Glad to see a familiar face. How's retirement suiting you? You obviously can't escape law enforcement."

"No, can't escape it," Michael replied and shook Alan's hand. "Glad to see you here so you can take over. I'm working cold cases right now, so this is far too hot for me."

"Boyd Olsen from the Southern Division was supposed to come but he had a family emergency and so it's me. Boyd was really upset that he couldn't come but family takes precedence. He remembered you from reading case reports at the FBI Academy."

"The Colin Murphy case, right? I hear it's used as an

example of how, despite everything, a case can go south fast."

"Exactly."

Michael felt bad that his last case was being used to teach FBI Academy recruits about bad case outcomes. "Unfortunately, you have to prepare yourself for the reality that the majority of stranger abductions are over before we even get notified."

"Let's hope we're luckier with the current case," Alan said.

"Yes, let's hope. There's a boardroom reserved for you, with all the relevant files upstairs. Come up with me and we can do a debrief on what we know and where the case sits currently."

After Conway was signed in, Michael led him to the elevator and up to the boardroom, all the while making small talk about the trip to Seattle from California and where he was staying while in the city. They arrived in the boardroom, which had been prepared with boxes of info from the old cold cases that police suspected might be linked, and one wall had been set up with cork boards and whiteboards so the SA could do his work. There was a projector and a screen on the far wall so Michael could do a quick presentation on the current case.

Which he did once Conway was introduced to Joe Mendez and Gord Fields.

He started the projector, which showed a PowerPoint presentation on the case he'd prepared while he waited for the SA to arrive.

The first showed a map of the woods where the abduction took place, with an outline of the presumed path that Aaron took when he escaped and was found fifteen minutes later, on the other side of the park. There were several traffic cams in the area, noted with a red camera icon.

The second showed the exact spot in the woods where the boys were smoking pot when the abductor arrived, where his 'unmarked police vehicle' was parked, just off a side road near the spot, and the items on the ground marked with numbers, including the backpack of Aaron, who escaped.

"Guy was sloppy. Should have taken the items with him to ensure the police didn't know for certain where the abduction took place," Conway said. "He's either green, or he's overconfident and let his guard down."

"Given that there was a similar abduction in the same general area ten years ago involving two boys of the same age, we are keeping the second as an option. Maybe news that we found the original burial site for Andy Owens got the perp reminiscing about old times, and he decided to try again."

"Could be," Conway said, nodding. He was leaning forward, his arms crossed on the tabletop. "Could also be a copycat, who liked the idea. That would explain why he fumbled the ball."

Michael nodded. "We have to keep that as a possibility."

He changed the slide and the next showed photos of both boys, taken from school photos the previous year, their names below the image. Michael did a brief synopsis of each boy, their families, their personal lives, before saying that both boys had been skipping out of school frequently, and that the families were struggling to keep them on the straight and narrow.

"This doesn't seem like a random abduction," Conway offered. "You're not just going to happen onto two young teens smoking pot in the woods, unless you followed them to the location. If they were being watched, that suggests the abductor was planning this. Even if he only picked the two that day, he had to have followed them into the woods with the intent to abduct them both."

Michael nodded in agreement. "My thoughts exactly. He picked them, followed them, intending to abduct them both. When Aaron resisted and ran, the unsub was unable to catch Aaron and so went back and took Ben. It's quite a risk, doing so. Aaron saw him up close and gave a pretty good description of him and the vehicle he was driving, the uniform he was wearing and the crest on the uniform. Based on that, we know that the uniform is old, from before the Washington State Patrol changed uniforms, and was either purchased online from a place like eBay, or it was the unsub's uniform to begin with. If that's the case, we're dealing with a current or former member of law enforcement, the Washington State Patrol. We have one of our techs reviewing all the security cam and traffic cam footage we've collected, looking for the vehicle to see where it traveled. We're checking with Washington State Patrol for the names of all former patrol members, who have retired in the past decade and are cross-referencing them to the description."

"Will internal affairs become involved?" Conway asked. "If one of their own, current or former, IA should be handling the inquiry into members."

Michael nodded. "Yes. We've contacted IA to get them checking on the schedules of all current Patrol officers who were in the area. They're also checking on all who retired, to cross reference against those who still reside in King County and neighboring counties."

"Good," Conway said. "What's next?"

Michael put up a map with the locations where the

missing teens of around the same age and gender were last seen for the past decade and a half. There were a dozen cases in total, from King County and surrounding counties.

"Based on the assumption that this wasn't his first abduction, I did a search on all the MisPers cases for the past fifteen years that match the general description of our two victims, Aaron and Ben. Young boys between the ages of twelve and eighteen. Over a third are from the SeaTac area, and more than half are in neighboring counties. If our unsub is currently or ever was in the Washington State Patrol at any time, he would be familiar with the roads and highways in the state. If so, he would also be aware of any and all traffic cams and security cams in the areas where he operates. He would have knowledge of police procedure. That means he's better than the average abductor."

"But he's screwed this one up," Conway said, rubbing his chin thoughtfully. "If so, he knows he's screwed this up and will be panicking. Which could mean he further screws up."

"One can hope," Michael replied and switched off the projector. "That's it for the update. The staff here are here to help you with any information requests you have or any equipment you might need."

"How many hours have passed since the abduction?"

"Almost ten," Michael replied.

Conway shook his head. "The fact the unsub screwed up might be in our favor. It might mean he's treading lightly and will be more careful, not doing anything until he thinks the heat has died down a bit."

"Or he killed Ben right away and has already disposed of the body."

"Either way, he's a dangerous man, and we have to find him as soon as possible," Conway added.

"I'm here to help you do exactly that," Michael said.

"Good." Conway stood and went over to the cork board and looked at the photos of the two boys that were pinned to the board. "I want to talk to Aaron as soon as possible. In the meantime, we need to review the security cam footage and see if we can track the vehicle."

"I'll get Gord to bring in the footage so you can watch."

With that, Michael left the room and went to where Gord and Terry were still working, watching video.

"Can you bring the footage you already have into the boardroom so Conway can watch?"

"Will do." Gord stopped what he was watching and shut down his laptop, then removed it from its power cord and followed Michael into the boardroom.

"Alan, this is Gord Fields with the Bellevue PD. He's the tech specialist and will walk you through the footage that we have so far."

Gord nodded to Conway and hooked his laptop into the system. Then, he showed the video of the vehicle leaving the park.

"We catch the vehicle here, but then lose it when it goes down a side road. Unfortunately, that's it for now. We traced the plates to a stolen vehicle, so it's a dead end, but it gives us some insight into the neighborhood where the suspect was when the vehicle was stolen. We're checking traffic cams of all the other roads that connect to this and will do a canvas of the neighborhood to see if anyone's security cams caught the suspect entering the area and then not leaving. If we can catch the SUV, we might be able to track him back, but so far, no luck. He could have ditched the SUV somewhere along the route and taken a different vehicle, but if so, we're screwed."

"Keep at it," Conway said. "That's important info on

who this suspect is. Without that, we're working blind. There are probably dozens of current and former Highway Patrol officers who could be suspects. It could also be that our unsub isn't connected to law enforcement in any way and just happened to purchase his uniform from the internet. Whatever the case, we need to winnow down the info and quick."

"I'd like to review the staffing records for the Highway Patrol for the past two decades, see if there have been any disciplinary actions against particular officers," Michael said. "If our unsub is a current or former patrol officer, I can't imagine he's got a clean sheet and excellent performance reports. There must be some kind of screw up."

"Good idea. I'll leave that to you while I check the traffic cam footage."

"I'm at your disposal," Michael said and raised his arms, pointing to the building. "Whatever you need, just say it."

"Good," Conway said and rolled up his sleeves. "I have a hunch those two avenues are our best bets at the moment."

Michael nodded and checked his watch.

He texted Tess to let her know not to wait up.

MICHAEL: *One member of the CARD Team just arrived and has been briefed. Going to stay and try to get some work done so don't stay up. Only one could attend so I'm the backup.*

She texted back right away.

TESS: *Okay. Understood. I'm meeting Kayla tomorrow. I contacted her and asked if she wanted to tell her story. She agreed. We're going to meet in the morning before her shift.*

MICHAEL: *That's good. Gotta go. Have a good evening.*

TESS: *Don't work too hard, but I know this case is important to you. See you later.*

He turned back to the room and watched as Alan sat in

front of the video monitor and watched the traffic cam feed, but his mind was still on Tess's interview with Kayla. Maybe she would be able to get something interesting out of the young woman. Sometimes, people clammed up in police stations and their minds were blank when it came to difficult memories. Talking to Tess might draw some important memories out of her.

Hopefully, Tess would get some good details. If not, there was always the video feed that Conway was reviewing. Maybe he would see something that would put them on the killer's trail.

They needed something.

Ben's life was hanging in the balance.

CHAPTER 23

THE TAXI DRIVER TOOK CURTIS THROUGH THE STREETS of Bellevue on the way to his mother's. The older woman was on the city's volunteer board administering to the city's homeless, and she was a church deacon, active in ministering to the local flock. She also lived alone after Curtis's father died a decade earlier.

In fact, it was through her that Curtis found quite a few of his own flock, so to speak. He helped on occasion at the yearly fundraiser baseball game, coaching one of the teams made up of boys who were in care through the local church. There were quite a few who had been on his radar, and he'd been watching them, taking note of where they lived, and who their foster parents were, so he could suss out any weaknesses and find a way into their lives without raising suspicion.

He taught a driver ed course, based on his previous experience as a trooper with the Washington State Patrol, and he also volunteered at the local youth center, cleaning and doing other miscellaneous tasks that the women who ran the center couldn't do or didn't know how to do.

They all praised him for his community minded nature, saying they wished there were more like him.

Yeah, no.

You don't know what the hell you're talking about, idiot. I am your worst nightmare...

Lucky for him, the women were trusting, despite the work they did and the experiences of the children they cared for.

You might think it would make them even more suspicious of the men who became involved with the organization, but it didn't. They were so run off their feet, always struggling to get enough funding to do their work, that any volunteer work was accepted without question and happily.

That was in his favor.

He kept his nose clean when with the kids and talked about his wife and his own family a lot. How he did his volunteer work, hoping he could prevent young boys from a tragic end.

Most of that was true, except of course, that he didn't really want to prevent a tragic end.

He wanted to be its cause.

The taxi arrived at his mother's house, a bungalow in a nice neighborhood in the north of the city, where he went inside, the door unlocked as usual. His mother had no idea what the hell was going on around her, lost in her happy make-believe world she lived in. She was currently in the back garden puttering around in her pots.

He went to the sliding door, which was open.

"You know, someone could just walk in and steal all the very nice electronics and costume jewelry you keep on display in your bedroom, Mom."

She stood up straight and shaded her eyes with a hand. "Oh, Curtis! It's you. Did I leave the door unlocked again? I know you always tell me to lock it, but I can't help it. What if the one of the kids I sit for come home early and I'm back here?"

"They have their own keys, Mom."

"But what if they lost them? Then what?"

"They'd come around the side of the house and find you here, that's what."

She only smiled, like he was just too worried about things that were never going to happen.

Well, they happen, lady. I make them happen...

"What happened to you?" She frowned and put down her trowel and came right over to him, raising a hand to look at his face, which was bandaged up. "Why are you wearing those scrubs?"

He glanced down and remembered the scrubs he'd been forced to wear at the hospital because the EMTs had to cut his pants off on the way to the hospital.

"I was in an accident, which is why I came by. Can I borrow the Audi? My Denali's totaled. Until I can get a replacement, I need something to drive."

"Of course. You can take it for good, for all I care. It's old and needs some gas, but there's enough to get you to the nearest station."

"Great. I'll take the Audi. Maybe we can get together Sunday for a barbecue? I have some ribs in the fridge we could cook up."

"That would be lovely," she said, smiling like everything was right with the world.

"I'll talk to Joyce, and I'm sure the girls would be happy to see you."

"I'll get you the keys," she said and went into the cool dim interior of the house. He followed her, thinking how easy it would be to just knock her over the head, take her bank card and get the money out of her account. She'd actually told one of the girls the security code when he had gone into the store to use the card to buy something for his birthday when she was sick. The two birthday months and years. How easy was that to remember?

He could take the card, get the money from the drive-through teller, and head for the hills...

Except, he knew that would just add more evidence for police to track him. If they found her dead, even if they didn't until the weekend, it would mean police would investigate the family, and that meant him.

The very last thing he needed was one more reason for his name to be looked at by police.

So, he resisted the urge to bash his mother on the head and take her bank card.

He'd have to find another way to get money out of his account and fast, so he could take off and start a new life somewhere.

Maybe instead of Mexico, he could try Southern California.

Yeah, he could imagine himself living in San Diego. All that sun, surf, and all those homeless people living on the streets.

Ripe for the picking.

Maybe farther north in San Francisco. It was the gay capital of the country, and there were lots of young male prostitutes who were always looking for their next fix.

He'd considered moving to San Francisco before, but he knew the streets and roads and mountains of Washington State so well, based on his years of patrolling them, that he hated the idea of moving somewhere new and having to start from scratch. Sure, there were lots of remote areas in California he could explore, places to hide, if needed. But nothing could compare to Washington State's wilderness for the hunter, whether one hunted game or humans.

He could drive south and arrive in SF the next day if he deadheaded it. If he didn't draw attention to himself, he could get there with no incidents and use his money to find a place to stay, get a new identity.

Start over.

He'd fucked up enough with the two latest boys.

Maybe a fresh start was just what the doctor ordered.

He'd have to go online and transfer all his savings to his private account, so he could access it without Joyce knowing.

He took the keys from his mother, gave her a quick peck on the cheek, and then went out to the garage where the old blue Audi awaited.

"Are you sure you're okay? You look quite banged up."

"I'm fine, Mom. Don't you worry. The doc gave me a clean bill of health."

"Okay. If you're sure. Should I call Joyce and see if there's anything I can do?"

"No, there's no need. I'll call you on Sunday after Mass."

She smiled like everything was just peachy...

He drove off and made his way to a local gas station that had fewer cameras around it. He checked his watch. Joyce would be at work, so he could go home, pick up his stuff, and then leave town. She wouldn't expect to hear from him until Sunday afternoon.

She'd wait and wait and wonder where he was. She knew that he was out of cell phone range up at the cabin and wouldn't be able to contact her.

By the time she started to really worry, maybe call

someone at the local PD, he'd have taken care of the boy, and would be south in California.

Starting his new life.

He could keep driving, and end up in Mexico, if need be.

Rents were cheap there. Rent boys were a dime a dozen.

Even better than SF or San Diego.

Yeah... Once he got everything pulled together, he could move to Mexico. The boy could stay at the cabin. As much as he wanted to go find the boy, have some fun with him, that would be a mistake, now that the police had the other boy in custody.

No one went to the old cabin, and it was remote enough that there would be no way for anyone to just happen onto it and find the boy.

He'd die alone from dehydration in a few days.

It wasn't what Curtis imagined when he planned to take the two boys, but whatever.

By the time the boy's body was eventually found, Curtis would be in Mexico, living it up on the beaches of Tijuana.

CHAPTER 24

THE AFTERNOON WAS A LONG SLOW SLOG, BUT THIS WAS what Grace lived for — old bones, a mystery of how the person died and when, and who they were.

Old bones because she'd always had a love of paleontology and had spent many a happy summer on digs in the Fossil Butte National Monument in Wyoming with her amateur-paleontologist-father. He'd encouraged her love of science and while he had hopes she'd become a PhD in paleontology, she chose instead medicine like him, wanting to look at current humans instead of dead dinosaurs, however interesting they were to her. Her mother was a nurse and had spent lots of time explaining how the human body worked and how to fix things that were broken and torn.

In the end, a course in forensic pathology sealed the deal and she decided that was her calling.

Unearthing dead people and determining how they died, how long ago, and if possible, who they were.

The almost-totally skeletonized remains laid out on the

autopsy table were from body #4 recovered from the Deep Lake site.

She measured various bones to determine an approximate age, which she put at between puberty and eighteen, but most likely closer to puberty since the rest of the body was on the small side.

The soil samples had been sent to the lab in the hopes that they could help nail down a post-mortem interval — the time since the body had been buried. Changes in the soil chemistry could indicate whether the body had been buried more recently or farther in the past. She didn't expect tests to come back quickly, as the lab was often backlogged with forensic tests and so she would have to make do with other clues.

One of which was the relative intactness of the clothing, which had barely degraded. That suggested this poor child had been murdered relatively recently, their body dumped in the past couple of years rather than a decade or more.

Grace examined the clothes, including a rain jacket, suggesting that the child had been abducted during the rainy season, which stretched in the Pacific Northwest from November to May. Summers were hot and dry, with little rain, so she doubted that the child had been killed in the summer months.

She checked the running shoes and saw they were a cheap brand rather than the more expensive brands that better-off families bought for their kids. The no-name jeans and t-shirt were likely a cotton-acrylic blend because both were still relatively intact. 100% cotton shirts and clothing decomposed much more quickly than fabric made with acrylic fibers. The underwear had been pulled down around the feet, suggesting that the child had been raped before or during the assault and strangulation. The ligature, the killer's signature mode of killing, was still around the skeletal remains.

Piano wire fixed with two pieces of wood.

Hair still hung in clumps from the partially skeletonized skull. The child had dark hair. A twelve- to sixteen-year-old boy with dark hair... Grace couldn't help but imagine what he looked like before he died, and it elicited a choke in her throat imagining the fear and pain he must have felt when he realized he was in danger.

She thought the boy might have been killed in the previous year, given the state of the clothing and the state of decomposition. Compared to the other bodies, this one was fresh.

After examining each piece of clothing and carefully removing them from the remains, she checked each bone for signs of trauma that might indicate whether the victim had been assaulted prior to death or had been a victim of abuse before the abduction. From what she knew about the other three victims from the Deep Lake site, they were all vulnerable children, who had been brutalized before they were murdered.

It made Grace sick that monsters existed who preyed on children who were already victims, but they were the easiest targets — vulnerable children and prostitutes.

The victims of choice for serial killers and pedophile monsters.

She sighed and examined the skull next, checking the teeth and noticing that there were fillings present in the molars. At least the child had some dental health care in his lifetime. They could send dental x-rays to dentists in the surrounding counties to check against their records. They might get a match quickly and then would know more about the victim and from that, Michael could do victimology and then construct a profile of the serial killer.

Alice took the skull and jaw to x-ray and sent them off to local dentists, leaving Grace alone to finish up her examination of the last set of remains. Once she was finished, she sat at her computer and reviewed the notes that were auto dictated into a document. She'd clean it up and then print off a copy for her paper file.

Her back ached after spending so much time bending over a site digging for skeletal remains or bending over an autopsy table examining the remains. She needed a coffee and to sit with her feet up for a while.

Maybe listen to some calming music and let her mind wander.

She checked her watch. It was late afternoon the day after she'd first gone to the Deep Lake site and started working on the remains. A lot had been accomplished since the excavator and homeowner had uncovered the first set of skeletal remains. They had two victims identified, and two who were still unknown.

Hopefully, the dental records would identify the victim. Grace thought he might be around fourteen to sixteen, and who she thought died earlier based on the extent of decomposition and skeletonization.

It may have been the very first body to have been buried, but like Michael, she didn't believe that it was the first child that this killer had murdered.

While she was removing her apron and getting ready to leave for her office, Alice came into the anteroom.

"The forensic team just called. They found more remains at the Deep Lake site using ground penetrating radar."

Grace stood up straight. "Good Lord," she said, shaking her head. "I thought they finished examining the site."

"This was on the neighboring plot of land where the house is. You can imagine that the homeowner is upset because two of the bodies are on his side of the property."

"I guess he'd be upset. It's one thing to find bodies on the piece of land you just bought. It's another to find them on your own land." She sighed and ran her hands over her aching back. "I guess I'm going to Deep Lake again."

"No rest for the wicked, right?"

Grace laughed. "You know it. I need a cup of java and a donut before I head down there. Where is Michael Carter when I need him?"

Alice smiled. "He'll probably be down at the site as soon as he hears there's more bodies."

"I think you're right."

She gathered up her jacket and keys and left the office, taking the elevator up from the autopsy suite to the lobby where she signed out before going outside to the parking lot where her vehicle was waiting.

The nearest Starbucks was a five-minute drive, so she'd go through the drive-through, get her donut and coffee, and head back to the Deep Lake site. She checked her watch. By the time she got to the site, it would be dark, and she would have to work under a series of spotlights. She could have just waited until the next day to attend the site, but she was eager to get going. Besides, all she would do at the house was think about the two sets of remains and who they were.

Better to go, spend a couple of hours digging them up, and then return home late, crash for eight hours, and return to the office the next morning fresh and ready to see what the bones said to her.

So, she did.

∼

THE DRIVE to the Deep Lake site was slow, due to late afternoon traffic, and so she arrived about a quarter of an hour after she planned, but when she got there, everything had been set up for her and she slid right into her place as the forensic anthropologist of record.

After slipping into her whites and donning her mask and goggles, gloves, and booties, she climbed down the slope to where the tent had been erected. She could see the bones before she even got there, sticking out of the dark wet mud. A femur, by the looks of it. The toughest bone and the hardest to break. Fully skeletonized.

This guy had been in the ground for quite a while. She adjusted the light and bent down to see that there were no clothes to speak of on the remains, so they had either degraded past recognition, suggesting that this body had been in the dirt for over a decade, or he was buried naked. She assumed it was another young male just based on the sex of the other four. If it was the same killer, he preferred young males just past puberty.

She checked the length of the bone and frowned. This one was an adult, based on the length. She began to remove the dirt from around the rib cage, hoping to find the sternal end of the fourth rib.

By the looks of it, the person was adult, as the costal cartilage at the sternal end of the fourth rib indicated it was a young adult rather than someone older. Maybe between eighteen to twenty-five. She would check the pubic symphysis to see if she was right, as that was another good way to age a set of remains.

As she thought, the symphyseal face showed ridge development that was characteristic of those nineteen to thirty-four. Taken together with the sternal end of the fourth rib, she wagered that the deceased was under twenty-five rather than between twenty-five to thirty-four.

She located the ilium, which was the upper portion of the pelvis, and noted it had a fine granular appearance and the absence of striations suggested that the deceased was between twenty and twenty-four years old when they died.

So, a little older than the other victims. What was that about? Did the person look younger?

Was it a murder of opportunity rather than one of preference?

Some serial killers had a preference when choosing their victims. In this case, it seemed the killer preferred younger male victims between the ages of fourteen and eighteen. Someone in their early twenties was out of the age range. Serial killers were also known to occasionally kill people who became inconvenient or who might have been a threat, rather than for sexual sadistic purposes.

That could be the case here.

Michael would be very interested in this victim.

She dug some more, removing the soil from the bones so that she could get a better idea of how the body had been lain down after death. Like the others, the victim was face down. Dumped. There had been trash placed above the body — an old carpet, which seemed to be a favorite of the killer. Probably meant to prevent animals from predating the body, masking the scent.

She took several photos of the remains once they had been fully exposed and then began the process of placing the remains in the body bag with as much care as possible to preserve any other evidence that might be present.

What she noted was that there was no ligature on this body, but from what she could see, there was evidence of a skull fracture. Whoever killed this person did so with a blow to the back of the skull with a heavy object.

She sat back and took a break, stretching her aching back. The victim was in a different age group. The killer used a different method of murder. But used the same burial grounds. The dead man was older than the other remains.

Perhaps it was someone inconvenient for the murderer?

Their first kill?

Michael would have some ideas.

Grace turned back to the skeletal remains in the ground beneath her knees and continued working, eager to hear his ideas.

CHAPTER 25

Michael watched the video feed. It was getting nowhere fast, and he was getting tired. He checked his watch. It was now six thirty at night. They weren't really making any progress, so he checked his cell and saw a text from Alice, the assistant who worked with Grace Keller at the King County ME's office.

ALICE: Dr. Keller wanted me to text you and let you know we found two more sets of remains at the Deep Lake property. This time, on the other side of the fence, in case you want to come and check it out. She'll be there late.

Michael frowned. He knew that the forensic team had employed ground penetrating radar to search the property where the other bodies had been found and had turned up nothing. Now, they found two more bodies on the other side of the property line.

That piqued his interest.

MICHAEL: Tell Dr. Keller that I will be there in an hour.

He turned to Conway and patted him on the shoulder.

"I'm heading out to the Deep Lake site. They've found more remains using ground penetrating radar."

Conway nodded. "I'll keep at this for another hour or two."

"Let me know if you see anything. I'll be up late, so don't hesitate to text me."

"Will do," Conway said and turned back to the monitor.

Michael left the tech room and went to the main office area. Mendez and Fields were deep in discussion about the map they were examining.

"Hey, Michael. What's up? See anything in the video footage?"

Michael shook his head and grabbed his jacket. "No, but Alan will keep at it. The forensic team found two more sets of remains at the Deep Lake site, so I'm heading south to check it out."

"Okay. See you tomorrow."

With that, Michael went down to the front lobby and signed out with the security guard. He took the Range Rover and drove south, taking Interstate 90 to Issaquah, making sure to stop at the local Starbucks to grab a latte for Grace. Then, he took a secondary highway due south. He arrived at the Deep Lake site in just under sixty minutes. The sun had set, and the yard was illuminated by bright overhead lights shining on the excavation site. A tent had been erected over the site, and he could see a white-suited Grace Keller seated beneath its cover. After he donned protective gear and climbed down beside her to watch, he held out the coffee.

"A latte for M'Lady."

She stopped what she was doing and turned to face him. "I already had one, but I'll never turn a second one down." She climbed back a few feet, removing her mask and goggles. "I was wondering if you'd show up. Should have known."

"You know I can't resist this forensic anthropology stuff," he replied and handed her the coffee.

"You're an eager student." She took the latte and had a long sip of it, sighing in relief. "You're a very good student, too, remembering that your poor teacher loves her latte."

"What have you got?"

She took another sip and then sighed. "Interesting. Male aged twenty – twenty-four, based on examination of the bones. Looks like he's been here for quite a while. Maybe older than all the others, based on the degree of skeletonization and the absence of any clothing and the consistency of the surrounding soil. Also, different method of killing him compared to the other four. This one's been struck from behind with a very hard blunt object. Caved in the back of the skull."

She went to the body bag and unzipped it, then pointed to the skull, which Michael could see when he stepped closer, taking care to stand on the blocks laid down so he didn't disturb the crime scene.

"Oh, I see," he said and nodded. "Yeah. Looks like it would have killed him pretty quick."

"Do you suppose it was an ambush? Came up behind and whacked him with a bat or crowbar? Can't tell if he was naked or his clothes all disintegrated, but we did find some rubber soles that look like they're from the bottom of some boots. Can't tell if they were still on him at the time he was buried or thrown in with the body, but he was lying face down like the others and there was an old rug placed on top of the body."

Michael nodded. "Same as the others, so it sounds like the same killer. Same location, same MO in terms of the position of the bodies and method of burial. Just a different age and method of killing. Could be his first, or it could be someone who he needed to get rid of. Until we know who it is, there's no way of knowing which."

"When I get him back to the office, I can send his dental x-rays out to see if we can ID him from those. There don't seem to be any personal belongings with him. No jewelry, watch, wallet. Just the rubber from the soles of whatever he was wearing on his feet."

Michael nodded, then sipped his own coffee while Grace went back to the remains and continued removing soil from around the body.

She worked for the next half hour on that body, and then stood, stretching and rubbing her back. "Jeeze but I'm getting old. Going to have to turn this part of the job over to Alice, but I hate to stop. I love this part. It's like finding buried treasure. I know that's morbid, and that I should feel bad for this man, whoever he was, and I do but this is like the start of a puzzle for me. I always enjoy it almost as much as I did digging up dinosaur bones with my father when I was a little girl. Almost as much."

"I imagine that was less morbid. Not likely murdered."

"Oh, we worked some areas with the remains of dinosaurs killed in the asteroid impact. Before he died, he went to a few locations and was really excited to find evidence of the K-T boundary and actual bones of dinosaurs." She smiled. "He would have loved the Tanis site in North Dakota, finding the fossilized bodies all stacked up on each other because of the tsunami from the impact. He died a few years too soon."

Michael smiled. Like father like daughter was a truism that applied to Grace and her father, the amateur paleontologist and physician.

Of course, that made him think of his own sons, and how much he was missing out being with them day in and day out. Yes, they had a father figure in the house, and he was glad of that. Julia's new husband seemed like a decent man, who treated the kids like his own, but still. He knew he was missing out important formative years in their lives. It made him consider moving to Tacoma, so he could live close by and share custody. Tess was at a stage in her career where she could work from home most of the time. If her book did well, she could maybe be a writer and freelance reporter, working from wherever she was.

They had talked about it briefly, and Tess indicated she would be fine if Michael wanted to move to Tacoma to be closer to the boys.

He'd have to really consider it. It would mean quite a commute for him — at least forty minutes to get from the King County Prosecutor's Office to the neighborhood where he would prefer to live. Doing that twice a day five days a week would be a pain, but if it meant he could be closer to the boys, he would do it.

Just knowing how close Grace was to her own father, how much of an influence he was on her choice of careers and how he encouraged her in her dreams made him feel sad about his lack of that with his boys.

He sighed and watched as Grace began transferring the bones into the body bag, being careful to place them in as close to their natural state as possible. When she was finished, she stood and stretched and then checked her watch.

"I'm calling it a night," she said and turned to him. "How about you and I grab a bite in Black Diamond on the way back? There's a good truck stop with famous French fries that I happen to like to indulge in now and then."

"Sounds perfect," Michael replied and smiled. He enjoyed their meals together, when Grace would regale him with tales of the various crime scenes she'd been at, and the numerous ways that people had found to kill each other over the years.

After removing their protective clothes, Grace got in her vehicle and Michael followed her down the highway to Black Diamond, and the infamous truck stop she spoke about. It was a huge affair, with dozens of huge rigs parked in the lot, some of them sleeping there.

The restaurant was like any you'd find across the state, with booths along the windows looking out over the lot, and stools at the counter. Grace found a booth open near the far wall. She removed her rain hat and raincoat, hanging it on the coat rack before plopping down in the booth.

"What a day." She glanced at the menu and placed it down quickly. "I already know what I want."

"What's good, other than the infamous fries?"

"It's all good. Whatever you like. There's meatloaf, and lasagna and spaghetti with meatballs, and dogs and burgers. Fish and chips. I've had it all."

Michael nodded and picked the same as Grace — a Western BBQ burger with onions, bacon, and gravy with the fries.

While they waited, Grace quizzed Michael on his theory of the case.

"So, what kind of monster are we dealing with?" She stirred some sugar into her freshly poured coffee. "Pedophile, of course. But what else?"

Michael shrugged. "Definitely a pedophile. Like most serial killers, he'll be a sociopath. Lacking empathy. Sees everyone as pawns to be manipulated. People to exploit. He won't feel any real emotion for them the way you or I would. They're objects. In fact, I suspect he's also a sadist. He likes the suffering. Hence, the garrote. Not a quick death, in other words. Prolonged."

Grace made a face of disgust. "What makes a person into a monster like that? What's your theory? Genes? Environment? Some mix of both?"

"Yes. To all three. Some people are born lacking empathy. They have bad experiences in childhood, and something breaks inside. They start liking to see suffering. First in animals and their siblings or friends. Then, they start sexualizing the violence. They may rape and stop at that. Or they may fantasize about raping their victims while they are killing them. Those are the worst, of course."

"You met many of that type?" Grace asked after the waitress brought their plates.

He nodded, and checked the burger, which looked as good as Grace promised. "Sadly, yes. Kincaid was one. A perfect example. Bad genes, bad home environment as a child. Tortured the neighborhood cats. Peeping Tom. Rapes. Sex murders. Pedophilia. He had it all."

"Jeeze, Louise," Grace said and chewed on a French fry dipped in gravy. "He was married to your sister, right?"

Michael took a sip of his coffee and nodded. "Unfortunately, yes. Luckily, he never hurt my nephews or my sister. He was using them as cover. It worked for decades. Right under our noses."

"Scary," she said and took a bite of her burger. "Sounds like this guy is like Kincaid. Likes them young. Sexual murders. We're at six dead so far. Who knows how many others are buried elsewhere?"

"Once we get some idea of who he is, we may be able to find more. I'm wondering if it isn't connected to the current case I'm working."

"You mean the abduction of the boy, Ben, and his friend? It was in the same area, right?"

"Same general area. Two boys. Just like Andy and Cory ten years ago. I can't help but link them, given it's so unusual for a perpetrator to try to take two victims at once, both male and in their early teens."

"So, you know he's still active."

"Yes, unfortunately. It means we have to find the sonofabitch and stop him before he kills again."

Grace sighed and held up her cup. "Here's to finding the sonofabitch and giving him the electric chair."

"No can do," Michael replied. "No death penalty in Washington State since 2018."

"Hmm." Grace eyed her burger. "I know the ACLU says that the death penalty is unequally applied, so maybe that's good, but still. You know that some people shouldn't be allowed to continue breathing the air with the rest of us."

"No comment," Michael replied with a slow grin. "I follow the law, and it's now the law."

"Good man," Grace said. "Luckily, I'm not judge, jury and executioner or I'd be glad to be the one to pull the switch."

Michael didn't reply, but he couldn't help but feel sympathy for her stance.

Hopefully, they'd find the monster who killed the boys and put him away before he could do more harm.

CHAPTER 26

When Michael arrived home, Tess was still up sitting at her computer, chewing her nail, and trying to think of how to end a chapter.

She quizzed him on how things were going before they went to bed.

"Another body?"

"Two, so far," he said as he stood at the bathroom sink and brushed his teeth. "They'll continue with the ground penetrating radar on the other side of the property line tomorrow. Who knows how many more there are?"

When he was finished, he climbed into bed beside her and switched off the light, before snuggling into her arms.

"What a long day," he said with a yawn. "Tomorrow will be even longer."

She smiled to herself. He was complaining but not really. He loved his job.

"Such is the life of a dedicated Investigator. But don't try and tell me that you don't love your job. I know you do, especially working with Grace at burial sites. Should I be jealous?"

"You should, you definitely should," Michael replied and tickled her. "But she did make me think of something and I wanted to talk to you about it. Maybe it should wait until tomorrow."

Tess frowned. "No, you can't do that. You can't bring something up mysteriously and then tell me to wait until morning. What? I want to know."

He sighed. "Grace had such a great relationship with her father. They spent a lot of time together, on weekends and holidays, traveling to geological sites to do excavations. It made me think of all the time I'm missing with Nathan and Connor."

That admission made Tess's heart squeeze. She knew Michael felt deprived of his boys. He'd spoken before of moving closer to Tacoma so he could share custody.

"We can move anytime you want. I think it would be wonderful to find a house with extra bedrooms so the boys could stay with us alternate weeks, or whatever you two decide works best."

"Are you sure? It would mean I would have to commute every day to get to work forty minutes. What about you? Could you continue to work from home?"

Tess nodded. "Yes. I could go into the office once a week when I'm back at work, after the book is finished. The rest of the time, I can work at home. Only need to go to editorial meetings when they're called. I can do Zoom if I need to talk to people. One thing the pandemic taught us is that we don't always have to be in the newsroom."

"Good. We should plan on it in the next year, okay?"

"Okay," she said and kissed him. They snuggled down closer and soon, she could hear him breathing deeply and regularly, a sign that he was already asleep.

She smiled to herself. He fell asleep so quickly.

In contrast, Tess lay awake for quite a while, thinking of Michael and his boys, and how Julia would take it if Michael asked for joint custody.

Tess had always assumed she'd be a mother one day but was so wrapped up in her job at the *Sentinel* that she figured it was a long way off. She'd met Nathan and Connor and they were nice enough boys, but would they accept her as their mother? Would they resent her?

She'd have to really try hard to be the kind of step-mother that she would like to have had if her parents divorced and her father remarried. Luckily, Tess never had to worry about that, but now, it would become her reality.

Maybe she would have to take up playing video games so she could relate to them. That seemed to be what the two boys were most interested in.

She finally fell asleep, her mind obsessing over what it would be like to have the boys half of the time.

WHEN SHE WOKE, it was still dark, and Michael was in the shower getting ready for his day. She went to the kitchen and made a pot of coffee and then sat and read over the headlines on her iPad to see what was new in the world.

Her cell chimed and she saw a text message from Kayla.

KAYLA: I'll be a bit late. Have to cover for a co-worker. Is 1:00 all right for you?

Tess texted back that it would be fine.

When Michael came into the room, she handed him a cup of coffee in a travel mug.

"I just got a text from Kayla that she'll be a bit late."

"Oh, yeah. See what you can get from her. She was pretty upset when police interviewed her. Ask her about

Chris's friends and acquaintances around the time that he went missing. Where he hung out, where he worked, where he stayed. Who he worked for. Every little bit helps."

"I will," Tess replied. "You going back to the Deep Lake site?"

"Yes. For the morning. Then, I'll spend the rest of the afternoon in the office. I think Alan Conway wants to do another press conference, see if we can get people jogging their memories for the time when Ben was abducted. Someone must have seen them enter the park. I suspect they were being watched. Based on where they were sitting when the perp confronted them, he wouldn't have just happened onto them. He followed them, which suggests he either saw them and was interested, or already knew they were his target."

Tess shivered. "It's scary to think these men are just hanging around waiting. One false move by some unsuspecting child or teen and they're gone." She shook her head and wrapped her arms around herself.

Michael slipped on his jacket and shoes. He slung his briefcase over his shoulder and grabbed his travel mug of coffee and a slice of toast with peanut butter.

"Gotta go," he said and kissed Tess briefly. "I'll text you to let you know when I'll be back. Maybe, if we're lucky, we can have dinner together."

"That would be nice. That is, if Grace doesn't monopolize you..." She grinned at him, and he laughed.

"I can eat dinner twice if I have to."

He kissed her once more and then left the apartment.

Tess sat in the kitchen and sipped her cup of coffee, imagining Michael sitting with Grace in some roadside BBQ place, chowing down on ribs. She wasn't really jealous of Grace, who was more Michael's mother's age than her own.

It was just fun to tease him about her.

SHE SPENT the morning reading over the latest draft of her manuscript, adding bits and pieces and revising a couple of chapters to get the timing straight. She had a shower and dressed, checking her watch to make sure she left the apartment with enough time to get downtown to the waterfront where she would meet Kayla to find a decent parking spot.

The traffic was heavy as she wound her way through the streets of downtown Seattle and over to Bellevue. She was lucky to find a spot a few blocks away from the cafe where Kayla would meet her.

The cafe itself was typical of what you'd find anywhere in Seattle — small, homey, with art on the walls. There were fresh baked muffins and cookies, as well as every kind of tea and coffee you could desire. There was a lunch menu with sandwiches and salads, so Tess selected a turkey sandwich on a bun and glanced out the window to see if there was room on the patio. Luckily, the sky was clear and so she went to the patio and selected a table under an awning. It would mean she could sit without a mask and enjoy her meal without worrying about the pandemic.

Finally, a young woman Tess recognized as Kayla arrived and came right over to the table. She had medium length brown hair and brown eyes, and was on the slim side, not much over five feet tall. She looked to be in her late twenties to early thirties, but Tess knew that she had a hard life on the streets.

"Tess?" Kayla said. "From the *Sentinel*?"

Tess pointed to the table. "Yes. Hi, Kayla. Are you getting lunch?"

"I'll go grab something and be right back," she said and put her backpack on the back of the chair. Tess watched as she went back inside and ordered some food. In a few moments, she returned and sat across from Tess, a cup of coffee in one hand and a sandwich on a plate in the other.

"I love their egg salad," she said and smiled. "Do you mind if I eat a bit first? I'm famished."

"No, please, go right ahead. I'm fine. I'll tell you a few things about what I'm hoping to do with the article and then we can talk more about Chris and your lives together."

Tess watched her eat, and while she did, Tess filled her in on the book she was writing, and her experiences with Eugene Kincaid.

"I read all about it," Kayla said. She wiped her mouth with a napkin. "That's why I agreed to talk to you. If anyone would care about Chris, it would be you. No one else did. Not at the time he went missing. There's probably no one but me who really cares now. I mean, I know the police care. They want to find out who killed him and all, but it's their job. His life mattered. Just because it was hard, doesn't mean it wasn't valuable just by being human. We should care about Chris and people like him."

Tess nodded, impressed with the impassioned speech about Chris.

She felt the same way.

"I agree," Tess said and took in a deep breath, thinking of all the victims she'd spoken to in the past few years, and all the ones she never had the chance to speak to. "His life did matter and it's a failure of our society that no one even cared when he went missing. He was too young to be on the streets living rough, and he was too young to die such a violent death. That's why I want to speak with you. I want to tell Chris's story. I want to tell your story, too."

Kayla shook her head. "Mine isn't as important. I figured my life out, but Chris didn't even have the chance. The killer took that from him, and I think he used the fact that Chris was a substance abuser to prey on him."

"I want you to tell me about the time you spent being homeless with him. Tell me all about how you survived and what people you knew — the adults Chris interacted with. Someone who knew him killed him. Someone he ran into during his last day."

Kayla nodded. "I've been thinking about that, trying my best to remember all the guys we knew on the street, and everyone Chris might have contacted."

She reached into her backpack and pulled out a folded and wrinkled piece of paper. On it, she had written a list of names. She handed it over to Tess.

Tess reviewed the list. There were single male names without surnames, and a few were obviously nicknames. Street names.

There were also a few names with surnames, and those would be useful. The nicknames might be useful for police who would have some idea of who the nicknames belonged to.

"Can I have this? Can I take a pic of it?"

Kayla nodded. "Sure. Take a pic. I want to keep that in case police talk to me again."

Tess flattened the sheet of paper and held her iPhone over the sheet, capturing the contents in a photo. She'd print it off later and show it to Michael.

If anyone could make sense of it, he could.

"My partner, Michael Carter, works with the King County Prosecutor's Office. He's on the task force looking into cold cases in the state. He'll be able to take these names and maybe track down some of them. Is there anyone you had a bad feeling about when you met them? Anyone you were suspicious of?"

Kayla frowned. "I don't know. I'll have to think about it. Some of them were pretty shady characters, drug dealers. Pimps. Some of them were community workers, at the shelters and youth center."

Tess nodded. "I'll give this to Michael. He'll be able to track some of these people down."

"Good," Kayla said. "Investigator Carter is nice."

Tess smiled. "He is. He really cares."

For the next hour, Kayla talked about her own life, which was harder than Tess could imagine, and Chris's life, which was worse, if possible. They really were abandoned children, left to fend for themselves, no adults caring enough to give them a place to sleep or food to eat. For half a year, they ate out of dumpsters behind restaurants, they slept under train trestles and bridges. They stole food from convenience stores and gardens.

When they were desperate, Chris was a drug mule, picking up packages of drugs and delivering them to those who distributed them on the street for one drug dealer.

Everything Kayla told Tess reinforced how there was a certain group of children who were society's cast offs. Children who had parents who didn't care for them or about them. Children who fell through the cracks.

Children who paid the ultimate price for being vulnerable.

It reinforced her decision to focus on crimes against children.

She would tell their stories.

CHAPTER 27

THE NEXT DAY, MICHAEL SPOKE TO DEAN BECKER about who lived in the house and when, assuring the man that his father wasn't a suspect, considering that he'd been in a nursing home for the past decade and a half after suffering a debilitating stroke.

"Phew," Becker said and wiped his brow dramatically. "I've watched a few of those shows on people who were wrongly convicted of crimes, and I don't want anyone to think we have a serial killer in the family. I grew up in that house, and so did my brother, but we moved out two decades ago and it's been empty for over fifteen years. I didn't want to do anything with it until my father passed. When he did and he left it to me, I figured it would make a great property for a hunting and fishing lodge, considering its location."

"Once we know more about the identity of the victims, we'll be able to develop a better idea of the kind of perpetrator we're looking for. Until then, we're just in the early stages of this investigation. I appreciate your willingness to help us."

Becker nodded, his hands on his hips as he watched Grace working under the tent.

"Gives me the creeps, honestly. I wonder if I shouldn't just sell the property and find a place somewhere else. The thought that there were bodies here for a decade makes me feel less like this is the dream house my wife and I have been planning."

Michael glanced around. "It really is a beautiful property, with all the trees and the river nearby. Shame to lose it."

"I might let it sit for a while and see what the response is to the find. It might be a bitch to sell if people find out a bunch of murdered boys were buried here."

For the rest of the day, Michael spoke with Grace after she finished recovering the last remains. There was a lot of evidence to sift through, and hopefully, some of it would help them identify the victims.

Then, Michael could get to work on victimology and then a profile of the monster who killed them.

Around three, his cell chimed, and he checked to see who was sending him a text.

It was Tess.

TESS: Just met with Kayla, Chris's girlfriend from when he went missing. Thought you might like to see this list. People they knew at the time, some nicknames maybe you could track down through local police. How's it going?

He opened the image she sent and saw the list of names. It would be useful, although he was sure the police had probably asked the same question when they interviewed her. Still, he could get onto the list right away and see what it turned up.

MICHAEL: *Almost done here. Will check the list out.*

TESS: *I figured you could use it. See you tonight?*

MICHAEL: *Count on it.*

He put his cell away and went over to where Grace was just finishing up, the last of the remains in body bags and lifted into the back of the van.

"Well, I'm done here. Going back to the office to check these out. You're welcome to come and see if you're interested."

"Thanks. I have a few lines of evidence to track down, but I might drop by tomorrow. See how things are progressing."

"Good," Grace said. She finished removing her protective clothing and slipped back into her raincoat. "Bring coffee if you come."

Michael smiled. "You know I will."

She smiled back and got into her vehicle.

Michael got into the Range Rover and followed her out to the highway. He smiled when he saw her go speeding ahead of him. She was no slouch in the driving department. Soon, she was lost in the traffic.

He could spend all day listening to her talk about her work, but he had his own to do and first on the agenda was to check out the list and see what sense he could make out of the names and nicknames.

There might be an interesting lead or two in it.

WHEN HE ARRIVED BACK at the Bellevue PD, he sat down at his assigned desk, checked his emails, and then turned to the document Tess had sent. He did a search using the police database, checking each name and nickname against its contents.

The search turned up a few names of interest.

Lee Turner — a known drug dealer, serving currently for possession with intent to distribute.

Joshua Boone — a pimp who was known to frequent the streets in Bellevue where prostitutes were known to stroll. He was currently free, and his residence was listed as Bellevue.

There were a few names he couldn't track down, but one caught his eye.

Curtis James Holloway.

Currently, a volunteer at the New Horizons Youth Center, located in a very seedy part of Bellevue, where a lot of the prostitutes and drug dealers worked, and where many homeless people spent their days. But what really caught Michael's eye was the fact that Holloway had been a Washington State Patrol trooper before retiring and starting his own business in security.

That just rang too many bells for Michael not to do a more detailed search on Mr. Curtis Holloway.

What Michael found made him excited, but he also felt a sense of dread at the prospect of the serial killer being law enforcement as they suspected.

From the looks of it, Curtis Holloway was an upstanding citizen, having fought in the war in Afghanistan and Iraq, and then worked as a State Trooper. Plus, he was a volunteer at the Youth Center.

Michael searched online for Mr. Holloway's public profile and found his Facebook page. His public pages looked innocuous: Holloway himself was ordinary looking, with a shaved head, a slight goatee, and dark deep-set eyes. He was forty-three and had been working at his own business since retiring from the State Patrol five years earlier. He was honorably discharged from the Army and from the State Patrol. He was a member of the local Catholic Church in an affluent Bellevue neighborhood. His father had been a powerful attorney in Bellevue.

Holloway had a wife and two daughters, who were currently in middle school.

No one — no one — would ever suspect him of being a serial killer, let alone a pedophile serial killer.

Yet, there Michael was, making that connection in his mind. He couldn't help it. Holloway was former Highway Patrol, and the abductor in the Aaron and Ben case had been wearing an old State Trooper uniform.

It didn't mean Holloway was the killer or that the two cases were connected, but it was just far too coincidental for Michael not to investigate it.

He would do some sleuthing before he went to Conway with his suspicions. The last thing he wanted to do was divert attention in the wrong direction. He'd do whatever research he could on Holloway and then go to them with his evidence, see what they thought.

It might be purely a coincidence, but Michael had a bad feeling.

He texted Tess to let her know that the list was very useful and that one of the names might be a key lead in the case. He didn't mention who, but if Tess was curious, she could figure it out on her own.

Holloway had worked in law enforcement. He was currently involved as a volunteer with vulnerable youth. One of the dead boy's friends mentioned his name when asked to think of Chris's associates from the time he went missing.

Michael needed to do some deep digging in Mr.

Holloway's life to justify bringing his concerns to the FBI Special Agent working the case.

He went back to the man's Facebook page and noted everything he could about the public profile — how often he posted, what he posted and who responded. He seemed most proud of his work with the Methodist Church, including hosting a yearly baseball tournament for troubled youth. There was a photo of him standing with several boys from a little league baseball team. Michael googled the event and saw that the boys ranged in age from ten to sixteen, which seemed to fit with the victims uncovered at the Deep Lake property so far. In one photo, Holloway stood behind three young boys in uniforms, the one in the center holding a trophy, his hands on the young boy's shoulders.

That sent a shiver of apprehension through Michael.

If Holloway was who Michael was beginning to suspect he was, all those boys were potential victims, or boys being groomed.

Michael checked Holloway against the database and saw that he had a clean sheet. No charges or convictions to speak of.

How could that be?

He did some further digging. The family was stalwart, with the sons going into the military and then into law enforcement or law itself, one uncle a criminal defence attorney in Tacoma and another a detective in vice, who retired a decade earlier.

With a family that deep into law enforcement, it would be easy to conceal minor offenses. Michael knew that in some cases, charges were dropped against the children of police officers, or officials in the legal system.

There had to be something in Holloway's past that indicated he was a serial killer in the making...

Finding it would be difficult if he did have family in high places in law enforcement. Michael loved his family in law enforcement, but he knew that sometimes, it was insular and protected its own.

He remembered how everyone was so shocked that Eugene Hammond aka Kincaid was a serial killer, considering how beloved Chief Hammond had been in the Paradise Hill community. That had kept everyone from even suspecting that Eugene could be a killer.

Everyone except Michael, but he didn't like Eugene for a different reason — Eugene preyed on Kirsten, his younger sister, who was far too young for an older guy like Eugene. Everyone else dismissed his concerns because Eugene was from such a good family. Kirsten was strong-willed and wanted to marry Eugene, especially once she became pregnant.

Michael had never liked the man and he ended up being right.

Now, Michael sat and stared at the photo of Curtis James Holloway with the same sense of suspicion bordering on certainty.

LATER, Conway came to his office, leaning in the doorway.

"What's up?"

"Hey, Michael. I know you have your own work in Seattle, but I'd really appreciate your help, if King County can spare you for the interim. The FBI will pay for your expenses if you have to stay overnight in Bellevue."

"I'm pretty sure my boss would insist on me helping,"

Michael said. "I'll give him a head's-up and let him know I'll be working with you."

Michael sent Nick a message, letting him know about the change in plans.

Nick replied right away.

NICK: *Yes, by all means, work with Conway on the case. With your expertise, you're the right man for the job. Keep me updated on any developments.*

MICHAEL: *I will. And thanks for the vote of confidence.*

Michael next sent Tess a message, letting her know he wouldn't be home until much later if at all. Luckily, she was flexible and understood that his schedule was never certain and could change on a moment's notice.

Such was his life. If he'd worried about working in the field with the FBI previously, he felt confident that he could handle whatever they had to deal with.

In fact, he felt like his old self again, perhaps for the first time since he found little Colin Murphy's dead body several years earlier.

He turned back to his files, eager for the hours of work he knew lay ahead. He was used to late nights, and knew he had to put them in during an abduction if they had a hope of finding the victim alive.

With each passing hour, that became less and less likely...

CHAPTER 28

BEFORE HE LEFT THE CITY, CURTIS WENT BACK TO HIS office to remove some cash he kept in the safe.

The office had been locked up for the long weekend and so he was pretty much left alone to do as he pleased. One of the security guards would make rounds and check on the office later that night, but he wasn't scheduled to do so for a couple of hours at least.

He went by his secretary's desk and saw that she had taken some messages for him while he'd been out, which she would have turned over when he arrived for work on Monday morning. He picked up the pink sheets and read them over.

Just the usual requests for shift changes from some of his workers.

A call from the repair shop where one of the company vehicles was in for a tire rotation.

And then one that piqued his interest and got his spidey senses tingling...

A Michael Carter, Investigator with the King County Prosecuting Attorney's Office called, asking about Curtis.

What the *fuck*?

He switched the television on and went to the local news station. He watched a repeat of the news conference from the previous day, showing several suits and uniforms from the Bellevue PD walked to a microphone and spoke about the abduction.

Beside the Chief stood a dark-haired former FBI Special Agent who was now working with the DA. Michael Carter. He had been on the FBI's Child Abduction Rapid Deployment Team before retiring.

Damn. Carter was already on his trail...

That was no good, and meant he had to rethink his plans.

He might just have to take a quick trip to the cabin and take care of the boy, bury his body somewhere so that there would be no link between them. Leaving for Mexico was only good if there was no suspicion about his connection to the abduction. If police had him in their sights, they would go hard looking for him.

He knew what they'd do — put out a BOLO and APB. Have people watching for his vehicle.

No. He had to rethink things.

What tipped them off?

Was it the goddamned uniform?

Jesus. Mary. Joseph.

Too many mistakes. He'd failed to secure the boy who ran, which meant that there was an eyewitness who could describe him. Luckily, he'd been smart enough to wear a wig but there was the decommissioned Highway Patrol vehicle. And there was the old uniform...

The accident was pure chance.

They didn't say anything about finding the dead man in

the garage, so they still hadn't found the body or the vehicle. That was good.

But if Michael Carter had called the office to talk about him...

He had to act and fast.

Before he could do anything, he got a text from Joyce. He knew he had to answer and put her off.

JOYCE: *Hey, hun, I know you'll be busy with Santiago until Sunday, but I thought you should know that police were here asking about you.*

WTF? A surge of anger went through Curtis. The bastards...

JOYCE: *Someone named Inspector Carter and Special Agent Conway. They wanted to know about your time in the Highway Patrol, and what you were doing now. I didn't say anything. You always told me not to talk to police without Gus present, so I didn't. I told them if they wanted to talk to me, I'd have to get our lawyer to join us, and they backed down.*

Thank God he'd coached her enough to never talk to police without their lawyer present.

JOYCE: *They asked to come into the house, but I said no to that, too. They didn't have a search warrant and were just asking questions about your time in the Troopers. But I thought it was strange. I know cellular reception is bad up there, but I hope everything's okay...*

He exhaled heavily, frustrated that the damn police were already on his tail.

Investigator Carter? The same Investigator Carter who had been so haughty on television at the press conference?

He'd been to the house?

What the fuck?

Who the hell was this Carter bastard?

He spent a few moments googling Carter, and came up with a LinkedIn entry, as well as several articles about Carter's involvement in several cases in Washington State. He was clearly a good law enforcement officer and had great instincts.

The profile said he was divorced, and was living in Seattle, while his ex-wife and two sons were living in Tacoma with their new stepfather.

He searched Facebook and came up with the profile of the new husband. There were pictures of the man, the ex-wife Julia, and the two boys. They lived in a wealthy neighborhood near Swan Creek Park in Tacoma.

One photo showed the two boys. The oldest boy, Connor, was dressed in a softball uniform holding a catcher's mitt, the catcher's helmet in his hand. He was a handsome boy, with light brown hair and a dimpled smile.

Almost old enough to be right for Curtis, but he usually liked them a few years older and more developed. Beside him was the younger boy, Nathan. Similar in coloring but clearly a few years younger.

He clipped the photo and decided to send it to Carter anonymously.

Yeah, that would make the man feel less cocky than he had appeared at the press conference...

He would have to find somewhere he could send the image to Carter that couldn't be traced and decided on the public library down the street. It had public access internet.

He could just send it to Carter. Or maybe post it to the King County Twitter account.

Yeah... that would do it.

Someone monitoring the feed would see it and google the image, find out it was of Carter's kids.

That would send a message.

On his way out of the city, he'd stop and post the image.

Then, he'd drive out to the cabin and take care of the boy. He'd clean up the cabin, remove all traces of the boy, then dump the body somewhere on the way. No one would be able to trace the boy to him.

This whole business had been one mistake after another, but if he was out of the state, it would be harder for them to track him down. If he was in Mexico, even better.

He knew a few tricks to avoid capture after working in the Highway Patrol for a decade.

He drove through the streets to the local library, and after parking in the underground lot, he went inside, a mask on his face, and sat down at one of the kiosks where patrons could access the internet. There were a few people in the library, and so he was free to choose one a distance away from the entrance. He logged onto the library's internet, and then went to the King County Prosecutor's Office Twitter feed and left a comment with the image clipped to the tweet.

He clicked send and then closed the browser and left the library as quickly as he could. He was wearing his wig, dark glasses and a mask so the only identifying traits would be his height and weight, but that was not enough to go on.

He left the parking garage and drove out of the city, taking the side roads to get to the cabin and the boy.

He had to work fast. Night was coming and he wanted to be out of the state as soon as possible.

With any luck, he'd be in California in the morning.

CHAPTER 29

MICHAEL GOT A TEXT FROM CONWAY THAT HE SHOULD come to the tech room to see some video footage.

Michael left his office and went right to the room to see Conway and Terry Rider bending over a screen.

"How does it feel to be pulled back in?"

Michael laughed at the Godfather reference. "What have you got?"

Conway stood up. "We found something interesting in a garage near the area where the boys were when Ben was abducted. Look at this," he said and showed Michael some footage of the interior of a garage.

There was an old model Ford with a push-bar and a broken rear signal light.

"That looks suspiciously like an old police vehicle, maybe used by the Highway Patrol at one time and then sold after it outlived its usefulness."

"Correct. What's interesting is what we found beside it."

He showed Michael more footage, which included a

man's body lying face down on the cement floor of the garage.

"Whoa," Michael said. "Who's that?"

"The owner of an abandoned vehicle, a man in his sixties, a widower who lives alone. The only reason we found him at all was that his son came by to drop off some groceries and when he wasn't in the house, the son checked the garage, which doubles as a workroom. Found him lying beside the strange vehicle. The man's usual vehicle was gone."

Michael shook his head. "Okay. So, we're thinking the abductor had a fender bender or something and so felt he needed to switch vehicles, picked this place at random, and when confronted, killed the owner and took the vehicle, leaving the other vehicle behind."

"Looks like the taillight was kicked out from the inside. Someone was in the trunk. We think it was Ben. Forensics are taking samples now and will compare to see if our suspicions are right."

Michael nodded. "Makes sense. So, the perp abducts Ben using his own vehicle, puts Ben in the trunk. Ben kicks out the taillight and so the perp stops to pick up a different vehicle."

"Yep. We've run the plates of the old Ford, but they come back to a stolen vehicle. The car's VIN has been removed. But it's a model used previously by the Washington State Patrol. Whoever this guy is, he's gone to a lot of trouble to hide his identity."

At that point, Michael knew he had to inform Conway about the list and his suspicions about Holloway.

"I think you should know about this," he said and pulled out the sheet of paper that Tess had sent him with the names of several men linked to Chris. "My partner spoke with the former girlfriend of one of the victims at the Deep Lake site and she gave this list of people connected to the victim."

Conway glanced over the list. "Okay. What am I looking at?"

Michael pulled out the photo and bio of Holloway and handed it to Conway. "Curtis James Holloway. Current owner of Sentinel Security LLC. Former Washington State Patrol trooper. Retired a decade ago after serving for only five years. Law enforcement family. Spent time in Iraq and Afghanistan."

"And you think this is our guy? Because of the trooper connection? There's lots of former troopers around."

"Yes, but this man was known to Chris Rogers, one of the victims at the Deep Lake site. Holloway volunteered at the local youth center, coaching baseball. He knew Chris."

Conway nodded his head. "That's interesting," he said, rubbing his forehead. "What else have you got?"

Michael shook his head. "Not yet, but I think we should give him some attention. I'm going to call his business number and see if we can arrange a meeting."

Michael took out his cell and dialed the number listed for the business office. After a few rings, a pleasant-sounding woman answered. He asked to speak to Curtis Holloway but was told that he wasn't in the office at that time.

"Please let him know that Investigator Michael Carter with the King County called. I'll try to get in touch with him later."

Michael ended the call and turned to Conway. "Care to drive out to his home and speak with him?"

"We could do that," Conway said.

"Good," Michael said and gathered up his papers. "I

think speaking to him would help eliminate him from our non-existent list of potential suspects."

They got into the Range Rover and Michael drove to the neighborhood where Holloway lived with his wife and two daughters. It was an upscale neighborhood in Bellevue with expensive houses and very manicured lots and green spaces. In other words, wealthy.

Holloway had his own business, so there was that, plus his heritage as the son of a long line of lawyers, judges and law enforcement.

"There's the house," Michael said and pulled up into the circular driveway. They left the vehicle and went to the front entrance, which was ostentatious with a large double door and on each side, twin lion statues.

Michael rang the doorbell and waited, holding out his ID as did Conway in case Mrs. Holloway was checking through the front peephole.

The door opened and a woman with blonde hair answered. She looked in her mid to late thirties and was wearing athletic wear, as if she had just returned from a run.

"Can I help you?"

"Special Agent Alan Conway, and this is Michael Carter, Investigator with the King County Prosecutor's Office. We were hoping to speak with your husband, Curtis Holloway. Is he home?"

"No, he isn't. Can I ask what this is about?"

"Can't say right now, Ma'am. Could we come in?"

Conway looked like he was planning to step inside, but the woman wouldn't let him.

"Sorry, but do you have a warrant? If not, I don't think so."

Conway smiled and glanced quickly at Michael. "No, we don't. This is just a friendly visit to ask your husband about his whereabouts in connection to a matter we're investigating. Can you tell me where he was on Thursday afternoon between the hours of ten in the morning and three o'clock in the afternoon?"

She frowned and appeared upset with them. "I imagine he was at work, like always. He owns a security business, as I'm sure you already know."

She raised her eyebrows.

"All right, Ma'am. You can tell your husband that we'll call back later tonight."

"He's going to be out of the city until Sunday, so you might as well not bother."

"Is he at the cabin?" Michael asked, wondering if he could trip her up by mentioning it. "I know he likes to hunt and often goes there with his hunting buddies."

"He's a hunter, in fact. A very good hunter. He often takes people into the mountains and hunts, acting like a guide. He does have a cabin, but he's not there."

"Do you know where he is? We really need to speak with him."

"That's none of your business," she said, and when she glanced sideways, Michael knew she was trying to hide the fact that he was, in fact, at the cabin. "I'm not answering anymore questions without our lawyer present if you don't mind. Good day."

She then closed the double doors in their faces, leaving them standing there, facing the wooden expanse.

Conway laughed and turned to Michael. "I guess that's a no."

"I guess so," Michael replied. "What do you say we take a trip out to the cabin? I saw on his Facebook public post that he and his buddies go there on the weekends to hunt. Might be a location that he'd keep a captive if he was into that kind of thing. I got the address from the tax info we have on him."

They walked back to the vehicle, and Conway looked uncertain. "You really think this is our guy?"

Michael took in a deep breath and shrugged. "I don't know, but he has the history with the Highway Patrol, and he knew one of the victims at the Deep Lake site. Boy was from Bellevue, went missing, never reported missing because he was homeless and a runaway from foster care. He was vulnerable, in other words."

"If so, he has a pretty good cover. The guy's active in his church, has a business, is married... I'm pretty new to this, but still... He's blinking red in my books."

They drove off, and Michael watched the house as they reached the end of the very well-manicured block. The wife was looking out at them, the curtain in the huge living room window pushed to the side.

"He is in mine, too. Call it a gut instinct. I can't help but think the two cases are linked. Andy Owens and Cory Dixon were from Bellevue and were about the same age as Ben and Aaron. There were three other boys around the same age at the Deep Lake site. My alarm bells are screaming, especially since Holloway was involved with the youth center in an area where a lot of vulnerable people live. I'll check with the staff there and see what they remember from the last decade. Any other missing kids, or kids they lost track of. Maybe someone will remember Chris."

"You have more experience than I do, so I'll let you take the lead. If you're sure you want to. I know you had a hard time of your last case with the FBI."

"I'm fine," Michael said and nodded slowly. "I feel good. I feel like I could come back and work with the team again. My arm isn't one hundred percent, but it's a lot better. Good enough that I was able to shoot a suspect in my last case and stop him from doing any more damage."

"That's good to know."

"As a matter of fact," Michael said and glanced over his left shoulder, deciding on the spur of the moment to make a U-turn. "I'd like to go to the youth center right now if you don't mind. I'd like to feel the staff out. See what they think of Holloway. See if there are any other missing boys of the appropriate age that they've lost track of. We still have three unidentified males from the Deep Lake site."

"Sounds good. You're the driver."

"I am," Michael said and performed a quick U-turn, going north towards the youth center, which was in the city's downtown, which in turn was a notorious stroll for prostitutes and drug dealers. The youth center was located a block east of the center, closer to the local high school. There was a playing field and baseball diamond nearby where he supposed the youth went to play on weekends and when the school wasn't using them.

The traffic was light, so they arrived in about five minutes and parked half a block from the center. Michael glanced at Conway, who looked as much like an FBI Special Agent as was possible, with the dark blue trench coat, dark aviators and tie.

"They'll know you're FBI from a mile away," Michael said with a laugh. He glanced down at his own clothes which were just a touch more casual.

Conway smiled. "That's who we are, so might as well look the part."

They walked to the entrance and went inside. There was a large recreation area, with pool tables, ping pong tables, and several foosball tables set up. Plus, a lounge area with sofas and comfortable chairs, a large flatscreen TV showing some recent series — looked like some fantasy series. Michael recognized it. The Witcher. About a man who hunted monsters.

Michael thought it was ironic that he was there to hunt for an actual monster. If he was right and Holloway was in fact the perp, the poor kids who frequented the center had no idea how close to a real live human monster they were.

Michael and Conway went to the reception area, where a woman in her forties sat, staring at a computer screen. From the ID badge on her sweater, he could see that her name was Sharon Burke. Youth Coordinator.

"Hello, Sharon?" he said and held up his ID. "I'm Michael Carter, Investigator working with the FBI. This is Special Agent Alan Conway. We'd like to ask you a few questions about a case if you have a few moments."

Sharon looked up and glanced at their IDs before raising her eyebrows.

"Is it about Chris?" She held a hand up to her mouth. "I heard they found his body at the Deep Lake site."

Michael nodded. "Yes. We're here because of Chris. Can we talk somewhere a little more private?"

"Right this way," she said and led them into a room in the back of the building.

Michael wasn't sure that talking to her would help, but he had a bad feeling about Holloway and wanted to know if anyone else felt the same.

CHAPTER 30

"So, I understand you're here to talk about Chris?"

Michael nodded and settled back in his chair across from a large desk where Sharon sat. Behind her was a window overlooking a paved basketball court. A dozen young teens played, passing the ball and doing layups.

"We are," he said. "We're looking into his life before he went missing, who he was involved with, to get an idea of why he might have been targeted."

Sharon took in a deep breath. "I've been working here for over a dozen years," she said. "When I first started, Chris was one of the youths who came here most often. He had a really bad home life and spent a lot of time just recovering from whatever hell he'd gone through at home."

"What can you tell me about his homelife?"

"His mother was a sex worker, who died of an overdose. Biological father unknown. His stepfather was disabled because of an injury that was not work related, so he didn't qualify for a disability pension. The father became a drug addict, was unemployed and took out his frustration on

Chris's mother and Chris. The home was chaotic, and Chris often went without food or clean clothes. No one cared about him, in other words. He looked after himself, got himself to school, and pretty much cared for them when they were passed out or too stoned to care for themselves. When he did get money, he bought food for them. Despite it all, he was a happy kid, at least on the outside. People liked him."

"Who was working with you at the time Chris disappeared?"

She frowned. "I'd have to go back and check," she said and opened a file drawer, removing a file. "We have a lot of volunteers who spend some time with us and then move on. Let me look. It was in 2010, right? I remember. It was rainy that February."

"No one reported him missing?"

She shrugged. "The kids come and go. They move away, move back home. All we can do is provide them with activities when they're with us."

She sat back at her desk and opened the file, flipping through documents. "Okay, here. In 2010, there were about a dozen volunteers, and several paid staff. If you want, I can give you a photocopy of this."

She handed Michael a sheet of paper. He took it and glanced at the document. It was a list of staff and volunteers with addresses and phone numbers beside them in different columns.

There, at the top, was Curtis James Holloway. He was listed as one of the top volunteers, who did hunting and camping expeditions with the kids who used the youth center.

"Tell me about those volunteers. What did you think of each one?"

She went through the list, and strangely, she didn't speak about Holloway, despite the fact his name was at the top of the list.

"What did you think about Curtis Holloway?" Michael asked. He glanced at Sharon to see her response. "I see he's the top volunteer."

She shrugged. "He gives a lot of his time to the center. He coaches a softball team, and he takes the boys on hunting and camping trips. I know the boys love it — especially the hunting and camping trips. He took them up to his cabin near Mount Rainier and taught them to shoot, and they bag some big game on occasion. He shows them how to dress a kill, how to cook it and how to look after their guns. It's male attention that most of the boys didn't get at home. Role model is how I see him."

Michael nodded. "Does he still volunteer?"

"Yes," she said and smiled. "As you said, he's one of our longest serving volunteers. He donates money to the center, and he gives us a lot of time. Honestly, I don't know what we'd do without him. Why?"

"I wondered why you didn't mention him first, since he's at the top of the list."

She frowned. "Do you suspect Curtis of being involved in Chris's disappearance?"

"We don't suspect anyone, or should I say, we don't rule anyone out at this point in the investigation."

"Curtis is married and has two daughters. He's a devoted father and husband. He's active in his church and community."

She said it like it was an affront to even consider that Curtis might be a bad person — a killer.

Michael glanced at the sheet and then handed it back to Sharon. "Could I get that copy?"

She took the sheet and went to a large copy machine in the corner of the office. After copying the sheet, she gave it to Michael.

"I hope you don't think Curtis is involved. Goodness."

"We don't think anything yet. Just doing our jobs." That seemed to satisfy her. Michael glanced at Conway and then back to Sharon. "Well, if there's nothing else you can think of, that's all we wanted to know."

They stood up and Sharon walked them out of the office and back to the entrance.

"Thanks for your help," Michael said.

Sharon clasped her hands together like she was worried. "I hope you find who did this to Chris. He deserved a better life."

"That's our goal. Find who did this and stop them from doing it again if we can."

They left the building and walked past the basketball court. The boys were running from one end of the court to the other, passing the basketball and shouting encouragement to each other.

The center clearly was a good thing, and very necessary for the boys who used it. He would hate to think that one of the most active volunteers was a serial killer, but he couldn't help but suspect it was true.

Was Holloway a wolf in sheep's clothing, preying on the vulnerable boys who frequented the youth center?

It made Michael angry that he could no longer trust anyone who worked with children. He knew that most people who volunteered to work with children were decent, giving people, but there were enough bad apples that he felt unable to look at a male volunteer with anything but mistrust and suspicion.

He hated it, but it was the truth.

"Let's go. I think we should check out Holloway some more."

"You're the boss," Conway said and got in the passenger side of the Range Rover.

They drove off, and Michael decided to go to Holloway's business office in case he was there and had given his wife a false story about his location. On the way, Conway was checking his cell for messages and held up his hand.

"You better pull over," he said.

"Why?"

"Just do it, okay?"

Michael frowned and pulled into an empty parking lot next to a local business. He put the Range Rover in park and turned to Conway.

"What?"

"Take a look," he said and handed Michael his cell. Michael accepted it and checked out the display. On it was the King County Twitter. One of the posts in response to the Amber Alert about Ben was an image of two boys standing in a school baseball diamond.

Nathan and Connor's baseball diamond at their school. The two boys were Nathan and Connor.

"Oh, my God." Michael's heart raced at the sight of his two boys, and the implication. "This is clearly a threat." He turned to Conway, whose face was serious, his expression dark.

"I have to agree."

Michael grabbed his cell and called Julia. When she answered, he asked her where the two boys were. It was late afternoon, and they should be both home from school.

"They're here with me," she replied, her voice sounding

confused. "Why do you ask? You're not seeing them until next weekend."

"There was a photo of them posted on a King County tweet about Ben's Amber Alert."

"What?" He waited as he knew she would be checking the Twitter feed for herself. "Oh, my God, Michael. What should we do? That was taken from our Facebook page. Is someone stalking us?"

He exhaled. "I'll call and have the Tacoma police send a cruiser by the house. You and the boys should go to a safe house the police have and don't tell anyone where you're going or why."

"Okay. Michael? What's going on? Tell me the truth!"

He took in a deep breath. "We're working the case in Bellevue involving the abduction of a boy from the city. Someone may be playing a prank on me, or it might be a legitimate threat. Whatever the case, I want you and the boys to be extra careful and safe until we know more. Police will work to track down who sent the post and image. I'll call you later, okay?"

"Okay."

Michael ended the call and immediately dialed the number for a detective working major crimes he knew in Tacoma. Josh Pope had been a cop in Tacoma for over a dozen years and seemed like a reasonable man and a very good detective. When Pope answered the phone, Michael filled him in on what happened and asked for police protection until they had a better idea of what was going on with the threat.

"Sure, Michael," Pope said. "I'll assign a patrol right now. I'll get victim's services to send a Victim Liaison Officer out to your ex-wife's house to help with the move to the safe house. They can stay there until necessary."

"Thanks for your cooperation, Josh. I really appreciate it. I guess someone took a dislike to me during the press conference, and are doing this to harass me, and hopefully that's all this is, but I want to make sure my boys aren't vulnerable."

"Understood. I'll call you if we have any update on the situation."

"I appreciate it."

With that, Michael ended the call and turned to Conway. "That's taken care of, at least. Now what?"

"Are you sure you want to keep working? I totally understand if you want to go to be with your boys."

Michael shook his head. "They have their mother and stepfather. If they're in the safe house, I'm sure they're okay. I want to find the bastard who sent that picture."

"Call the guys in your tech office. They have the expertise to find out who did this."

Michael dialed the number of the King County Sheriff's Office and spoke directly to one of the technicians in the computer crime unit.

"Can you check and see where the picture was uploaded and when? See what IP was used to upload it? That kind of thing?"

The tech replied that they already had someone on it, and that it shouldn't be too difficult to identify the computer that posted the image.

"Call me when you find out," Michael said.

He turned to Conway. "After we check out his office, I think we should take a trip out to Holloway's cabin near Mount Rainier. See if he's there."

Conway shrugged. "You're the boss, but do you really want to drive all the way there? He might not even be there."

Michael keyed in the location of the cabin, which he'd obtained from a search of tax records. "It should take us less than two hours to get there. We can be back by eleven if he's not there."

"Okay," Conway replied and pointed ahead down the street to a Starbucks. "Drive on. Can we stop and get something at Starbucks on the way? I'm in dire need of coffee and some grub."

Michael pulled in and ordered an Americano for himself and an espresso for Conway as well as some sandwiches. Then, he took Interstate 90 south and east on the way to the cabin.

He didn't know if Holloway was there, but if his instincts were right, he was.

And so was Ben...

CHAPTER 31

CURTIS ARRIVED AT THE CABIN JUST AS THE SUN WAS setting and the last rays of sunlight filtered through the tall trees surrounding the property.

He parked the Audi and went to the garage where he kept his tools and hunting gear, the door secured with a large padlock. Inside was what he came for — his collection of weapons, a toolbox filled with cash that he'd squirreled away in case he ever needed to run, and a suitcase filled with several changes of clothes, personal items in a shaving kit, and several wigs he could wear to hide his identity.

There had been many nights he'd lain awake beside Joyce, wondering what he'd do if his secret life was discovered or if he found out police were on his trail. It would happen eventually. He had been operating for years in the counties from King to Pierce. By his count, he had six victims and another one waiting in the cabin. Now, police had dug up all six of them. It was only a matter of time before they discovered some forensic link to him, some scrap of DNA or fiber evidence, or video feed.

The biggest mistake was the crash. If he hadn't gone for

that stupid cup of coffee, he'd be free and clear. Now, he was twenty-four hours behind schedule.

Dammit...

He would have picked up the laundry, dried it, and he would have been on his way.

Now, the uniform was at the police station and could be linked to the vehicle that was registered to him. The Denali was in the police compound, waiting for him to claim it.

Was that why Carter and his FBI counterpart had gone to Joyce?

They suspected him?

If so, it was all over but the cleanup and escape.

Curtis gathered up everything he had prepared for his escape — the metal case with the fake ID and money, the clothes, the disguises, the weapons, the burner phone, the iPad. He placed everything into a large duffle bag and placed it in the back of the Audi.

When that was done, he pondered what to do about the boy. He'd survived the night, but clearly, he had to be disposed of. Sure, he could leave the boy at the cabin, and he'd eventually die of dehydration, but that would take days. At the same time, if he took too much time to dispose of the boy, he might delay his getaway.

Discretion was the better part of valor, or so the saying went. It might be best to get a head start on his trip south and leave the boy.

Yeah... That's what he'd do. He'd just get the hell out of Washington State. He'd take less-traveled roads south and east, maybe I-90 to Ellensburg, then south on I-82, before taking I-97 all the way south to come out at Pismo Beach, CA. It was a sixteen-hour drive, and with any luck, he could drive eight hours straight, sleep a few hours in Klamath

Falls, Oregon, and then make it to Pismo Beach after another eight hours of travel.

He'd spent some time at Pismo Beach as a youth, and thought it was as good a place as any to regroup before he drove even farther south to either San Diego or Tijuana.

There would be good hunting in Tijuana...

He spoke pretty good unaccented Spanish, and could blend in.

He went into the cabin, glancing inside at the boy, who was lying exactly where he'd left him, on his side, his feet and wrists tied together behind him.

"You're lucky I'm leaving the state. If I had time, we could get to know each other better, but sadly, I have to leave and fast. You may or may not be rescued. I figure you'll die of thirst in a day or two from now. So, you better say your prayers and ask for forgiveness for anything you've done wrong. Not that I believe in God, or anything. There can't be a loving God or why would he leave you here to die?"

The boy frowned at that, and his eyes filled with tears.

Yeah, it was a cruel truth, but it was the truth, nonetheless.

He went to the cupboards in the kitchen and packed up a bag of canned goods and some dishes, so he could stop and eat without having to show his face at any restaurant. The Audi had a full tank of gas, and that would get him at least to Klamath Falls.

He grabbed some blankets from the chest of drawers, and a pillow, so he could sleep in the Audi, and then left the cabin, loading up the back of the vehicle and then strapping himself into the vehicle. He started up, then drove down the gravel road to the main road that led out of the deepest part of the woods, back to one of the main highways. The drive took twenty minutes, and the entire trip, he encountered no traffic.

It was when he was stopped at the intersection to the secondary road leading back to the highway that he saw a dark Range Rover approach. He waited to see where it would go, and when he saw the turn signal indicating the vehicle was turning left, he glanced at the occupants.

Two men, both appearing to be in their thirties, and the driver...

The driver was none other than Investigator-Fucking-Carter.

What the *fuck*...

As the vehicle drove by, taking the road into the woods, Curtis had to decide how to respond.

He could just drive on, take the highway south, and hope he was able to elude the police. If Carter was on his way to the cabin, he'd find the boy, and the boy would tell him that Curtis just left less than twenty minutes earlier.

Carter might even make the connection between the Audi he'd passed and Curtis.

Then, Carter could alert Highway Patrol to be on the lookout for a blue Audi.

Crap.

He had no choice. He had to turn around, follow the vehicle back to the cabin, and then take care of the problem.

He had his hunting rifle in the back, and lots of ammo. The sun was setting but he had night vision goggles to help see in the dark.

So, instead of taking the highway south to Ellensburg as planned, he pulled a U-turn and drove back up the secondary road behind the Range Rover — far enough back that Carter couldn't see him but close enough that he'd be able to park somewhere out of sight, get out his weapon and night vision goggles, and pick them off, one by one...

THE ROAD back to the cabin was winding, the trees on each side of the road making the drive claustrophobic. The sky was getting darker, and it was getting harder to see the road ahead, but Curtis didn't want to turn on his headlights. He didn't want Carter to detect an errant flash of his headlights behind just in case Carter was driving slower than Curtis.

He stopped the vehicle and removed the night vision goggles from the duffle bag holding his weapons and ammo. He hoped the battery held out, but if it didn't, he had the charger cord in the duffle bag and could use it to charge it up. He placed the goggles on, and glanced around, noting how much better he was able to see the road. There was a steep embankment on one side of the road and the last thing Curtis needed was to veer off the shoulder and end up hopelessly stuck in the ditch.

On he drove, slowly up the winding path back to the cabin, hoping that Carter hadn't stopped on the way and would discover he'd been followed, but so far, so good.

When he finally arrived near the cabin, he stopped the vehicle, got out his weapon, and crept through the woods so he could get a decent vantage from which to observe. He stopped at a fallen tree and knelt behind it, resting his rifle on the trunk. He saw that the Range Rover was parked near the garage, and the door to the garage was open. Someone was inside the house. The headlights provided illumination, and the effect of the night vision goggles was magnified.

Was it Carter?

A man came out of the house, and it wasn't Carter. He had his arm around Ben.

Curtis hesitated. He took in a deep breath and committed to his plan.

He pulled the trigger, but just as he did, the man bent down when Ben collapsed and the bullet missed its target, slamming into the wooden garage with a resounding crunch that was audible from where Curtis was.

The man must have realized what happened and pushed Ben down, both of them ducking behind the Range Rover. The man called out, then Curtis saw something peek out from the top of the vehicle's hood.

A gun...

The bastard thought he could defend himself against Curtis. Of course, he didn't know Curtis had night vision goggles.

"Carter!" the man called out. "Shots fired!"

At that, the lights in the house blinked out, and Curtis laughed to himself. Carter really thought that turning off the lights would help him escape?

All Curtis had to do was sit in wait for one or both to come into view and he could pick them off one after the other.

The first miss was just unlucky.

He wouldn't make the same mistake twice and he had a duffle bag filled with ammo...

CHAPTER 32

THE DRIVE TO THE CABIN IN THE HILLS NEAR MT. Rainier was slow-going, because large potholes filled with water from a recent rain pock-marked the roads. Michael's Range Rover could handle the rough roads, but he took them slowly so that he didn't slide off one of the narrow shoulders into the deep ditch on either side of the narrow lane.

"You sure this is the way? Seems pretty inaccessible. These roads haven't been maintained very well."

"Yes, I checked Holloway's records, and this property was listed as his. I assumed this was the cabin he went to on his numerous hunting trips. Lucky for us, his wife likes to talk, even when she's trying not to. Her denial made me suspicious."

"I had the sense she'd like to tell us more but was holding back."

"I think so," Michael said and slowed for a sharp turn. When he rounded the curve, the road ended at yet another narrow side road leading north. As he turned right, another vehicle was turning left onto the road they just left.

He frowned and wondered who would be traveling in this part of the park at this time of night.

"What kind of vehicle was that?" he asked Conway.

Conway glanced back over his shoulder.

"Looks like an old Audi of some make."

Michael considered. According to the records he'd seen, Holloway owned an SUV and a Volvo Station Wagon, but that had been in the driveway of the Holloway house, so he wasn't using it.

He drove on. If Holloway was at the cabin with hunting buddies, it could be someone leaving.

Or Holloway himself. If so, they'd find out soon enough.

The road led on deeper into the woods, the elevation increasing as they drove up the side of Mount Rainier. Night had fallen fully, and the headlights on high beam lit up the forest on either side of the road. The only people who would be hunting at that time of the night were hard-core types using night vision scopes and goggles.

That thought sent him back to Kincaid and his night vision goggles, that he used when spying on Michael and Tess, and which allowed him to shoot Michael in the shoulder with the crossbow. If only Michael hadn't run into the forest after the man, things would be very different. No telling how they would have turned out, but he would be uninjured and would more than likely still be in the FBI and on the CARD Team.

Funny how even so, there he was, working with a new member of the team who replaced him.

Doing the same work that he would have been doing if things had turned out different that day...

They finally arrived at the cabin, which was located at the end of yet another side road that penetrated the woods by a few hundred feet.

The cabin itself was rustic, with wooden clapboard siding, and a wrap-around deck. There were no lights on inside, and for a moment, Michael began to wonder if he had been wrong about Holloway coming out here. There was no sign that anyone had been at the cabin. If there had been tracks, they were washed out by the recent dump of rain.

Michael parked the Range Rover in the driveway and the two men got out and walked up towards the house.

"The garage door is unlocked," Conway said and pointed to the garage beside the house. Sure enough, there was a side door, and it was open.

"We should check it out." Michael removed his flashlight from the back of the Range Rover, and the two went over to the garage. Michael went in first, shining the light into the pitch-black interior. There was no vehicle inside, but there was a large workbench with shelves and a tool cabinet. Beside it was a gun locker used to keep hunting rifles secure, but it was empty.

If Holloway had been there, he'd taken all his weapons with him.

Which was not a good thing. He'd have to inform the Highway Patrol that Holloway was armed and considered dangerous, so they'd approach with extra caution if they did manage to find him in the state or trying to leave it, which was what Michael suspected.

On a shelving unit beside the workbench were several boxes for night vision goggles. Michael recognized the brand. When he picked one of the boxes up, it was light, which suggested that wherever Holloway was, he had night vision lenses with him. There were several others, so Michael took one set and hung them around his neck. They might come in handy. He took a pair for Conway as well.

Perhaps Holloway did go hunting, but somewhere else. Or perhaps he took the night vision goggles so he could better navigate the back roads on his way out of the state...

Whatever the case, he showed Conway the box.

"Looks like our friend is prepared for battle. The gun cabinet is empty. He has an arsenal with him and the ability to hide and watch his target undetected. We better be careful just in case he expects us. I have these, though. Just in case." He handed the goggles to Conway, who took them and then hung them around his own neck.

"Do you think that was him leaving the cabin in the Audi?"

"Could be. It isn't registered to him, but who can say whether he rented it or borrowed it? That could have been him. Doesn't seem like there's other cabins up here, at least nearby."

Conway nodded and went to the door. "I'll go check out the house."

"I'm going to call the Highway Patrol, let them know to be careful, given what we've seen here."

With that, Conway left the garage, and Michael took out his cell. He started to dial the number for the Highway Patrol, but unfortunately, the reception was poor, and he couldn't get a signal.

He was just about to walk out of the garage when he heard Conway call out.

"Carter — in here!"

Michael could tell by the sound of Conway's voice that he'd found something important.

Was it Ben?

He ran out of the garage and saw that the light was on in the house. Conway had broken the window beside the door and had climbed inside. The front door was open.

Michael rushed inside. "It's Ben," Conway said, kneeling beside the boy, cutting the ropes that restrained him. "He said he's been here since he was taken."

"Oh, God," Michael said and knelt beside them. He looked in Ben's eyes and smiled. "We got you, bud. You're going to be okay."

Ben nodded; his eyes wide. "I thought I was going to die."

Michael went to the sink and turned on the water. He poured Ben a cup of water and brought it over. "Here," he said and handed Ben the glass. "You need this."

He watched while Ben drank the glass of water, and in his eagerness, the water spilled out from the corners of his very dry mouth. The boy looked pale, and his hands shook as he held the cup to his lips, but he was alive.

It was a better outcome than Michael could have hoped for. Ben was fourteen, a few years older than Connor, and all Michael could think was how he would feel if Connor had been abducted and held captive for days. He felt a sense of tension ease out of his body as they helped Ben stand up. The boy was a bit wobbly on his feet, but they would take him to the ER and get him some IV fluids, a good meal and a good night's sleep.

That would fix him up. He'd be traumatized by his experience, but he would live to overcome that trauma.

Michael would make sure of it.

"I tried to call for backup, but my cell isn't getting enough signal. How about yours?"

Conway pulled out his cell and tried but shook his head. "No luck. We gotta get out of here. Get Ben to a hospital."

"Sounds good. You put him in the Range Rover. I want

to check the rest of the house out, see if there's anything that will let us know where Holloway is going."

"He said he was leaving the state," Ben said, his voice sounding stronger.

"How long ago did he leave?"

Ben shook his head. "I don't know. It's like a blur to me. Not long before you came."

Michael turned to look at Conway. "That was him turning onto the road," Michael said. "We better be careful."

With that, Conway helped Ben out of the house while Michael did a cursory examination of the cabin. It was a wreck, with old furniture and most notably, several drop sheets stained with what looked like blood on the floor and table.

It would be a good place to either butcher game – or take captives, sexually assault them and then murder them.

Michael figured that the only reason Holloway hadn't done so with Ben was because he knew police were on his trail.

Michael checked his watch. It was now eight thirty, and it would take at least an hour and fifty minutes to get to Newcastle, where the boy lived.

He was just about to leave the cabin when he heard a loud crack and froze. A gunshot.

"Carter! Shots fired!"

Michael grabbed his sidearm and switched off the lights, his heart rate increasing at the realization that it was Holloway on the road and that the man had followed them back and was sitting in wait. He had the advantage of being able to hide in the woods.

And he probably had a set of night vision goggles.

Holloway would be a formidable opponent because of

the goggles, even though Michael and Conway had their own. He slipped on the goggles and went to the window and peeked out, taking care not to present too much of a target. From his vantage, he could see Conway and Ben on the ground behind the Range Rover. Conway was holding Ben down with one hand and was holding his weapon out, peeking out from the back of the vehicle. It looked like Conway had slipped on his own goggles.

Michael crept through the cabin, looking for a back exit. There was none, but he did find a large sliding window in one of the bedrooms. He opened it, and jumped out, landing hard on the ground and rolling into some bushes.

There was no telling where Holloway would be, but if he had to guess, the man would be circling around, trying to get a better angle on Conway and the boy.

Michael would have to outmaneuver Holloway, but given the darkness and his night vision goggles, he was almost equally matched with his opponent. He would go a bit deeper into the woods behind the cabin and circle the property, trying to outflank Holloway and get an angle on him before he was able to shoot Conway and Ben, but it would be difficult.

Michael crouched low and crept into the underbrush.

There was nothing else to do but try...

CHAPTER 33

Crap...

Curtis had the advantage, but both men were trained in law enforcement and knew he was armed. He'd have to flank the one cop, who was currently hiding beside the vehicle, with a very disoriented boy under his arm. Curtis didn't think the vehicle was armor-plated, so they would be vulnerable to bullets — especially the double-bullet cartridges he used to load his weapon.

The bullets could kill a moose.

A human without real body armor would be a sitting duck.

To his surprise, the man got into the vehicle and started the engine. Did the idiot think he could drive away without getting shot at?

He took aim but just when he was getting ready to pull the trigger, a shot whizzed by his head, impacting a tree a few feet away. He moved in response and therefore, his shot went wide, striking the back of the vehicle near the bumper instead of the passenger side.

What the *fuck*?

Was it Carter? Where was the bastard?

He glanced around the yard to see if he could find the tell-tale silhouette of a man in pale green, but there was nothing. Wherever Carter was, he was well camouflaged.

The bullet aimed at Curtis had been far too close for comfort, so he crept along the ground until he found a fallen log and placed his rifle on top of it, then peered at the cabin through the scope. By the time he had the cabin in his sights, he could see that the vehicle had backed down the driveway. He took aim and fired, aiming for the driver's side and the pale image of the man who was driving. He thought his bullet appeared to hit its target, and while the vehicle kept driving erratically, backing out of the lane, it went down an embankment, the rear of the vehicle first.

Curtis wasn't certain whether he'd killed the man or merely injured him, but whatever the case, the vehicle had been rendered unusable. At that point, it was merely a matter of sitting in wait until the boy and Carter made their presence known.

He could pick them off, one by one...

He waited, but there was no movement and although he scanned the area around the cabin, he saw nothing from either the vehicle still stuck in the ditch or from the woods.

Where the fuck was Carter?

He got up and crept through the underbrush, bending down low just in case Carter could see him.

How had Carter been so accurate to almost hit Curtis?

Did the man find the extra pairs of night vision goggles Curtis had for his hunting buddies when they joined him?

If so, it wouldn't be quite as easy to pick them off as he had suspected...

Damn.

He should have thought to take the other pairs of

goggles with him, but he never expected that anyone would be on his tail this quickly. He never expected anyone to come out to the cabin.

He really fucked this hunt up right from the start. Should never have picked two boys at once. That had only worked once before, back when he moved to the local area.

Now, as he crept through the woods trying to find Carter, he regretted the day he decided to follow the two boys and take them both.

He'd failed to secure them right away, and the one boy — Aaron — got away. The boy would have been able to give police a good description of him, and even if he was wearing a wig and aviator glasses, there was still the uniform, the vehicle, and his general weight and height.

Next, he'd gotten in the accident, and had left behind evidence that the police could use to tie him directly to the abduction. The uniform was an old Highway Patrol version that the state stopped using a few years after Curtis left. He drove an old patrol vehicle that had been decommissioned, but a lot of the public bought them at auction, getting a good price. It was a badge of honor among some of the men who fancied themselves as pro-cop types to drive a decommissioned Patrol SUV.

He thought he saw the outline of a person moving in the distance, and so Curtis crouched low behind a thick cedar trunk and hid for a moment, before glancing around it.

Nothing.

If it was Carter, he was out of sight.

Damn...

The woods were thick around the cabin, and it was difficult, even with the night vision goggles, to see anything. All he could do was find a vantage and wait. Sooner or later,

Carter would have to try to go to the vehicle, and when he did, Curtis would take his shot.

Then, he could go to the vehicle and finish the job.

Part of Curtis debated with another part — the more rational part.

That part of Curtis said, *get to your vehicle and get the hell out of Washington State*. His instinct was to run.

Carter didn't have a functional vehicle. Curtis could just leave them and escape. By the time they were able to make it to civilization, he would be near the border. He had money. He had a disguise. He had false papers. He had a clean vehicle.

The other part, the part that felt like he'd fucked everything up far too much, doubted that instinct.

He had to stay and take care of business...

So, instead of circling back and just taking his vehicle and getting the hell out of the state, he waited, taking in a deep cleansing breath and trying to calm himself. He needed to be totally in control so he could focus and get a good clean kill when Carter did eventually appear.

From his position behind the tree, he could see the cabin, the lane, and the vehicle, with its rear end in the ditch. They would need a tow truck to get it out of the steep incline. No way to drive it out.

Of course, that was when it started to rain.

They were at a higher elevation and often, when the clouds rolled in, the cabin and surrounding forest were thick with it.

That was the case at the moment. The cloud hung on the side of Mount Rainier and felt like fine mist on the exposed skin on his face.

Unfortunately, the night vision goggles he used were not thermal, therefore, the rain and mist had the effect of scattering the light which the night vision technology magnified. Back when Curtis had purchased the goggles, he'd picked the night vision versus thermal imaging, because the thermals didn't provide an accurate depth perception, which was required for hunting. Thermal imaging goggles provided you with better image of a target, but night vision gave you a better sense of the actual distance to the target. Since he was buying several sets, he decided on the night vision. The cost was high, but he'd written it off as purchases for his business. His hunting buddies enjoyed the use of the goggles, and none of them could really afford to buy them for themselves.

One even joked that they could use them to hunt humans and went on about a crime show he'd seen in which a hunter used night vision lenses to chase down victims.

Curtis laughed. *If only they knew...*

Curtis sat with his back against the tree and considered. Given the rain and the difficulty seeing anything in the thick mist, it might be better for him just to bug out.

Get his vehicle and drive south.

Sure, Carter would eventually sound the alarm, if he hadn't already, but cellular reception was poor on the side of the mountain. If Carter had to walk out, it would take him hours and Curtis would be long gone.

Yeah...

You had to change plans when the conditions on the ground changed. That was one lesson he learned from his years in the military, even if he wasn't in a combat role.

Curtis wanted most of all to get south, get to Tijuana, and start a new life using his fake ID.

He was young enough and smart enough that he could soon be living well in Mexico where the US dollar was worth a lot, the cops were corrupt, and the rent boys were easy pickings. Mexico had one of the highest homicide rates in the world.

There were so many unsolved homicides because the police were both underpaid and underfunded, and those who weren't, were corrupt.

He could have free rein if he was in Mexico...

He made his way back through the woods towards the road where he left his vehicle, planning on driving back down the mountain and onto the Interstate that would take him south to Oregon and freedom.

When he arrived at the spot where he'd parked his vehicle, he stopped in his tracks.

It was gone...

Goddamn, but Carter had managed to find it and take it. Curtis checked his pockets, and he had the keys, so Carter must have hot-wired it.

It was an old Audi and wasn't equipped with the anti-theft devices of modern vehicles built after the mid-1990s. His mother had kept it up to date, ensuring regular maintenance, and the vehicle drove like a charm. But that meant it was vulnerable to hot wiring. No doubt Carter would know how to do that.

Damn.

Now, there was no other choice but find Carter and stop him.

Curtis turned back to the woods, determined to go back to the cabin and find Carter before he was able to escape. If not, Curtis would have to find another vehicle and get out of state, but that would mean he wouldn't have his new papers, his cash, or his other possessions that would make life easier on the run.

He couldn't let Carter get away...

CHAPTER 34

MICHAEL MADE IT TO THE OTHER SIDE OF THE WOODS where the road diverged, leading to another part of the mountain. That was where Holloway parked his vehicle — an old blue Audi that looked like it was from the early 90s.

When he checked the vehicle, there were no keys in the ignition. Holloway was careful enough to take them with him when he went into the woods. However, Michael had one trick up his sleeve. He knew how to hot-wire a vehicle, having been taught it at the Academy in case he was ever in the situation where he needed a vehicle fast.

He checked the road and woods for signs of movement, and when he saw none, he opened the door, which Holloway had thankfully left unlocked, and sat in the passenger side. He opened the glove box and searched for some kind of implement he could use to break the ignition lock cylinder. A screwdriver was the best tool, but when that was unavailable, anything that could wrench the cylinder out of its place could be used. He found nothing that he could use in the glove box, so he popped the trunk and went to the back, searching for something he could insert into the ignition cylinder and break it loose.

There — in a toolbox that Holloway had in the back. A nice flat head screwdriver would do the trick. Back in the driver's seat, he inserted it into the ignition cylinder and pounded it in, then turned it, hoping that it would start the vehicle. The screwdriver would damage the ignition cylinder, but it could start the car that way.

Failing that, he would have to break open the ignition and hot wire the starter.

As luck would have it, the screwdriver failed to start the engine, so he had to break open the housing that enclosed the wiring. Once done, he used some wire cutters in the toolbox to snip the wires providing power to the car. When that was finished, he did the same to the wires providing power to the starter.

Bingo...

The engine started. He drove down the road with the lights off and his night vision goggles on, intending to circle back and go to the Range Rover, which had backed into the ditch. There was no telling what he'd find when he arrived, but he hoped Conway and the boy were both still alive. If so, he would get them both into the Audi and drive down the mountain until he got cell reception and could call for an ambulance and police backup.

When he reached the side road leading to the cabin, he saw the Range Rover still stuck in the ditch. The lights were pointing up into the rain, which was coming down steadily, the wind blowing it in sheets that made visibility too difficult to manage the night vision goggles. He stopped the vehicle and got out, creeping along the tree line until he was behind the vehicle. Just when he was about to check inside to see if the boy was all right, a bullet whizzed by his head and struck the tree next to him. He ducked down, and edged back deeper into the woods, his night vision goggles back on because the rain was partially hindered by the canopy.

He scanned the woods across the street to see if he could detect Holloway but saw nothing.

Whatever the case, Holloway saw him and was able to almost hit him from wherever he was hiding.

What could he do now? The last thing he wanted was for Holloway to get the vehicle and take off.

"Carter! Is that you?" his voice came from the darkness. It was Conway.

"Yes. Are you and Ben okay?"

"Yes," came the reply. Then, Michael saw movement beside him a few feet deeper into the woods. It was Conway and Ben, a large blood stain on Conway's upper arm.

Conway was injured.

"I'm hit, but I'm okay. He got my arm. I think the bullet missed my bone. I have a makeshift tourniquet on it."

Michael went over to where they were crouched behind a fallen tree. He removed his night vision goggles and patted Conway on the other shoulder.

"I have Holloway's vehicle. If you can make it there, we should try to take it and get the hell out of here. I'll lay down cover while you go to the vehicle."

"Okay," Conway said and motioned to the Audi a few dozen feet down the road. "We'll go through the woods until we're even with the doors and you can fire over top of the vehicle while we get inside. I'll leave the door open, and you can get in."

"Sounds good," Michael replied and led the way to the edge of the wood next to the vehicle. He stopped and held up his weapon, pointing it above the Audi and towards the area where the last bullet had come from. He'd shoot several times in several directions just in case Holloway had left the location.

"On my count. Three, two, one. Go."

Conway and Ben bent down and climbed down the ditch and then up to the side of the vehicle. When they got to the car, Ben got in the back seat and Conway got in after him. As Conway said, he left the driver's side door open.

Michael shot several times above the top of the Audi while they did and then he ran to the door and jumped inside, sliding the vehicle into reverse, and gunning it, the vehicle's tires throwing up gravel as it went down the road. Several bullets whizzed by the car, and one struck one of the tires, which led to the Audi careening across the road.

Michael tried to pull a quick U-turn so he was facing down the road, and then gunned it again, driving as fast as he could away from the property.

He heard another couple of bullets striking the car and then the scrape of the tire rim on the road, indicating they had another flat. It became increasingly difficult to steer the old Audi and finally, the car slid sideways and came to rest at the base of a tree, the front-end crunching.

"Get out, get out," he called to Conway and Ben. "We have to hide."

They left the car where it came to rest, the two blown out tires making it impossible to drive. Hopefully, they were far enough away that Holloway couldn't see them.

"Into the woods," Michael called. "Get in deeper. Follow me."

Conway hopped behind Michael, and it was then he saw that Conway had been struck again, his lower leg taking a hit.

"Are you okay?" he asked Conway.

"I'm hit."

They stopped beside an old tree stump and Michael examined the wound. The bullet had pierced Conway's lower leg. Michael took off his jacket and then removed his shirt, ripping some fabric so he could create a make-shift tourniquet.

While he tied it around Conway's calf, he turned to Ben. "You good?"

Ben nodded, but the boy was breathing hard, no doubt adrenaline getting the better of him.

When he was finished tying the fabric around Conway's calf, Michael slipped his jacket back on and took out his cell to check the reception. It was still poor, and he couldn't get a signal.

"We have to move farther down the mountain if we want to call and get help. Can you walk?"

He searched Conway's face, who stepped gingerly onto his injured leg, wincing. "I don't think I can manage."

"Here," Michael said and offered his arm and shoulder. "I'll help you. Ben, you help Special Agent Conway on the other side."

The three of them were all soaked from the steady rain. It dripped into Michael's eyes.

"Good," he said when they managed to make it a few feet, Conway holding onto their shoulders. "Let's go. Keep low. We stop every twenty feet and listen, to see if Holloway is following."

"Okay."

They began their climb down the side of Mount Rainier, with Conway in between Michael and Ben. Michael kept his weapon at the ready. He had an extra clip in his pocket if he needed it. He hoped Holloway would just give up and try to leave the state, but neither of them had a working vehicle. There was no telling what he'd do, in that case.

One thing was certain: they had to get help and fast.

For the next half hour, they made very slow progress, stopping every twenty steps and listening to see if they could hear anyone following. So far, so good, but the reception was still terrible, and Michael couldn't get a signal on his cell.

Then, as Michael was glancing around the forest, Conway collapsed and fell to the ground. Ben stumbled and stopped before falling on top of the man.

"What's the matter?" Michael asked, kneeling at Conway's side.

"I don't feel good," Conway said, and closed his eyes. Even in the dim light, Michael could tell Conway had lost a lot of blood and was getting weaker.

"You stay here," Michael said. "Ben, you stay with Special Agent Conway. I'll go down the mountain and see if I can get a signal and call for help."

"How will you find us?"

Michael glanced around, unsure of what to say. He knew they'd been walking east and north, down the face of Mount Rainier for at least thirty-five minutes. He'd be able to give the police a rough coordinate of where Conway and Ben were, but they'd need to search, and it was still raining hard. It would be difficult to find anyone unless the weather broke without a big search party. Given that Holloway was still on the loose, it would be dangerous as well.

"I want to come with you," Ben said, his voice sounding panicked. "Don't leave me here. He's still out there."

Conway shifted on the ground, a grimace on his face. "Take the boy with you. I'll be fine. Put some branches over me to hide me from Holloway in case he comes by. Besides,

I have these," he said and pulled out his sidearm and slipped on the goggles, showing the sidearm to both Michael and Ben. "I'm a crack shot, so if I see the bastard, I'll get him."

"Are you sure?" Michael asked. He glanced around and saw some fallen branches, the leaves dried. He picked a few branches up and placed them over Conway, to hide him from view. They might offer some cover from the rain as well as prevent Holloway from easily seeing him. The underbrush was thick where they were. In the dark, even with night vision lenses, he would be hard to see.

"We'll come back," Michael said. "I promise we'll come back and wait with you."

Conway nodded and waved Michael on. "Go. I'm not going anywhere."

Michael took in a deep breath and put his hand on Ben's shoulder. "I'll stop every twenty steps and check the signal. Hopefully, we'll get one soon and we can go back to stay with Special Agent Conway."

Ben nodded and did what Michael suggested, staying a step or two behind Michael as they made slow progress down the side of the mountain and through the woods. Michael checked three times and each time, his cell showed that there was no signal. He glanced up when he saw light overhead. Good, the clouds were thinning, and the moon was a white glow behind the clouds.

"Let's go," he whispered to Ben. "Keep your head down and stay close."

Maybe, they could get a signal and escape. It might mean leaving Conway alone on the mountain, but the most important thing was getting Ben to safety.

Even Conway would agree with that.

CHAPTER 35

Tess waited for a text or call from Michael that evening, but there was nothing. He'd said he might have to stay overnight, but usually, he'd call if that was the case.

It wasn't like him not to call or at least text, but despite texting him numerous times, there was no response. She grew more and more worried as the time passed, until finally, when her watch read ten thirty, she called the Major Crimes Unit at the Bellevue Police Department to speak with one of the detectives on the abduction case.

She got hold of Officer Gord Fields, who was in the office working late. She introduced herself and said she knew Michael was working with him and Detective Joe Mendez.

"I've been trying to get hold of Michael for the past hour, but he hasn't responded. I was wondering if you knew where he was. It's not like him not to respond to his texts or calls."

There was a pause at the end of the line and Tess heard papers flipping. "Ah, Michael's out with Special Agent Conway. According to my message from him, they were going to speak with the family of a suspect who lives in Bellevue, but beyond that, I'm not sure about their plans."

"Is the Medical Examiner finished with the Deep Lake site? I was wondering if maybe he went there, but I haven't had any problems with cell reception when he was there."

"I think they're finished at the Deep Lake site. I know they're processing evidence right now, so I'm pretty sure the ME is done."

"The thing is, my calls all go right to message, and none of my texts have even been seen. That suggests that either his cell battery is dead, or he's out of cellular range. That could only mean he's in the mountains somewhere. Is there a site where he might go that is out of cellular range?"

"Not that I recall," Fields replied. "Our suspect lives in Bellevue. As you understand, I can't say anything beyond that. The last location I know Michael was attending was at a private residence in Bellevue. After that, I would expect him and Conway to either come back here or shut it down for the night, depending on what they decide."

"Okay, thanks. If Michael does arrive at the station, please get him to call me right away."

"Will do."

With that, Tess ended the call, but she wasn't satisfied.

Michael wouldn't let so many hours pass without at least texting.

She sat back down at her computer and began searching for whatever information she could find on the Holloway man that was mentioned in the list of people Chris had known from a decade earlier when he went missing.

Curtis Holloway.

She googled Holloway. He owned his own business monitoring construction sites with a fleet of vehicles and a staff of former police and military types, who patrolled private property to protect against theft and other problems. It seemed like something a former Highway Patrol officer would be interested in.

She went to Holloway's Facebook page and looked at the photos of the man. They included images from his community work as a volunteer at the local youth center in Bellevue. It also included several images of him posing with the body of a deer he'd shot, and the location tagged was near Lonesome Lake, on the slopes of Mount Rainier.

She called Fields back, chewing on a fingernail, anxious that someone should be more concerned about Michael's whereabouts.

"Hi," she said when he answered. "Sorry to pester you, but I gave Michael a list of people Chris, the boy who was murdered, knew around the time he went missing. One of the men on the list was Curtis Holloway. He's a former Highway Patrol officer, and is a big volunteer with troubled youth, especially boys. He takes them hunting and coaches ball. I'm not saying he's the killer, but Michael said one of the names on the list I gave him might turn out to be a key lead. I think he meant Holloway. His Facebook profile shows he has a cabin near Mount Rainier. Maybe Michael went there to check it out? It could be why he isn't answering his cell or texting if the coverage is bad."

"Thanks for the info. I'll check into it and get back to you if I come up with anything, but I don't think you need to worry. It could be that his cell battery died, like you said. But I will check, so thanks for calling."

With that, the call ended, and Tess was left to sit and stare at the television, feeling helpless that there was absolutely nothing she could do about anything.

While she was searching on a Reddit thread about the bodies found near the Deep Lake site, the land line phone rang. She answered it, and it was Julia, calling from Tacoma.

"Michael isn't home," she said. "He's at work. I've been trying to get a hold of him all evening..."

Before she could finish, Julia interrupted. "Michael hasn't told you. Someone posted a photo of our boys on the King County Twitter feed. Michael saw it as a direct threat to him and so we're in a safe house right now, with a police officer providing security."

"Oh, my God, Julia... I'm so sorry. I didn't know. Michael hasn't contacted me since earlier today. I had no idea."

"I was calling in the hopes of learning more about what's going on. I've tried calling him several times, but he isn't answering his cell."

"I know," Tess replied, sighing. "I haven't been able to contact him either. I spoke with one of the detectives working the case, but he had no idea where Michael was either, nor could he get through to his cell. I'm worried."

"So am I," Julia said. "I mean, I feel safe enough, but maybe Michael isn't safe, if some nutcase is threatening us."

They spoke for a few more moments and then Tess promised to call Julia — and vice versa — if either of them heard from Michael — or the police.

She ended the call, and sat staring at her screen, not really seeing anything.

Someone threatened the boys?

Was it the killer, angry that Michael had spoken about him? Michael was trained as a profiler and had provided the police with a profile of the suspect. During the press conference, he said it was likely someone in his late forties, who had been with law enforcement at one time. He was knowledgeable about police procedure and likely fit in quite well with his community. In other words, no one would suspect him. He might be married, but the marriage was just cover for his darker interests, and he would be a pedophile and would be hiding his sexuality.

Maybe the killer had watched the press conference and was angry at the way Michael described him, deciding to threaten Michael as a way of getting revenge.

Sociopathic killers often involved themselves in the cases, either by joining search parties, or providing tips to police. Or taunting police.

This seemed to be the case with the man who abducted Ben.

At least Julia and the boys were safe.

FOR THE REST of the evening, Tess did her best to keep her mind occupied while she waited for Michael to finally call or text, but it wasn't easy. When midnight came around, she was startled when her cell rang, and she grabbed the phone and checked the caller ID.

It was Officer Fields.

"I'm calling to let you know that we're sending a unit up to the location you mentioned, just to be on the safe side. I'll let you know if there's anything to report once our guy contacts us."

"Thanks so much," Tess said, exhaling heavily. "It's just not like Michael to go so long without even texting to let me know when he'll be home or if he'll be late. He always calls or texts. Always."

"I understand," Fields replied. "I tried both Michael's cell and Conway's, but no response, so it's better to be safe than sorry. Like I say, I'll call back if we get any new information."

"Thanks," Tess replied. "If Michael contacts me, I'll make sure he calls you to let you know he's okay."

"Great."

They ended the call and Tess sighed, glancing at her watch, and then switching the channel on the television, hoping to find something that could distract her from what was occupying her mind — fear that Michael had been hurt.

Or worse...

CHAPTER 36

MICHAEL AND BEN CONTINUED DOWN THE SIDE OF THE mountain. Every time he stopped, he placed a marker on a nearby tree so he could find his way back to Conway. All he had in his pockets were plastic evidence bags and so he ripped them up and pounded them into a tree at eye-level with a twig broken from a nearby branch, so he'd see it when they came back to Conway.

Michael was glad that the rain had stopped and that the clouds had parted. The moon was bright enough to provide some illumination. At the same time, it also made them more visible to Holloway if he was following, so Michael made sure to keep low, trying to use the dense undergrowth of the forest floor to keep as hidden as possible.

He stopped after another twenty steps, his hand on Ben's shoulder, and held up his cell, checking for signal but it was still showing no bars. The cabin was so remote and in such an inaccessible location that the reception was terrible.

"Nothing yet," he said, patting Ben's back. "We have to keep going." After he attached a piece of the plastic evidence bag to the closest tree, they went on.

They took another twenty steps and stopped again, but still no luck. This went on for at least two hundred more steps before his cell showed one bar.

"Bingo," he said and tried to send a text to Mendez and Fields at the Bellevue PD.

MCARTER: Shots fired, and Conway is injured. Send an ambulance and backup at this address immediately.

He tapped send and waited, hoping beyond hope that the one bar of reception was enough for the text to go. Thankfully, it did, so he next tried to call Mendez.

The call failed to go through, so he still didn't have enough signal for voice calls. He sent another text immediately, to Tess.

MCARTER: Tess, I'm okay, but I'm having problems with cellular reception. Will update you later. I'll be really late.

He sent that off and the text was successful. He knew Tess would worry, but there was nothing he could do that would really allay her fears. He just wanted her to know that he was still alive and aware that she would be worried because he hadn't contacted her for so long.

"Let's get a little farther down the mountain and see if I can get a call through," he said to Ben, who was kneeling quietly beside Michael. "Are you feeling well enough?"

Ben nodded. "I'm hungry but I'm okay."

"Good. You're strong. You're doing really well. Not much longer and we should get good enough cell signal that I can make a call."

He attached another piece of plastic to a nearby tree and then they went another twenty and then forty feet and he finally had two bars of reception.

He stopped and dialed Mendez again.

The call went through.

"Michael!" Mendez said when he answered. "We were trying to get through to you all night. You're up near Mount Rainier? Holloway's cabin?"

"Yes. Conway's been shot. I had to leave him in the woods and come down the mountain to get reception. I have Ben with me. He's okay."

"Great. We're on the road and have a Chinook chopper and a rescue team on the way."

"Fantastic. Holloway is armed and has night vision goggles, so he'll be difficult to find and he's a threat. He has no transportation so I imagine he's still near his cabin, but where exactly I can't say. Somewhere near my coordinates if you can pinpoint my location."

Michael read off the GPS coordinates.

"Got it," Mendez said. "Sending them now to the crew. How's Conway?"

"Shot in the leg and shoulder. I put a tourniquet on his leg, and he was still alive when we left him, but I suspect a bone was hit and so he couldn't walk. That's all I can really say. Hopefully, Holloway hasn't found him, but he couldn't keep walking with his wounds. We'll go back to Conway's position and wait for you."

"Sounds good. Take care, and we'll be there as fast as we can."

He ended the call and checked the location on Google Maps to see how far away the nearest road was. He had considered taking Ben there, in case they could flag down a passing motorist, or at least be more accessible once the police arrived, but it was too far.

Sending a Chinook helicopter was great — it meant that help would arrive much sooner than if they had to rely on roads, since the location was so inaccessible.

"The road's too far to walk," he said to Ben, and pointed

to the location on his Google Maps image. "We should go back and wait with Special Agent Conway. We need to keep low, and as much under cover as possible."

Ben nodded, and so Michael led the way, moving from one clump of brush to another, hoping that Holloway was no longer tracking them. He tried his best to go in the exact direction he took from Conway, checking for the pieces of plastic he'd left on the trees as landmarks on the way so he could find his way back.

Sure enough, within about half an hour, he found Conway still lying under branches.

"Damn glad to see you," Conway said when Michael lifted the branch off him. "Was wondering if I'd be here all alone all night."

Michael helped Conway into a more comfortable sitting position and checked his wounds. "I called for an ambulance and backup. Mendez said they're sending a Chinook in, so search and rescue is on its way."

"Great," Conway replied, gritting his teeth when he tried to move his leg. "I like nature and all, but I'd rather spend the night in an ER, thanks."

Michael smiled and turned to Ben. "Ben, I want you to stay with Special Agent Conway. I'm going to scout around, see if I can find a good place to watch for the rescue team so I can flag them down. They'll have IR technology to find us, but I'm hoping I can also find a spot to watch in case Holloway decides to come looking for us."

"I don't want to stay here," Ben said, his expression pleading.

"You should. I'm going to be within fifty feet of this location, so don't worry. Besides, Special Agent Conway has a sidearm and can protect himself and you in case Holloway shows up."

"That's right, kid," Conway said, trying his best to sound humorous. "Like I say, I'm a pretty great shot. Just sit down here beside me and keep quiet. Put a branch over yourself so the bastard can't see us if he happens by. Carter — you good with that weapon you have?"

Michael smiled. "I'm better than before, so there's that. Hopefully good enough."

Michael placed the branch over Conway and adjusted the one that partially hid Ben from view and then began to circle the location, ducking down low, his night vision goggles on.

He didn't know exactly what he was looking for — some position or easily-climbable tree he could use to survey their location in case Holloway was in the area. Search and rescue used both night vision and infrared technology to locate people in the night, but it was a very big mountain. They would have to start from the location of the cabin and fan out, but hopefully, when Michael called Mendez, they would be able to use the GPS location coordinates he gave to find them.

He was heading north and west of Conway's location when he heard a shot ring out and could almost feel the air move beside his face as the bullet whizzed past him, slamming into a tree beside his position. He immediately fell to the ground and rolled onto his back, holding his weapon in front of him, pointing in the direction from which the bullet came.

He saw nothing but the green glow of light on the trees.

Wherever Holloway was, he wasn't visible. Michael rolled onto his belly and began crawling along the ground, trying to keep as close to the underbrush as he could, but it was sparse where he currently was. He finally stopped near a bush of some kind and tried to crawl under it as much as possible, the thorns on the blackberry vines scraping his face in the process.

He lay there, his weapon held out in front of him, night vision goggles giving him a view of the local area, waiting, but he saw no movement, nor did he hear any sound except the breath of wind in the trees above him.

If Holloway was smart, he'd get the hell out of the forest and go into hiding. There was nothing he could do now except escape, so Michael was surprised that he had continued to pursue them. It suggested he wanted to kill them all to make sure they didn't live to tell the tale. He didn't know that Michael had successfully contacted law enforcement and that help was on the way.

Long moments passed, and Michael glanced at his watch, checking the time. It was now after one in the morning. By his reckoning, it would take the Chinook less than half an hour to get to their location, so he should be hearing it soon. That would likely scare Holloway off.

Michael debated about what to do. He'd promised Ben that he'd stay close, but he also didn't want to see Holloway escape. In the end, he decided to return to the cabin in case Holloway had gone back. He got up from the underbrush and glanced around the forest, checking in case Holloway was nearby but he saw nothing.

He kept a mental picture of where Conway and Ben were and used that to find his way to the woods surrounding the cabin. He stopped and watched the yard, noting that the light was still off, so if Holloway returned, he was smart enough to leave the lights off. He knelt in silence at the edge of the woods and listened but heard nothing — not a crack of branches under foot that would signal the presence of someone else.

The silence was eerie…

Then, he saw movement at the side of the cabin and a greenish figure came into view. Michael prepared to take the shot, but at the last second, Holloway dropped down and the bullet missed. Now, Holloway would know Michael was there.

Michael crept around the back of the cabin, keeping low, trying his best to stay as hidden as possible. He watched for signs of Holloway but saw nothing. He stopped and waited, listening for any sound that would indicate Holloway's position, but the wood was silent.

Then, the distant sound of a rotor. The Chinook was approaching.

Hope filled Michael that maybe, Ben and Conway would be rescued, and this nightmare would end.

He heard the crunch of brush in the distance and turned to check out the location. A brief flash of green signaled Holloway's position. Michael raised his weapon and checked the area but saw nothing he could identify as a person.

Holloway must have realized help was coming and he had to get the hell out of there, fast.

All Michael could do was follow, in the hopes of finding him and stopping him before he escaped completely.

He didn't want the bastard to escape justice.

CHAPTER 37

CURTIS SAT AT THE BASE OF A HUGE CEDAR AND CAUGHT his breath, his back against the trunk. Sweat dropped down his brow and fell down his face beside the night vision goggles.

He had to decide.

Stay and fight? Maybe take out Carter in the process?

Run and hide?

He decided to run and hide. What he really wanted was to get the hell out of Washington State and start over somewhere new.

He took in a deep breath, wiped his jaw, and crept along the ground, keeping low, his rifle at his side. He had first decided to find Carter and shoot him. If Carter knew he was the killer the police sought, everyone would soon know, and Curtis would have an even more difficult time escaping. It would be difficult no matter what, but he was a skilled outdoorsman and survivalist, having spent many a weekend with his buddies from Highway Patrol in the woods on the foot of Mount Rainier, toughing it out. Even if he managed to find and kill Carter, he would still have to find his way through the forest, locate a vehicle, and get the hell out of Washington State as fast as possible if he hoped to evade capture.

That meant he had to go back to the garage at the cabin and get some more gear so he could spend a few days in the wilderness if necessary.

He needed something to hide his heat signature. He had a mylar blanket in the garage along with some MREs and a water purifier. He could use that if he had to camp out for a few days until he found a vehicle that he could hot wire. After checking the local area out for signs of life, he went to the Audi and grabbed his bag, then made his way around the back of the cabin to the garage's side door. Once inside, he found the mylar blanket and stuffed it in the bag on top of the MREs and other items he'd need if he had to camp out for a few days on the side of the mountain.

He left through the side door once he felt he had enough to survive.

He dropped his weapon and bent to take it, and when he did, he heard the unmistakable sound of a gunshot and heard the whizz of a bullet passing him, slamming into a tree a few feet away.

Almost got him.

The sound of a helicopter in the distance filled the air. Immediately, he realized that somehow, Carter had been able to contact law enforcement.

The bastard...

They were on their way and that meant Curtis had little time to escape. Throwing caution to the wind, he slipped his arms through the handles of the duffle bag and crept around the side of the cabin.

He had no intention of being caught or killed and so the only choice was to run.

Without hesitation, Curtis hoofed it through the forest, not caring if Carter heard him. He had to get into the thicker part of the woods and as far away as possible as soon as possible or else it would all be over. Carter would have to give chase, but in a match between the two men in a battle of wilderness survival, Curtis knew he would win.

As he ran, he thought about the near-fatal mistake he'd made when he took the two boys the other morning. He had already seen Aaron around the youth center a few times, and he knew the moment he saw Ben that he wanted the boy. When he saw them the other morning, leaving school grounds and heading towards the park, he knew what he wanted to do.

He wanted them both.

It was a spur of the moment decision, and he wasn't as prepared as he should have been, nor as careful, and so he'd made mistake after mistake.

The mistakes had to stop.

He took out his compass — an old one that relied on the earth's actual magnetic field and not GPS—and used it to find his way towards an RV campground nearby. There would be vehicles there he could take, and if he had to, he wouldn't hesitate to kill the occupants and take a camper. In fact, that would be the best plan because he'd have a place to sleep on the road when he had to rest.

The campground had individual parking spots surrounded by woods, so it would be a matter of finding one that he could break into, kill the occupants, and then take off.

That was his plan.

By his reckoning, the campground was a few miles to the north and east of his cabin. If he could evade Carter, he could make it there in an hour or two depending on the terrain and be on his way south.

Thankfully, the clouds had parted, and the moon shone down brightly, illuminating the forest around him. With the night vision goggles, he could easily maneuver through the thick underbrush, jumping over tree roots and fallen logs with relative ease.

The sound of the chopper intensified, and he figured that would draw Carter away from his trail. If Carter was smart, he'd save himself and not pursue Curtis. He had the boy, after all.

That would be a win for the man.

Curtis intended to deny Carter a collar. He would prefer to go down in a hail of bullets than spend the rest of his life in custody. As a former trooper, a veteran, and a pedophile child killer, he would spend the rest of his life in solitary to protect him from the other prisoners.

No, that was no life for him, and so he was preparing himself for whatever happened next.

His hope was that he found a decent camper, easily took out the owners, and was driving south on the Interstate within a few hours.

He checked his compass once more, and figured that he was on the right track, and given the time that had passed, he might be less than a mile away. There was no way to be sure, and he might miss the place entirely, but he knew the general vicinity of the campground. If he could make it to the road leading to the campground, he'd be able to find his way there. It was a risk, but it was all he could think of unless he had to resort to carjacking some lone driver on the road, taking the vehicle after killing the driver and dumping the body in one of the deep ditches on either side of the road.

Yeah. That was one option, if he managed to get to the road and was unable to find the campground.

He decided to try and climb a tree and see if that afforded him a better view of the forest, so he could check for the campground. He stopped at one towering fir, and after dropping the duffle bag to the ground, he jumped up and grabbed a lower branch, then managed to lift himself up onto the branch, thankful for all the years of workouts and pull-ups he'd done to condition himself for just this moment.

He climbed up the fir, using the branches to get higher and higher until he was about twenty feet up. He turned and glanced down the side of the mountain and saw the campground in the distance. Luckily, there were lights in the campground positioned around the entrance and throughout the various services, such as outhouses and water stations. They made the campground stand out against the vastness of the mountain and forest covering it.

It was a good thing he checked his position, because he was definitely not on the right path. He'd have to adjust, but he was confident that if he stopped halfway and checked again, he'd be able to make it to the campground in under an hour.

He climbed back down the side of the tree, and adjusted his path, taking a more eastern route than he was initially taking. He'd stop again in a few hundred yards and check again.

When he reached a slight decline in the forest floor, he picked another fir with an accessible lower branch, removed the hockey bag, and climbed up the side of the tree. From his position, he could see the campground was much closer, but he could also see the chopper hovering over a position back closer to the cabin. They must have found Carter, Ben, and the other cop.

There was nothing Curtis could do about that, so he tried to shrug it off, climbing back down the tree to the forest floor. He picked up his duffle bag and slipped it back on when he felt something slam into his back. He fell to the forest floor and realized that he'd been hit by a bullet.

Carter...

Damn the man. He was so close to the campground. Another half hour and he'd be there. He was quiet for a moment, trying to feel if he was injured but no. He didn't feel any pain. He removed the duffle bag and checked and sure enough, there was an entry point in the fabric. Inside, the bullet had impacted the metal container that he used to store his money and valuables.

Thank God for that...

Whatever the case, he had to either stay and fight or run.

He ran.

CHAPTER 38

Michael followed in the direction Holloway went, staying as far behind as he could to avoid being detected, but close enough that he could hear Holloway crashing through the brush, the dry twigs cracking under the man's feet.

The man was desperate.

Michael hoped that the chopper was on its way to find Conway and Ben. That was his first concern, but he didn't want Holloway to escape. If the chopper was busy rescuing Conway and Ben, he was on his own and couldn't stop chasing the killer.

He wanted to catch Holloway and bring him back to face the music.

He wanted justice for all the killer's victims.

Because the undergrowth was so thick, it was almost impossible to see much except a silvery-green outline of the trees with the occasional brighter spot from the moon on the forest floor. It was enough to maneuver safely, but he was really running blind. His hearing was a better detector of Holloway's position than the night vision goggles. If he could come close enough to the man, he could get off a shot, but if it was dark, it was difficult to imagine seeing him if he was hiding in the underbrush.

He stopped and listened, waiting for some sound that would indicate that Holloway was ahead. His own breathing was the loudest sound, so he took in a breath and held it, hoping that would help. Sure enough, he heard the crack of brush to his three o'clock position. It had to be Holloway.

He went in that direction and did his best to avoid making a sound, but it was difficult as the ground was still dry enough even with the recent rain to crack under his boots.

All he could do was continue to follow Holloway in the hopes that he would be close enough when Holloway became visible so he could take a shot, disable the man, then hold him until back-up came and took him away.

Michael didn't want to kill Holloway, although the man deserved death for all the lives he'd taken, but that wasn't Michael's role. His role was to bring the man to the justice system and let it do its work. He didn't want to kill Holloway, but if it came to it, he would take the shot and do his best not to kill the man. He knew that in the end, it was his life or Holloway's.

Yes, Holloway wanted to escape, but only so he could continue his serial killer lifestyle somewhere else.

These men didn't change.

They would go on killing as long as they could.

They had to be stopped.

Michael continued, stopping every so often so he could listen for Holloway. Each time he stopped, he heard sounds in the distance, and they seemed to be getting softer and softer. Holloway was getting away.

He stopped once more and waited, listening for the tell-tale sound, but heard nothing.

Did he lose the man?

Was Holloway hiding somewhere nearby?

Michael crouched down beside a huge cedar and caught his breath.

The only thing to do now was wait. If Holloway was nearby, he was likely doing the same thing — hoping Michael would make a move so Holloway could shoot him.

Michael scanned the forest in front of him. Nothing moved. There wasn't even a whisper of wind through the trees.

Then, he heard the unmistakable sound of brush crunching behind him.

He held his weapon out and rolled onto the ground on his side, so that he ended up on his stomach, his weapon pointing towards the source of the noise.

There, a dozen feet away between two fir trees, was Holloway, his back to Michael.

Michael sighted Holloway and pulled the trigger.

The bullet struck Holloway but failed to bring him down.

Instead, Holloway took off running.

Michael struggled up and chased him, his weapon still drawn and pointing ahead, but Holloway was zigging and zagging through the trees and Michael was unable to get a shot off.

He searched the forest ahead of him, but there was no sign, and the only thing he had to go on was the sound of brush being crushed. It sounded like Holloway was at his nine o'clock position, and then straight ahead, then his three o'clock and then nothing.

Michael stopped, not wanting to become a target

himself. He crouched down in some brush, and wished he had better camouflage.

There was nothing but silence.

"Give it up, Holloway. There's nowhere for you to go. Police are here, and they have a surveillance drone and chopper with IR tech. They'll find you. Surrender now and save your life."

There was only silence in return. Not that Michael really believed that Holloway would surrender, but he wanted to offer so that he could justify shooting the man if it came to it.

"Fuck you."

The brush crackled again in the distance, and the sound grew dim as Holloway decided to run.

Michael shook his head and took in a breath. He was going to have to give chase. Holloway would make them both play out this cat and mouse game until the end.

So be it.

Michael took off again, keeping low, his weapon ahead of him, his night vision goggles scanning the forest ahead of him.

Where did the man think he was going?

He tried to keep as low and as close to the tree trunks as possible to hide his position in case Holloway was merely waiting for him in an ambush. He stopped and listened once more, and there was nothing but silence.

Did that mean Holloway was lying in wait for him to emerge again?

He heard a crack of brush, closer than he expected and taking a chance, he leaned around the tree trunk, his weapon extended and there, beside a tree, was the unmistakable outline of a man.

Holloway, his weapon extended.

Michael fired, just as Holloway did, and luckily, Michael ducked back behind the trunk as the bullet flew by, missing him by inches.

He sat with his back against the tree trunk, breathing fast, listening for any sign that Holloway was running, but there was no sound.

Finally, he heard a groan.

Holloway had been hit. A sense of elation filled Michael, but then he tempered that with doubt.

Was he really hit or was this a feint, meant to draw Michael out into the open?

Michael waited, not willing to go to check just yet. He listened and heard movement in the underbrush. It was faint, like someone crawling along the ground.

Then sound stopped.

Was Holloway just lying there, waiting for Michael to show himself?

Michael refused to give Holloway an easy target.

He waited. He checked his watch and saw that it was now close to two in the morning.

Holloway had either decided to lie in wait, or he was injured and couldn't run.

He waited. Time passed, the moon moving across the sky, hiding behind a bank of clouds so that the forest around him dimmed. Michael listened for any sound from Holloway, but there was nothing. He checked his watch again and another twenty minutes passed.

Holloway was either so injured he couldn't move, or he was gone.

Finally, Michael decided he had to check. He got onto his belly and crawled around the massive trunk, with roots so thick he could hide behind one. He peered around the tree and saw the outline of a body on the ground about fifteen feet away. Almost exactly where he'd seen Holloway when he took the shot. Holloway hadn't moved much from his position — maybe a few feet but he wasn't under cover.

He was just lying there on his stomach, his arms on the ground beside him.

Michael got to his knees, his weapon still drawn, and waited but Holloway didn't move an inch.

He stood and still no movement from the man.

He took a few steps closer, ready to take another shot, but nothing.

The man had either given up or was unconscious.

Or dead...

He took another step but if Holloway was conscious, he wasn't making any move to raise his weapon or try to get away.

Michael went to his side, his weapon trained on Holloway, but still nothing. He removed his night vision goggles and stared down at the man, whose own night vision goggles were off and were on the ground beside his head.

His eyes were open and staring straight ahead.

Michael knelt beside him and put his fingers on Holloway's neck to check for a pulse, but there was nothing.

He was dead.

A sense of relief flooded through Michael, and he sat on the ground, allowing himself a moment to catch his breath and be thankful.

He hadn't intended to kill the man, but at that point, it was kill or be killed.

He picked up the weapon Holloway had been carrying and removed the backpack from the man's body. Just in case.

Then, he took out his high-intensity flashlight and

started to signal to anyone who might be near and could come to the rescue.

For the next fifteen minutes, he flashed the light on and off, and soon enough, he heard the unmistakable beat of the rotor as a chopper closed in on his location.

When it arrived overhead, the rotor wash blowing the trees and leaves around him, a voice came over the speaker.

"Inspector Carter? Is that you?"

"Yes," Michael responded. "I have Holloway. He's dead."

"Roger that. We'll dispatch a team to your coordinates from a nearby clearing. They should be at your location in fifteen."

"Thank you."

The chopper turned and left, and the forest was once again silent around him. He stared up at the space between the tall firs where the chopper had been hovering and now, with the clouds parted, he could once again see the stars.

He leaned back against a nearby tree trunk and closed his eyes.

CHAPTER 39

WITHIN FIFTEEN MINUTES, MICHAEL HEARD MEN approaching, their boots crushing the underbrush.

"Carter? You there?"

It was Mendez, his slight accent unmistakable.

"Over here," Michael said and stood up, a sense of relief flooding through him. "Holloway's dead. How's Conway? How's Ben?"

Mendez approached, his flashlight trained on Michael and then pointing to the forest floor where Holloway's body lay.

"They're both good. Conway's on the way to a hospital, but he'll be fine. He'll be non-com for a while, because the bullet probably shattered the bone in his lower leg and maybe his shoulder, but he'll survive. Ben is happy to be going to the hospital for a check. He's dehydrated and scratched up, but he's alive. This is a big win."

"It is," Michael said and shook Mendez's hand. "I was afraid Holloway was going to get away. I was lucky to catch him before he could."

Mendez glanced down at Holloway's body. "You were

more than lucky. You were well-trained and good at your job. You sure you don't want to go back and work for the CARD Team again?"

Michael smiled and shook his head. "No. I like cold cases, but damn. I'd like to get one that's actually cold instead of these hot cases they keep sticking me with."

Mendez laughed and they both watched as two men with a body bag rolled Holloway into it and then carried him off in the direction they came.

"Let's go. I expect you'd like a drink after all this, but we have some paperwork to do before that."

"I'd like to call my partner and let her know I'm still alive."

"First things first, am I right?"

Michael nodded and gave Mendez a smile. "You got that right."

They walked through the woods until they came to a clearing a few hundred feet away from where Holloway was shot. While they watched, the chopper came into view and lowered a stretcher meant to lift the body into the interior.

The two officers with Search and Rescue secured Holloway's body in the stretcher and then signaled to the chopper to raise it. The rotor wash made it almost impossible to speak so they stood and watched as it drew up and was brought into the chopper's cargo hold.

"You're next," Mendez said to Michael. "Get in and let's get the hell off this mountain and back home."

"I thought you'd never ask," Michael replied. He climbed into the stretcher when it came back down, and after being fastened in with a safety belt, he held onto the ropes while it was raised and brought into the chopper. He climbed out once inside and took one of the four seats next to the stretcher, which was fastened to the side of the bay.

Next up was Mendez and then finally, the two other rescue officers.

Finally, the chopper took off and they headed straight to Bellevue.

While Michael was watching out the window, he took out his cell and called Tess.

It was now three in the morning, but he knew she'd be worried.

"Hey," she said, her voice sounding tired but happy at the same time. "You're okay?"

"I'm fine. A bit worse for the wear, but generally uninjured."

"What's the status of the bad guy?"

"He's dead, and Ben is safe."

"Oh, thank God," Tess replied, her voice sounding relieved. "I was so worried. What happened? How did Holloway die?"

"Can't say just yet, but I'm fine and apparently, my shooting arm has almost fully recovered."

"Okay," Tess said. "Understood. You took the shot that killed him, in other words."

"In other words," he replied. "We'll talk when I get back home. There'll be a debrief and I'll probably get some food, but then, I'll be home. Can't say exactly when. Get some sleep."

"I will now that I know you're safe," she replied. "Bye. I love you."

"I love you, too."

He ended the call.

Beside him, Mendez smiled. "You married?"

Michael smiled back and shook his head. "Not yet. But soon, I think."

"You should count your lucky stars this ended the way

it did and marry her as soon as you can. Life is short. In our line of work, you never know what's going to happen."

"You're right," Michael said and nodded. "I will."

With that, they flew through the darkness in a comfortable silence, neither man wanting to fight the noise of the rotors overhead.

WHEN THEY ARRIVED BACK at the Bellevue PD, after the chopper landed and they disembarked, Mendez and Michael watched as the body was put in a waiting hearse to be driven to the local ME's office for the post-mortem.

"Of course, we need to debrief you and do all the paperwork. I think we can do this quickly, so you can go home and get some rest. We can do more of the work tomorrow, but I want to get a statement from you while your memory's fresh. You up for it?"

"Yes," Michael said and followed Mendez back into the building. They took the elevator to the Major Crimes Unit offices and then went to the back conference room where the task force had its papers and maps spread out.

Michael flopped down on a chair and rubbed his face, glad to finally be back in his familiar surroundings.

"Can I get you a soda? Maybe something to eat? There's a vending machine with sandwiches and chips."

"Yeah, a sandwich would be good. Let me check what you've got."

They went to the vending machine in the break room and after selecting the roast beef, and a bottle of water, they went back to the conference room and sat down.

"Tell me what happened, start to finish. I'm recording so we can get a transcript ready."

For the next half hour, Michael went over what happened from the time he and Conway arrived at the cabin to when Mendez and the other rescue officers found him. They went through all the paperwork required after an officer-involved shooting, taking his sidearm and having him sign the written statement.

Then, Mendez walked Michael to the front entrance. "We'll get one of the patrols to take you home. Come back tomorrow afternoon or evening. I'll be here and we can talk more."

"I will," Michael said and extended his hand for a shake. "It was a pleasure working with you."

"Thank you," Mendez said. "I'm glad you were with Conway instead of some other cop who didn't have your training."

Michael sighed. "I would have liked to bring him back alive, so he could face the courts, but that wasn't in the cards. He wasn't going without a fight."

"It is what it is," Mendez said. "I'm sure there's no question that you did the right thing, considering he shot at you several times and injured Conway."

Michael nodded and watched as one of the patrol cars drove up to the front and waited for him.

"See you tomorrow," he said and went down the stairs.

"Later today," Mendez corrected with a laugh.

"Yeah, that's right. Later today."

He got inside and gave the patrol officer his address and then sat back, his eyes closed, enjoying the quiet of the ride back home.

❧

When he got back to their neighborhood, after crossing Lake Washington on the Evergreen Point Floating Bridge, he unlocked the front door and went inside. The lights were on, and Tess was waiting, dressed in her nightgown and robe. Relief was clear on her face when she saw him.

"There you are," she said and came to him, her arms open wide. "Thank God, you're okay. I was so worried..."

They embraced and kissed, and Michael held her tight, emotions finally overwhelming him. He was so damn glad to get out of the forest and back home.

"You need to marry me, soon," he said, his voice filled with emotion.

She smiled. "You name the date and I'll be there."

He laughed and kissed her once more, thankful that he had her.

The next day, after sleeping in and spending a good solid hour with Tess, telling her everything he could about the events of the previous day and night, he used her vehicle to drive back to the Bellevue PD.

When he arrived back in the Major Crimes Unit office, he was greeted with a round of cheers from the officers working there.

"There he is," Gord Fields said. "The man of the hour. Welcome back, Carter. You thinking of joining the force and working with us full-time?"

Michael laughed and shook his head. "Not on your life. I'm supposed to be working cold cases. Get that — cold cases. Not ones where I have to take out bad guys with a bad shooting arm."

He shook hands and enjoyed some good-natured banter

with the other cops as they peppered him with questions about the night. Most of them had probably already read the preliminary statement about the shooting, but still wanted more intimate details.

"We'll have lunch," he said and waved them off. "I have some paperwork to get through."

He went into Mendez's office and sat down, then heaved a sigh of relief.

"How's Ben?"

"Good," Mendez said and came around, then sat on the front of his desk, facing Michael. "He went to the ER, was checked over and spent the night just for observation. He'll be in soon for questioning, but we wanted him to have a good sleep, some food and rest before we questioned him further."

"What about family?"

"They're with him," Mendez said. "He's been through a lot and will need a lot of care and attention over the next few years, but I know the social workers and Victims Services reps are committed to working with him and the family."

"Good," Michael said. "He's the one I care about the most in all this. Has he had a chance to see Aaron?"

"Apparently, they already visited at the hospital. Ben is on his way over now for an interview."

"That's good news. He's been through so much. What about the other victims? Have they been identified yet?"

"We're sending the DNA of the unidentified remains to several DNA databanks, hoping we can get some forensic genealogy to help track down their identities. The Department has some money set aside, and since this is such a high-profile case, I was able to get the top brass to approve the expenditure. We should have something in several weeks, depending on the results."

"Good," Michael said. "It will be nice to close a few cold cases and missing persons cases.

Michael looked around. "What about Holloway's family? I imagine it's been a real shock for them to learn the truth about him."

"Apparently, still in denial. It will be hard for them to process everything."

"Yes, I feel bad for them. What now?"

"Now, we meet with the team, go over everything, and you go on leave for a few days. A week if you want. You need to talk to your boss and figure out the details, but we've got the case from here."

Michael nodded. A week off sounded like just what the doctor ordered.

A week at the cabin up north, overlooking Puget Sound — just him and Tess and the sound of water on the shore.

Yes, that sounded like just the medicine he needed to get back to his old self.

He took in a deep breath and waited for what was to come next, the memory of the cabin's view of Puget Sound keeping him going.

CHAPTER 40

GRACE SAT AT HER DESK IN THE AUTOPSY ROOM AND read over her notes from her latest autopsy, a cup of coffee in her hand.

The last of the skeletal remains from the Deep Lake site had been processed and were now tucked away in their respective boxes to await being claimed by family. Barring that, they would be cremated and buried in unmarked graves on cemetery property owned by the County.

She read the latest news about the Deep Lake serial killer on her iPad that morning and noted that a GoFundMe campaign had been initiated for the burial and headstone for one of the murdered teenage boys – Chris Rogers.

Chris was one of the first victims of the Deep Lake Killer, as he was being called. The boy with the parry fracture in his left arm and the Wyoming belt buckle. Murdered a decade earlier, his body buried beneath an old carpet and load of garbage. A boy who never had a real chance.

She clicked on the link to the GoFundMe page and made a decent donation.

At least she'd help him have a proper burial, complete with headstone.

That was money well-spent.

Alice poked her head in the room from her own office. "Got some results back on the oldest victim. You'll be really interested in this. DNA match. You should call Michael Carter."

"Let me see," Grace said, holding her hand out to receive the papers Alice was holding. "I'll call Michael and let him know."

Grace took the sheets of paper from the Forensic Sciences unit and checked them over. Sure enough, there was a DNA match from the oldest victim at the Deep Lake site.

Twenty-seven-year-old David Bridges, a former Washington State Patrol officer. Quit soon after graduating, giving no explanation other than an email. Except for the DNA, there was nothing to identify the remains. There was no dental work to ID him, so they were lucky to be able to extract some viable DNA from the demineralized and liquefied bone powder, using DNA-binding magnetic beads.

She picked up her cell and dialed Michael Carter's number, knowing that he would be most interested in getting the information as soon as possible. Not that there would be any trial regarding any of the murders, but at least the families of the victims would finally know what happened to their loved ones.

"Hey, Michael," she said, smiling at the sound of his voice. "I have some results you might be interested in. We have a positive DNA identification of the older remains at the Deep Lake site."

"Grace, you read my mind. I was just going to call you and see if I should drop by bearing gifts, to see what you've managed to come up with while I was on the side of the mountain."

"I read all about your escapades. I thought you were working cold cases, not hot ones. What's up with that?"

Michael laughed. "So, what's the ID?"

"His name is David Bridges, a former Washington State Trooper, who quit in his first year. Guess who he was in the academy with?"

"Let me guess – Curtis James Holloway, recently deceased."

"The very one," Grace replied, shaking her head. "His body was the first to be buried. Do you suppose Holloway thought he'd found a good dump site because he patrolled that area and used it from then on? Does that mean that there aren't more bodies to be found elsewhere?"

"You're doing my job for me, Dr. Keller," Michael replied. "I'm not going to stop looking for any links between Holloway and missing young boys and men in any part of the state he might have frequented. He returned from the war in 2007. That leaves thirteen years during which he could have been killing. I suspect there are more than the six we've found."

"You're the expert," Grace replied. "Just thought you'd like to hear the news hot off the presses."

"We have IDs on all the remains?"

"Yes. Names and dates. The final report is being prepared for your office as we speak."

"Good," Michael replied. "If you could fax me the report when it's done, I'd be grateful. Just wrapping up the paperwork right now on the cases."

"What's next for you?" Grace asked. "Going to keep working cold cases or are you going to go back into the FBI? Seems you did a pretty good job at finding and rescuing a child victim."

"Nah," Michael said with a sigh. "I realized how lucky we were to find Ben and get him out safe. It's a tough job. Besides, I like working cold cases. There's reward when you're able to solve old cases and bring closure for the families."

"Well," Grace said and placed the report's first page on the scanner. "The scans are going to come through to you right away."

"Thanks, Grace. Appreciate the call."

"You're welcome. I've enjoyed working on the Deep Lake cases with you. Don't be a stranger."

"You know I won't."

Grace ended the call, smiling as she thought about him showing up in her autopsy suite or at a crime scene in the future with a cup of latte in his hand.

She scanned the three-page report and sent the images off to Michael in an email.

Then, she leaned back in her chair and stretched her back.

Alice stuck her head back into the room. "We got a call. There's a body in a dumpster in downtown Seattle off Aurora."

"Geeze Louise, I guess it's true that there's no rest for the wicked. Pack up. Let's go see what's up."

When she saw that her email to Michael had sent successfully, she stood and grabbed her jacket and case, then left the office, eager to find out what poor person was dead in a dumpster off the most notorious prostitution stroll in the city.

Just one more victim of the violence endemic to the drug and prostitution trade.

At least six families would finally know what happened to their loved ones.

That made her job, as hard as it was at times, rewarding.

She wouldn't give it up for anything.

CHAPTER 41

Tess walked along the waterfront, a cup of coffee from Starbucks in her hand.

It was one of her favorite places to go, when she wanted some fresh air and exercise. Today, she was meeting with Kayla to wrap up her story on the serial killer who had been operating in Washington State for the past two decades undetected. He'd had six victims so far; perhaps more once police did more checking. Would have had another if Michael and the other officers hadn't persisted.

Michael was going to join them for a coffee and to give Kayla an update on the case. Tess arrived at the spot where she would meet them—a small set of benches overlooking Elliott Bay, not far from Michael's workplace at the City Attorney's office.

Michael had taken a week off and they had spent it in their cabin overlooking Puget Sound, across from Whidbey Island. Michael had needed the time off, to decompress and process everything that happened to him.

Tess had been worried it would be traumatic to have to

spend so much time in danger, considering everything, but he seemed remarkably well and in good spirits.

Perhaps being able to do the work he used to with the FBI's CARD Team, successfully stopping a serial killer and rescuing a victim, would help heal the wounds from his experience with Blaine Lawson and the unsuccessful rescue of little Colin Murphy.

Michael's partner from the FBI, Special Agent Conway, was recovering back at his home in California. A bone in his lower leg had been shattered by the bullet, and his shoulder had been injured, so he would be on medical leave for months while he recovered. Mendez and the other detectives from Bellevue's Major Crimes Unit had done their work to close the case, and Michael was finishing up the paperwork and closing the old cold cases tied to Holloway's murders.

All in all, things had turned out much better than they could have. Holloway's last two victims survived, and he was now six feet under in some cemetery outside of Bellevue. Tess's article detailing the case was in its last draft, and today was meant to wrap things up and give Kayla an update on the case connected to her old boyfriend, one of the victims. Michael was still checking other cases for links in case the current count wasn't complete.

Michael arrived a few minutes later, and as usual, was early. He had a cup of coffee in his hand and bent down to give her a quick kiss before sitting beside her on the bench.

"You picked a nice day for a meeting here," he said and glanced around the waterfront. "Lucky for a break in the rain."

"That's why I wanted to meet Kayla here. It's more casual, and I felt that she'd feel more comfortable instead of at the *Sentinel's* offices."

"Good idea," he said and then he sat up. "Oh, I was able to get something for her," he said and reached into his pocket, withdrawing a plastic Ziplock bag with something inside. Tess recognized the bag as an evidence bag from the police. "I was able to get this released so we could give it to Kayla."

He handed it to Tess, and she examined it. Inside was the belt buckle with the word Wyoming and a cowboy riding a bull, his hat in hand.

"This is what identified Chris," Tess said, holding it up to examine it more closely.

"Exactly," Michael said in reply. "If it hadn't been for her coming forward and providing us with what he was wearing, I doubt if we'd know it was him. He has no family, and no one even cared that he was gone or had reported him missing. He would have remained just one of the dozens of missing persons whose fate we have no idea about."

Tess nodded. "Do you want to give it to her?"

"You can," Michael replied.

Just then, Kayla walked up and stopped in front of the bench. "Hello," she said.

Michael moved over and pointed to the spot between them. "Have a seat."

Kayla sat between them and sighed heavily. "I read that Chris's case is closed."

"Yes," Tess said and handed the belt buckle to her. "Michael was able to convince them to release this to you, since there's no one else to claim Chris's possessions."

Kayla took the package and glanced at it, taking a minute to compose herself. She opened the bag and removed the belt buckle, turning it over almost lovingly in her hands.

"Chris loved this. It was the one thing he had from his

family that he loved." She closed her palm around it and turned to Tess, her eyes filled with tears. "Thank you for this."

"You're more than welcome. Thank Michael. He advocated on your behalf."

"Thank you," Kayla said to Michael. "I'm so glad I have this. Can I find out where his remains will be buried?"

"Yes," Michael replied. "The remains will be cremated and buried in a common grave, but you can get the coordinates so that you can visit the site. There will be a headstone that commemorates all those whose remains weren't claimed."

Kayla nodded. "I wish I could afford a separate burial, but I'm just getting by myself."

"I understand," Tess said. "Have you considered a GoFundMe? I could write an article about Chris, his life and death and the case, and put up a GoFundMe campaign. You might get enough to bury him or put his remains in a crypt."

"That would be wonderful," Kayla said. "Thank you for offering."

"No problem," Tess said and squeezed Kayla's arm affectionately. "I'm happy to tell Chris's story and help."

Kayla smiled and wiped her cheeks. For the next half hour, Michael gave her as much of an update on the case as he could, but now that it was closed, most of it was public knowledge. When their coffees were finished, they walked back to the parking lot and said their goodbyes.

"Thanks for everything," Kayla said and gave Tess a quick hug.

"You're very welcome. I'll text you the details about the GoFundMe."

Kayla nodded and then shook Michael's offered hand awkwardly.

"Do you need a ride back to work?" Michael asked. "I'm heading back to the office and could drop you."

Kayla shook her head. "No," she said with a sad smile. "I think I'll walk. It's such a nice day and I need the fresh air but thank you for offering."

Then, Kayla walked away.

Tess turned to Michael. "You going back?" She glanced around and saw his brand-new Range Rover in the parking lot.

"I am, but I'll be home early tonight. Maybe we can head out to the cabin and spend the weekend there."

She smiled. The thought of spending the weekend at the cabin sounded perfect.

"I'll see you later."

With that, they parted ways. Tess walked along the waterfront to the *Sentinel's* offices, the last rays of the sun a warm orange glow on the horizon.

ABOUT THE AUTHOR

Susan Lund is an emerging author of crime thrillers and romantic suspense. She lives in a forest near the side of a mountain in the beautiful Pacific Northwest with her family of humans and animals.

Join Susan Lund's newsletter to get updates on her new crime thrillers.

http://eepurl.com/dAfi6j

ALSO BY SUSAN LUND

Made in United States
North Haven, CT
19 April 2025

68115975R00173